ALEXANDER McGREGOR
LAWLESS

Black & White Publishing

First published 2006
This edition published 2014
by Black & White Publishing Ltd
29 Ocean Drive, Edinburgh, EH6 6JL

1 3 5 7 9 10 8 6 4 2   14 15 16 17

ISBN   978 1 84502 745 2

A CIP catalogue record for this book is available from
The British Library.

Typeset by RefineCatch Limited, Bungay, Suffolk
Printed and bound by Grafica Veneta S. p. A. Italy

Acknowledgements

Every work of fiction depends on facts. Somewhere in the creative process, parts of real people and events inevitably intermingle with imaginary ones. Sometimes the distinctions are obvious. At others, even the person doing the creating isn't sure where the fine line separating the two has been drawn.

Lawless journeys at times between fact and fiction and a few of the characters actually exist. Some are half true and others, thankfully, are completely make-believe. In every case, the dialogue is pure fiction.

The book was inspired by certain actual events encountered during research for a previous book, *The Law Killers*, and experiences soon after its publication. In that sense, it is a fictional sequel.

It could never have been written without the help, advice and encouragement of a number of people and I am deeply indebted to them. My particular thanks go to:

Ex-Detective Chief Superintendent Tom Ross and Dr Doug Pearston of the Scottish Police DNA database; the governor and staff of HM Prison Perth, especially Steve Kinmond; Petra McMillan, Paul Gunnion and Gordon Dow, all of whom helped one way or another to put this book on the shelf.

The fine staff at Black & White Publishing always deserve more praise than they receive, so, hopefully, this makes amends – my particular thanks go to the magnificent Patricia Marshall. On this occasion Alison and Campbell have to be singled out for a unique combined contribution to the main character, as well as for their guidance.

Above all, my gratitude goes to my wife Christine for her helpful suggestions, editing skills and understanding. None of the following would have been possible without her.

For Gavin
who makes me proud

1

He'd seen his name in print often enough above newspaper stories but it looked different on the spine of a book. He still wasn't entirely convinced that he and the Campbell McBride described on the jacket were the same person. According to the blurb, he was a distinguished investigative reporter and an authority on crime. Now he'd turned author and, what was even more unlikely, the book had become something of a best-seller. OK, maybe it wasn't *War and Peace* but thousands had seemed to want to read his account of the catalogue of murders that had taken place in Dundee, the town he used to call home.

During that afternoon of the signing, he had worked his way through an unexpectedly long line of people wanting his name on their copy of *The Law Town Killers*. Some were old acquaintances – even a couple of ex-girlfriends – a few were amateur detectives but most were just curious. Maybe they thought that getting the author's signature would make the book more collectable.

McBride saw it differently – sign as many as you can and that way they're less likely to lend the book out to friends who should be buying their own copy. At least that was the theory. But they could be a bit contrary in that city of contradictions.

As the queue gradually evaporated, McBride became aware of a middle-aged man hanging back, waiting to be last. He was small and spruce, his salt-and-pepper beard close trimmed. Not carrying any extra weight. Clothes sensible, matching. Not cheap – maybe expensive. He held the paperback protectively to his chest – not like a reader, more the way a professor would before he delivered a lecture. Perhaps he wanted a long chat about forensics or a complicated dedication. Either way, he was going to take up time.

When there was no one else left, the precise, uncluttered figure approached and his body language definitely wasn't that of a fan. He was controlled but agitated. There was none of the usual uncertainty of what to say, no half-smile or hesitant attempt at a handshake. Spreading the book open, he held his fingers over the start of one of the chapters.

'Your book's shit and this is the biggest pile of it – just like yourself.' The words were chiselled out but the voice was measured, soft – just loud enough for McBride to take in but not for anyone passing the table. 'You couldn't be bothered doing any proper research, could you? Or were you just talked out of it by your pals in the police?'

Before McBride could look up or think of a sensible response, the troubled man had turned away and was walking towards the main door of the store. Ten seconds later, he had vanished into the throng of shoppers that packed Murraygate every Saturday afternoon.

Even if he'd been inclined to, McBride knew there was no point going after him. That part of town was the commercial backbone of the city. The shoppers always came at you like a football crowd and, with seven days to go before Christmas, sanity had deserted them. It was said that, if you stood under H. Samuel's clock long enough, everyone in Dundee would pass you by. That day, they seemed to be going round twice.

McBride had prepared himself for possible confrontations with the family or friends of some of those he'd written about. It was inevitable, he reckoned, that he'd cause offence somewhere. He'd revived a lot of old memories that some would have struggled to bury and his resurrection of the facts wasn't going to make him the most popular guy in the country as far as they were concerned. He would have felt the same if he'd been one of them and he'd resolved to be apologetic and sympathetic. He would respond with unaccustomed gentleness. But, when the simmering anger spilled from the man at the end of the queue, there hadn't been an opportunity for saying even a holding, 'Sorry you feel that way.' How could he placate someone who apparently didn't want to listen?

When he looked at the book still open in front of him, he was surprised to discover that the chapter wasn't among those he'd mentally noted as the ones most likely to stir up trouble. In fact, if he'd been forced to choose the least offensive, the chapter staring back at him would probably have been it.

It was textbook straightforward – young man strangles girlfriend after argument . . . abundance of evidence . . . arrested within hours . . . jailed for life . . . end of story. The killing had only made it into the book because the victim had been a policeman's daughter. If such a thing as an open-and-shut murder existed, the death of Alison Brown and the subsequent despatch to prison of Bryan Gilzean for her slaying constituted it.

3

So why had the brief episode with the troubled man who had come to Waterstone's bookstore to make a point left him with such an irrational feeling of unease? He told himself it was because he would have preferred a longer, less considered outburst – something he could have dealt with, apologised for.

The world is full of bampots, he reflected. Forget it. But he knew he wouldn't.

2

The Fort bar out in the posh Broughty Ferry suburbs never seemed to change. Same sports trophies in their glass cases out of reach along the back wall of the 'public bar. Same groups crouched over the domino table. They played for pennies but the concentration matched anything you'd see at the blackjack tables in Monte Carlo.

Next door, in the discreet lounge, the thirty-somethings were starting to negotiate. The people were the clones of the ones who gathered there before McBride had left town twenty years before – only the faces had changed. The conversations had never altered. They tried to sound relaxed, casual, but the small talk was the usual evening mating call. You could tell the ones who weren't picking it up. They looked hopefully over at the door every time a newcomer came in just in case a better prospect had arrived.

The Fort had always been the best bar in town, even if some of the women could be a bit choosy. At least no one was ever going to bottle you there. John Black saw to that. He was unlikely to be described with any accuracy as 'genial' by those who coupled that word with 'host' but the outward gruffness concealed an unexpected generosity and he was a soft target for a good cause. The owner of The Fort had also learned the first lesson of being a successful publican – to make every customer feel like you knew them.

'Saw your picture in *The Courier*,' he told McBride. 'Best-seller, eh? Never knew Dundee had spawned such a bunch of murdering bastards.'

McBride had no idea if the short figure behind the bar had the slightest inkling about who he was, beyond what he'd read in that morning's paper. Did he remember their conversations when McBride had been a young reporter on *The Courier*? Then there was the night John Black had put him into a taxi when, by rights, he should have called the police after the drunken brawl . . . He'd feel his way.

'I was going to do a chapter on Dundee United – the day they murdered Dundee 5–0 back in '64 but there was no real mystery in it. Good side annihilates crap side – what's new?'

Black took the bait. Football, or more accurately, Dundee FC, obsessed him almost as much as making money. Life lost much of its meaning the day the team was relegated, leaving their hated rivals as the city's sole representatives in the Premier Division.

'Lippy asshole,' he flashed back. His language had all the old finesse. 'You didn't learn any manners all that time in London then, you little prick?'

'So you remember? I was sure the old dementia would have kicked in by now,' smiled McBride, extending a hand across the counter, which was warmly grasped.

'Who's going to forget a celebrity like you? Your name was never out of the papers for long enough. If there was trouble anywhere, you were up to your neck in it – just like years ago 'cept some paper was paying you fancy money

6

to write about it. In the old days, you were the trouble. If it wasn't the drink, it was putting a leg over the wrong woman. Maybe you still are?'

McBride felt an unexpected flush spread up from his neck. He quickly raised his pint glass and drained the contents, taking longer than necessary in the hope the redness would disappear. When he finally put it back on the counter, he forced a laugh. 'Straight to the point, eh, John?' He wondered if it was one of his random jibes or an unusually subtle attempt to ask about his marital status.

'You find out there's no future in that carry-on – maybe some of us just take longer to get the message than others. More to the point, when are Dundee going to do the decent thing and sell off Dens Park to United for a training pitch?' It was an obvious change of subject and he knew the pub owner would pick up on it. That was another talent John Black had acquired in his years behind a bar. He'd learned when topics should be dropped, directions altered – that the customer was always in charge of the conversation.

What was the point in going into it all, anyway? McBride thought to himself. A crowded Saturday-night lounge bar wasn't exactly the most tranquil of settings for a cerebral exchange about the state of his marriage, even if it still existed in some recognisable form.

Not for the first time since returning to Dundee, McBride became aware of a feeling of melancholy creeping over him. The town had changed – almost beyond recognition in some parts. So had a lot of the people. Now there were bioscientists with English accents rubbing shoulders with the old-time trade unionists. Wine bars were opening up and the council couldn't pull down some of the empty housing estates fast enough. Out in the suburbs, high-priced villas were springing up on every available plot of ground. There was a whiff of prosperity in the air. But nothing could alter the memories, the distant echoes that could still seep slyly into your head when your back was turned.

He wondered if Caroline had ever returned and tried to imagine where she would have gone if she'd found the strength to come back. Would she have revisited all the obvious places or would the recollections have overwhelmed her the way they were starting to do to him? The only thing left in Dundee for her – for them both – was the precious spot where they'd taken Simon's ashes all those Decembers ago. That was probably the best reason to stay away.

He asked himself if he would make the journey to that peaceful place where she'd shed so many tears before he departed again for London but he still struggled for an answer. He'd never been there without her.

Caroline, sweet Caroline. He walked on every crack in the road – she read Annie Proulx and put the handbrake on when she stopped at traffic lights. But, magically, for ten years, it had worked. Then he went away and, when he came back, it was over. He still wasn't sure why.

3

When the phone rang, McBride was on the floor of his hotel room. He was wearing purple shorts and battered Nike trainers and his body ran with sweat. For the previous ninety minutes, he had jogged through the rain in the awakening centre of town. He stopped trying to reach his toes and stretched out to pick his mobile from the bedside table. Janne from his Edinburgh publishers always had a smile in her voice and he pondered if all Danish women sounded that way, even on wet Monday mornings.

When McBride informed her he was in his hotel room, half naked and sweating, she queried why he was also breathless.

'Not what you think or might like to think,' he fired back. 'Anyway, I thought it was the Swedes who thrived on all that sort of stuff.'

Janne giggled. 'I bring news of "fan mail" – some of it from ladies, perhaps. Should I send it on or won't you be able to contain yourself? I could open it up but maybe you won't want me to see what colour the knickers are?'

'I'll risk it. They'd probably be too small for you anyway.

Come to that, I was never that sure you Scandinavians actually wore such things.'

Janne sighed in mock indignation. 'We're not all bare-bottomed Scotsmen in kilts. Give me five minutes and I'll get back to you.'

She rang off.

When she called again, exactly five minutes had passed and this time Janne was wearing her Miss Efficiency hat.

'Right. Sorry – no knickers. There are nine letters in total. Six say, "Well done" – can't imagine why – two are requests for you to speak – one of them a Rotary Club and the other, which I know you'll like, is a young wives' group who say they try to attract interesting men to entertain them. The last one is a bit more unusual. In fact, it's not nice at all. Says, in effect, that you're a bit of a tosser and you got one of the chapters all wrong. You're accused of helping to keep an innocent man in prison and it says you've been hoodwinked, just like the police. Do I bin it and just post on the others or do you want it for your scrapbook?'

McBride knew the answer to the question he was about to ask but he asked anyway, his mood of light-heartedness dissipating. 'Does it refer to the story about the bloke who strangled his girlfriend with his tie?'

'Yes – Bryan Gilzean and Alison Brown. According to the letter, he's doing life. By the by, did I say the note is beautifully punctuated, very neat and without a spelling mistake – unlike the work of some authors I know!'

It was McBride's turn to be businesslike. 'Never mind the rest of the stuff,' he said, suddenly brusque, 'I'll pick it up next time I'm through. But let me have the complaining one. Can you get it off today?' He rang off before he became aware of his rudeness. He knew he had work to do.

If he'd still been a staff man on one of the nationals, there wouldn't have been much of a problem. The news desk would have him pencilled in for an assignment somewhere and the air tickets would have been booked in his name and awaiting his return. He would have caught the plane and stayed away until the final word of his 'scintillating' prose had been filed. Then he would have come home and waited for the next trip to the airport. Life didn't present too many dilemmas. You followed the news and everything else fitted in round about – or sometimes it didn't for the unlucky people who shared the ordinary, static parts of your nomadic existence.

But, now that he freelanced, McBride could make choices. The one facing him in his room in the Apex Hotel was straightforward. It should not have taken any time at all. He should have showered, dressed and checked out. He should have left his bags at reception and spent the afternoon catching up on the changing face of Dundee. Then he should have caught the early evening flight out of Riverside Airport back to London. He should not have returned to his native city for another ten years.

Instead, McBride called the airport and cancelled his seat on the plane. It made no sense but he did it because he couldn't stop himself. The voice inside his head told him it was irrational and pointless to remain in the city but, down in the pit of his stomach, the other voice, the one he always obeyed, told him it had been inevitable from the moment the insistent stranger had walked quickly away from him in Waterstone's.

McBride consoled himself with the thought that his seemingly illogical act had much to commend it. He was following his instincts and they rarely let him down – it was paying attention to these same instincts that had so often helped to put his byline on the front pages. There were also old contacts and new places in Dundee he could visit. Besides, the reality was that he was in no particular hurry to return to London after the way he'd left it.

Sarah had moved her stuff out of the flat but she continued to appear on the horizon at inopportune moments. The rows had begun to last longer than any of the highlights of their short existence together. The only redeeming feature of the increasingly hostile exchanges was that she had not taken the threatened hammer to his pride and joy – the midnight-blue, carbon-fibre Trek bike which was capable of carrying him almost as fast as the speed of sound. Her restraint had almost certainly not been prompted by any compassion, he reflected, but by self-preservation. It was one of the few sensible decisions of her life.

The more McBride considered his current state of affairs – romantic and otherwise – the more logical his decision to remain in Dundee became. Hell, it was even starting to look like a good idea.

There didn't seem an obvious starting point for the mission he was about to embark upon so retracing his footsteps looked as good an option as any. It was also the only one he could think of. That afternoon he called again at Waterstone's.

Gordon Dow was the kind of man any bookshop chain would want as its manager. He had conducted a love affair with books all his life and could put an affectionate hand on any one of the thousands of volumes on his shelves without having to wonder where it was. He was on first-name terms with every regular customer he had ever had and he received a nod from everyone worth knowing in the city – even those who didn't read. But he did not know the man who had waited so patiently in McBride's book-signing queue two days earlier. He had, however, spoken to him just an hour earlier.

That was another thing about the lean, sensible-eating manager – he never missed a bit of drama in his own shop, no matter how minor, and he had witnessed Saturday's exchange.

'What's going on with you two?' Dow wanted to know. 'You're in here asking about him and he's just left after enquiring about you. Is there something I should know about this relationship? Anyway, he's left you a love note. Said I should give it to you if I saw you again and, if not, to send it to your publishers for you to collect.'

He handed over a small brown envelope he retrieved from a drawer under the till. McBride tore it open and read the single sheet of paper inside, turning his back on the store manager who was unashamedly trying to read the contents over his shoulder.

The message was brief and to the point – much the same as the conversation its writer had had with McBride on the Saturday afternoon. It read:

Dear Mr McBride,
Please accept my apologies for my comments when I spoke to you at the book signing. My son is innocent but I am aware his incarceration in prison has nothing to do with you. My rudeness was prompted by a sense of frustration. Forgive me.

It was signed 'Adam Gilzean'.

McBride passed it to Gordon Dow who could read the page of a book in ten seconds. He devoured the words at a single glance. 'So, that was Adam Gilzean – it makes a bit of sense now. He wrote to the papers practically non-stop after his son was put away. It was always about how the lad was as pure as the driven snow and was doing time for another man's crime. If I remember correctly, he even tried to rope in his MSP to take his side – fat lot of good that was going to do, even with a strong case. But, with all the evidence there was against his boy, it was just peeing in the wind.'

McBride stuffed the letter in a pocket. He patted the part of his jacket where it lay. 'It's well put together,' he told the bookstore manager. 'The man's not an idiot. In his letters to the papers, did he have anything to say other than that he'd been with his son on the night Alison Brown was killed? If I remember correctly, when I went through the stuff when I was writing that chapter for the book, that was his main contribution at the trial.'

Dow had total recall. 'Nope. That was it,' he said. 'His son couldn't have done it because he'd been with him. He *would* say that, though, wouldn't he? What father wouldn't?'

McBride nodded in silent agreement. 'What about the forensics? Do you remember if there was anything special that came out afterwards?'

Gordon Dow did his best to shake his head and shrug his shoulders at the same time. 'Don't ask me. It was an open-and-shutter as far as everybody was concerned. What are you getting so worked up about it for?'

McBride wished he knew the answer himself.

'Have you any idea where Adam Gilzean lives?' he asked although he was unclear what he would do with a positive answer.

'No. I'd heard he moved to another house someplace but don't ask me where.'

McBride was on the point of leaving when Gordon Dow took his arm and led him across the floor of the bookstore. 'What do you think of that?' He swept an arm towards the main window of the shop.

Two assistants were piling dozens of copies of McBride's book on top of each other for a front-of-store display. Above them a large board proclaimed, 'The No. 1 Bestseller'.

'The figures just came in this morning. Bet that makes you feel good,' Dow said expectantly.

McBride's nod could have been more enthusiastic. 'Yeah,' he replied, 'but not as good as you lot who are making most of the dough. You won't mind if I reduce your profits a tad by taking one of these?' He picked a copy of *The Law Town Killers* off the top of the stack. 'I've got some reading to do,' he said as he headed for the door.

4

It didn't take him long to remind himself of all the details of the chapter entitled 'A Final Romance'. It was an unspectacular tale of two people in their mid twenties who had loved with a passion and warred with just as much fervour. You could write a love song about their highs and horror story about their lows. When they quarrelled, everyone in the same sombre blocks of flats in Clepington Road where Alison Brown resided and where Bryan Gilzean spent most, but not all, of his time, heard about it. Sometimes you would think the folk two streets away were probably tuned in as well.

On Alison's last night on earth, she had again shouted out in anger. Then she fell silent and the eavesdroppers imagined her rage had once more given way to sexual fulfilment – which was indeed an inevitable feature of their making-up scenario.

It wasn't until they read *The Courier* the following day that they discovered her sudden loss for words had not been the result of any loving embrace but a consequence of having been throttled. She had been found that morning by a friendly neighbour who had called to enquire if Alison would be interested in a shopping expedition later in the day. There had been no response to her knock and the neighbour tried the door handle. Finding it unlocked, she entered and walked hesitantly into the living room.

Alison would not be going to the shops that day or any other. She lay, quite serene but very dead, on the floor beside the sofa she had saved up so hard for and which she had finally been able to afford a week or two earlier. Her pallor practically matched the colour of the soft white leather of the Italian-made settee but her make-up might have been applied just an hour earlier. Her clothing, in co-ordinated shades of terracotta and cream, was all neatly in place and she was still wearing her brown, strapless, high-heeled shoes. She could have been ready to welcome visitors – except she had long ago stopped breathing because of a tie which was knotted tightly round her windpipe.

Before expiring, it looked like she'd enjoyed a drink. A bottle of white wine, with only two inches left in it, sat on a low table beside two glasses, each with their contents unfinished.

Within an hour of the unfortunate neighbour's grisly discovery, scene of crime officers in their white paper suits and masks were swarming all over the small flat that was meticulous in its neatness except for the corpse on the floor.

A post-mortem indicated that death had probably occurred around 11 p.m. on the previous evening – which was around the time her raised voice had been heard coming from the flat. Forensics were the clincher. Gilzean's semen had been found inside Alison and a hair from his head was on the tie. The wine bottle had been wiped clean but his prints were on the glass.

McBride continued to reread the words he had written some twelve months previously and found the subsequent

17

arrest, trial and conviction of Bryan Gilzean just as inevitable as he had when composing the chapter. It was a fairly simple conclusion based on the facts and a view that was obviously shared by the police who had arrested Gilzean within hours and the High Court jury who took only fifty minutes to unanimously find him guilty.

Apart from an abundance of forensic evidence, he had no believable alibi, was known to be hot-headed and was liable to be quarrelsome with a drink in him. And, on top of this, there were enough witnesses to testify how frequently the couple could be heard arguing. As homicides went, it verged, just as he had remembered, on the mundane – it was as uncomplicated for the investigating officers as it was undemanding for those who sat in judgement on Bryan Gilzean.

He had been given the mandatory sentence of life in prison, with a recommendation that he should serve a minimum of fifteen years before being considered for parole. It seemed a reasonable enough tariff in the circumstances.

McBride fell asleep. It was just a few days before Christmas and he was in a hotel room in Dundee when, by rights, he should have been occupying a warm corner of his local in Maida Vale. For the first time that week, he slept well.

5

McBride woke at seven o'clock precisely the following morning, as he did every day. He never needed an alarm clock, a call from hotel receptionists or their automated equivalents. He just woke at seven o'clock, no matter what time he had gone to sleep, who lay beside him or where in the world he was. He nodded his head seven times on the pillow and followed this by tracing the number seven on his forehead before turning over to go to sleep and he believed this routine was what caused him to rouse with such exactness. But, when he was too drunk to remember the procedure or so wrapped in a pair of delicate arms that such behaviour would have prompted questions, he still started each new day at 7 a.m. which was frustrating on the days he didn't want to.

It had an upside. Unless he had company and the option of other forms of exercise, he invariably pulled on his jogging kit and put in a few miles before breakfast, which was never much of an occasion for him anyway. McBride had a schizophrenic relationship with running. Even after doing it for a dozen or so years, he could not make his mind up if he actually liked it. He knew with absolute certainty, however, that he could not function fully without it. It aided his body, of course, but it was what it did for his head that kept taking him out in every kind of climate. He had a simple formula – the more there was on his mind, the more miles he consumed. Usually he found his answers before exhaustion overtook him.

That morning, he fought with the wind all the way through the harbour area and kept on going, with the river by his side, until he'd passed Broughty Castle. Then he turned and headed back. Altogether, he covered ten miles but there weren't any answers because he didn't even know the questions.

When he plodded back into the Apex, a small package awaited him at reception. The Jiffy bag bore the frank mark of Black & White, his publishers, and the handwriting was unmistakeably Janne's. Without pausing, he slid it open and pulled out the contents. The first item to appear was pair of knickers, black, lacy and extremely brief. Janne's sense of humour, like her complexion, glowed. She would have experienced a moment of blissful triumph if she'd been present to see the look on the receptionist's face.

McBride contained himself until he was back in his room before poring over the letter. Janne's description of the anonymous communication was accurate. It was word and punctuation perfect and the computer-produced message was quite unambiguous:

> Your book may be factual, Mr McBride, but that does not mean it contains 'facts'. Bryan Gilzean most certainly did not kill Alison Brown. I know this beyond doubt.
>
> If you are the investigative journalist we are led to believe, you should investigate more and

believe the idiots in the police less. They are easy
to hoodwink.

My message to you is that it could be productive
for you to review the 'evidence' on which you based
your words.

Of course, there was no signature. McBride folded the single
A4 page and slowly replaced it in its white, rectangular
envelope, the front and rear of which he inspected three times
though he knew before he did so that it would be a pointless
exercise.

He also knew that, in order to 'review the "evidence"', he
should begin in the building where, many years earlier, he
had devoted endless hours to absorbing the kind of facts any
would-be investigative reporter would require if he wanted
to flourish away from his home town.

6

The walk to the Central Library in Wellgate filled McBride with an unexpected sadness. It took him only four minutes but, in half that time, he experienced the kind of feelings that had made him want to leave the town in the first place.

For half the population it was boom time. They earned good money in the new industries that had replaced the spinning and weaving of the jute that had once been imported from India and Bangladesh, occupied fine houses and holidayed abroad, sometimes twice in the same year. Their offspring attended either of the two expanding universities that were beginning to acquire international reputations.

But, alongside the throng of students who strode through the city centre to lectures or coffee shops, knowing where they were going for the rest of their lives, there were other young people with less to fill their time, less to look forward to. Skimpily dressed girls with pinched faces pushed baby buggies when they should have been attending school. Instead they were adapting to motherhood at the age of fifteen. They wandered aimlessly with one hand on the buggy and spoke to their clones on mobiles held in the other – all of them contributing to the statistics that made Dundee the teenage pregnancy capital of Europe.

The largely unidentified fathers of the tots gathered in groups in the shopping centres, their acne, tattoos and earrings making them indistinguishable from each other. The only time the mothers and fathers apparently got together was to share a needle or produce another occupant for the baby carrier. Few of them worked or ever would.

Except for the phones, it had been the same kind of mind-numbing existence for their parents. Most of those in the prams were assured of an identical future. In anybody's language, it wasn't going to be much. So much change, yet so little.

Dundee had a heart as big as a football pitch but it ticked the poverty and deprivation boxes every time. Nobody took the blame and only the brain-dead believed the adolescent baby-makers were truly responsible for their plight.

When he walked among them through the shopping centre on his way to the library, McBride felt the sense of injustice he had forgotten he had for his fellow Dundonians. Maybe it was his conscience about the lopsided forms of life in his home town that was inexplicably coaxing him towards the belief that there might be a different kind of injustice taking place. He was beginning to feel like a missionary.

Was this what all of this was about – trying to compensate for some kind of guilt trip at leaving them behind? he asked himself. He forced images into his mind of himself cycling alone along a hot Mediterranean coastline, an easy breeze at his back. It was his usual technique for dispelling uncomfortable thoughts.

The local studies section of the library was almost empty, save for three student types earnestly making notes from a tower of books in front of them and a prematurely elderly woman who'd come in out of the cold.

'How can we help you, Mr McBride?' The female librarian was neither so pretty that you'd remember nor so plain you'd forget but, because of the size of her breasts, no one was ever going to describe her as ordinary. Her name badge, sitting above the more than ample chest, said she was called Elaine.

McBride was surprised by how she'd phrased her question. Even his old classmates would have had trouble recognising him after so long. Then he remembered that those who worked in libraries also read papers, especially when the news was about people who wrote books.

'If it isn't too much trouble, can you point me in the direction of the old, filed copies of *The Courier*?' McBride replied, not sure if he should acknowledge the recognition or give her one of his practised lines. He decided to do neither and instead tried to smile modestly, an unfamiliar experience.

When he pored over the files moments later, he resisted the temptation to begin reading the news that had happened more than three years earlier. People had been known to spend entire afternoons devouring column after column of historic events when all they had wanted was to confirm what the weather had been on a particular day.

He leafed his way quickly through the dry, yellowing pages of the paper until he came to the issue chronicling the report of the High Court trial of Bryan Gilzean. It could not have been more ordinary and was exactly as he had remembered it when he had ploughed through a *Courier* of the same date many months earlier, in the Colindale branch of the British Library in London, when preparing the chapter about the killing of poor Alison Brown.

He read the report of the first day of the proceedings three times to be sure he had not missed anything and repeated the process for the second day. Unless you counted an unexpectedly risqué photograph of the winner of the annual Forfar Young Farmers' Club beauty princess competition on the opposite page, nothing jumped, or even crept, out at him. He wondered if there was much point scrutinising the happenings of the third and final day of the decidedly routine trial of Bryan Gilzean but turned the pages to it anyway.

He was quite correct. There was nothing particularly enlightening to read there either. He was riveted, however, by what was absent. Removed from the report, which recounted in detail the finding of guilt and subsequent sentence of life imprisonment, was what he presumed from the layout had been a photograph of someone involved. Of much greater interest was another extraction. Cut from the body of the main text were several sentences from the middle of a long-winded testimony by a forensic scientist witness.

Both removals had been carried out with surgical precision and almost certainly by someone using a razor. There was no indiscriminate butchery or lack of regard for the rest of the article. Whoever had carried out the meticulous operation had gone well prepared for the task in hand. It was deliberate to the point of fastidious. The same result could have been more easily achieved simply by ripping the paper at the relevant section. That was what someone with less precise habits would have done.

McBride stared blankly at the page for a full five minutes, trying to make some kind of sense of what he had stumbled upon. Then, aware that his lack of movement was beginning to attract the attention of the now-bored students, he quickly flicked over a handful of pages, afraid his discovery might be shared by others.

Back at the reception desk, Elaine was also eyeing him suspiciously. In spite of his innocence, he experienced pangs of guilt and knew that, if the file was examined after his departure, he would inevitably be blamed for its defacement. It only made him feel more furtive and anxious to hoard his find.

He tried to appear casual. 'Hi again. Thanks for that. Fascinating things, old newspapers – I could spend weeks here,' he said with another attempt at a coy smile. He avoided adding the obvious 'especially if you were here'. Instead, he tossed in what he hoped sounded like a conversation-making afterthought. 'Do you get many folk in digging about in your files?'

She smiled back, trying to make the old joke sound original. 'Nostalgia isn't just a thing of the past, you know. It's an endless procession, especially after your book with all the would-be Rebuses who have read it coming in to look up the facts for themselves. Some right dodgy types too. Did you get everything you wanted?'

McBride lied, ignoring another chat-up opportunity: 'Absolutely.' He wasn't about to disclose the existence of the treasure trove he had unearthed, even if he hadn't the faintest idea if it had any value at all.

Outside, sleet was swirling along the freezing corridor of Murraygate. The buskers had disappeared and the buggy-pushers without money hurried to God-knows-where.

McBride also moved quickly. He had urgent business in his old newspaper office.

7

Richard Richardson never knew whether he liked his name. All his life, folk had joked about it. At school they called him Double Dick and pubescent girls sniggered at the thought of what that could mean. He pretended to be offended but inwardly hoped they would believe he had been blessed.

As he grew older, he realised there were other benefits to having had such unimaginative parents. Few forgot his name though some occasionally got it wrong and referred to him as Dick Dickson.

When he decided to become a journalist, he faced a dilemma. Should he use his own name on articles and risk further ridicule or change it to something more mundane? He decided that unforgettable was best and every story he ever wrote in *The Courier* carried the exact words his birth certificate bore.

It would not have mattered what he called himself. Richard Richardson was a legend in local journalistic circles and not just for his odd handle. He received Christmas cards from half the police force, most of the publicans and every dignitary. His appetite for fine food was surpassed only by his taste for cigarettes and outlandish neckties. It was a constant source of irritation that ash from the former frequently dropped into his food or, worse, on to his tie.

He also wrote magnificently. When Richard Richardson was of a mind, only a handful of reporters in the country could match his insight. Even fewer had his elegance with words.

Campbell McBride and Richard Richardson had started on *The Courier* within days of each other and had rapidly become ferocious rivals and bosom friends. They fought dishonourably for the best stories and worst women and mocked each other's work. When they wanted to drink, which was often, they did it together. After they returned to their respective flats, they reread the articles each had in that day's paper. Sometimes, they scrutinised them three times. There was no greater tribute they could pay each other. Of course, they never spoke of such things.

The job offers to move away from Dundee came from the same national newspaper on precisely the same day. One post was in Glasgow, the other in London. It did not matter to the *Daily Express* which of them took which position. The nation's biggest-selling daily wanted both of them but in different cities.

McBride always knew that, when the call came, he would respond with alacrity even if he had to feign initial hesitation to help jack up the money on offer. Richard vacillated too but for different reasons. His head told him to start packing his bags but his heart desperately tugged the other way. He loved his home town.

McBride chose London and moved away. His great friend and rival stayed. They never knew how things would have turned out if, that day, the *Express* news editor had offered two jobs in the same town when they could have gone together to seek their spiritual and financial fortunes in a far-away place.

In the twenty or so years since, they had met only twice – once, in the early days, when McBride had persuaded his old sparring partner to spend a long weekend in London and then when Richard learned Simon had died. He had heard the news shortly after arriving for work one morning and by early afternoon he was with McBride and Caroline in their home in Kent. He had not even gone home to pack a bag or change his tie for a black one before catching the midday flight south.

As time passed, the regular exchange of phone calls became less and less frequent until they stopped altogether. They had not spoken for almost four years. It was not anyone's fault – it just happened.

When McBride had arrived back in town to sign books, he had fully expected to witness Richard charge his way to the head of the queue to unleash a volley of good-natured barbs. His non-appearance prompted the celebrity author to leave messages for him at every likely venue where he could have been expected to turn up. There was no response to any of them.

Now McBride was waiting to greet him in the reception area of *The Courier*'s offices on the Kingsway city bypass and wondering how he would explain to his old friend and rival why he wanted to scrutinise back copies of the paper.

He could tell him the truth – that he was desperate to solve the mystery of the missing sentences that had been razor-cut from the one in the City Library. But old habits die hard. Every journalistic instinct he had acquired told him that you never parted with a bit of intrigue to anyone who might make use of it before you did – especially when it was the kind that made hairs stand up on the back of your neck. And, unless he had changed, Richard Richardson, whose dictionary did not include the word scruple, would shamelessly have availed himself of every detail. Furthermore, he would have been proud to have boasted of it.

When the lift doors slid apart, it might have been a time machine that had opened up. The man who exited and was walking eagerly across the highly polished floor, hand extended to greet McBride, had made only one concession to modern times. He did not have a cigarette in his hand – not because he had stopped smoking but because a foolish law prohibited him from contaminating his workplace. Apart from that, Richard Richardson had remained in a time warp. The sleeves of his shirt were still turned back to midway between wrist and elbow, the collar was unbuttoned and the nightmare necktie, unaccountably smudged with ash, was loosened. He even wore grey shoes, which had not been fashionable twenty years ago or at any period in history.

'God, you've aged,' he roared at McBride. 'Has it really been thirty-five years since I saw you?'

McBride had been prepared for a jibe. 'No. Judging by the clothes you've got on, it was only yesterday. Still wearing the safari-suit at the weekends?'

'Still the smart-ass, I see,' Richardson replied quickly. 'At least I continue to get my name in the papers. Can't say I've noticed much of yours of late – unless, of course, you count the free plug we gave you and your book. Haven't read it yet, by the way. I'm holding off for a couple of days until the price is slashed and it hits the bargain shops. Might even wait until next week when I'll be able to pick it up in Oxfam.'

The exchanges continued all the way up in the lift to the editorial floor, normal conversation commencing only when McBride looked directly at his companion for the first time and asked, 'How are you, Richard?'

He did not expect the response he received. 'Crap. But who wants to hear that?' Richard struggled with a smile and unexpectedly put an arm round McBride's shoulder. 'Look, sorry about not picking up on any of your messages. I'd heard you were going to be making an appearance in Waterstone's but I had to go out of town on a job. By the time I got back, I assumed you'd left. I was going to give you a bell in London in a day or two. Anyway, great to see you – we'll grab a pint later. In the meantime, are you going to tell me what's brought you to the great citadel of truth where pale-faced scribes toil for a pittance?'

McBride shook his head at the line he'd heard Richardson use a dozen times. 'Can't beat the old ones. Actually, it's the old ones I've come to see – not your collection of decrepit women but *The Courier* files.' He tried to sound casual. 'Any chance of half an hour in the file room?'

There was practically a click when Richardson's head jerked round. 'Easily arranged, old son. Anything special I can help you with?' It was his turn to appear laid-back.

McBride shrugged. 'No. Thanks all the same. I just want to have a look at some old stuff I did for the paper years ago for a bit of a feature I'm trying to work up. Nothing very exciting, I'm afraid.' He knew Richardson hadn't been convinced but it was as much as he was getting.

Five minutes later, he was alone in an extremely cold basement room surrounded by the history of a city. Everything worth recording, and much which wasn't, about what had happened in Dundee and the surrounding area was contained in the once-white but now ochre pages of the bound volumes that were stretching before him. He quickly located the one he required and feverishly flicked over the pages until he came to the murder trial report of Bryan Gilzean's case.

Although he hadn't been sure what he'd expected to find, he was disappointed with what was there. As he had suspected, the largest extraction had been a photograph of Alison Brown, evidently taken when she had been a bridesmaid at a wedding. The other piece of the report, which had so meticulously been removed from the file in the Central Library, could not, on the face of it, have been more ordinary or unexceptional. Had they not been so precisely sliced out, the missing three and a half sentences could have been selected at random.

McBride gazed at the words in bewilderment, even reading them out aloud to make sense of why someone had gone to such extremes to excise them. He gave up after several minutes, even more baffled than when he'd seen them for the first time. Taking the notebook he never left home without from his jacket pocket, he carefully copied every detail of the text into a new page.

The expunged passage, which started midway through a sentence, read:

> . . . though this is not unique. These activities happen from time to time and can be confusing. Care has to be taken to ensure a dispassionate analysis and conclusion. It wouldn't be the first time someone got it wrong and it won't be the last.

The words were those of Dr Christopher Rae, a forensic scientist, and had been spoken by him during his testimony for the prosecution. He had examined the corpse of Alison Brown and his evidence had been instrumental in the Crown achieving such a swift and unanimous guilty verdict. He could be said to have been Bryan Gilzean's executioner.

McBride studied the context in which the expert witness had used the words and noted that the doctor had been speaking generally, making broad references to the removal of DNA samples and the need to avoid contamination. The information didn't help.McBride shook his head in frustration once more, closed the file and replaced it on its metal, utilitarian shelf. Then, before he found himself sharing the same fate as brass monkeys, he left the silent, bone-chilling file room.

Back upstairs, the air-conditioned newsroom was a hubbub of chatter and ringing telephones. More than fifty reporters and sub-editors, all starting to write and package the words that would appear on the next morning's breakfast tables, were in varying stages of stress. Later the same day, the different editions of the paper would be gathered and taken away to be given their own place in the file room.

Richard Richardson was just submerging himself in a think piece about the extravagances of the Scottish Parliament, a theme he explored at least once a month. It did not matter how often he wrote about the subject, there never seemed to be a shortage of material. He looked up, still deep in crusader mode, as McBride approached.

Double Dick's eloquence occasionally deserted him. 'See those bastards in Edinburgh?' he said with venom. 'They spend our dosh like water. And what do we get for it – sweet Fanny Adams. They're a shower of useless pricks – and that includes the women.'

He remembered who was with him and the red cloud lifted. 'Sorry, Campbell, old son, you have no idea of these parasites. They get me going every time. Find what you wanted?' He was getting interested again.

'Yes – more or less,' McBride replied with an air of offhandedness. 'It was useful to remind myself why I was the star man in the old days.'

Richardson almost growled. 'Star man, my backside. Good to see you still have a sense of humour. Anything else you need before we kick you out?'

McBride had hoped to hear that. 'Thanks for reminding me. Can I have a couple of minutes on a terminal to check something on the Web?'

'Help yourself – but, if it's porn you're after, forget it. Our systems are crawling with firewalls.' Richardson pointed at a row of blank screens awaiting the arrival of the evening shift. 'Take your pick.'

McBride chose the one furthest away. Then he accessed a little-known people-tracer website and keyed in the name Adam Gilzean. Five seconds later he had his address.

Richardson, meanwhile, had reverted to his jackboot assault on anyone associated with Holyrood and barely lifted his head as McBride, his mission completed, approached.

'That's at least two pints you owe me,' Richardson said into his computer screen. 'If you've no objections, I'll collect them tonight.'

'You're on. Still The Fort?'

'Where else? I'll be released from the salt mine about eight. Now, piss off and let a real star get on with illuminating the masses.'

Two seconds after the lift doors closed behind McBride, the man he would be sharing a drink with rose from his desk and moved quickly to the computer terminal which had just been vacated. His fingers ran expertly over the keys and swiftly clicked on Internet Explorer's History icon to learn which page had last been accessed.

8

By the time the two were reunited in The Fort, 8 p.m. was long past and McBride was growing weary. He had revisited all of Dundee FC's European Cup triumphs with John Black, who, if pressed, would probably have been able to name every family member of every player in each of the teams. He was a human encyclopaedia on the matches. Click the remote and he moved instantly from game to game, effortlessly replaying in precise sequence every one of the moments when his beloved Dark Blues swept up the park. Listening to him may have been tedious but it was at least restful. It was not necessary to speak, even if there had been an opportunity. All that was required was an occasional nod in appreciation or a sharp intake of breath at the beauty of what had taken place on the football pitch.

Richardson barged through the swing doors at the exact point when Dundee had scored their eighth goal against Cologne on the way to the semi-final, a memory that always brought Black close to the point of breakdown. Sometimes he was forced to turn his back on his listener lest the tear welling its way to the surface was detected.

The emotion of the moment was lost on Richardson, who was loudly apologising about his lack of punctuality while still ten feet away. 'Forgive me, old son,' he called out over the heads of a group who were also squeezing their way to the bar. 'The bastard sub-editors who masquerade as journalists were playing their usual little game of not understanding some of my finer phrases, which is hardly surprising given their lack of education. You'd think they'd find jobs more appropriate to their abilities, like on a building site.'

Long before he arrived at the counter, McBride was aware of the heavy smell of tobacco smoke fitting like an invisible shroud over Richardson. He may have been running late but he'd still found time for a last cigarette outside before joining the other forced abstainers inside.

'Real good of you to turn up, Richard,' said McBride, elaborately pushing back his jacket sleeve to look at the time. 'Just in time for a nightcap.'

'OK, sorry, sorry. Want a whisky to go with the pint I'm about to get you?' he offered by way of compensation.

McBride shook his head, declining the short and in resignation at his friend's lateness. 'Haven't touched the hard stuff since I started trying to run marathons. We finely honed athletes have to watch these things.' He knew this would trigger a predictable response and was not disappointed.

'Christ, another marathon bore. I remember when you used to have two fags going at the same time in the office, usually when you were struggling to find one of your "masterly" intros to a story. Some of them were that laboured you went through the best part of a packet.'

It was McBride who was first to break off the cut and thrust. 'So, what's all this about you feeling crap? This is not the "Tricky Dickie" I used to know. Some woman been giving you a hard time? Or is it a case of you not giving them a hard enough time? Have you considered Viagra?'

McBride's sparkling wit did not meet with the expected response. His drinking partner flushed and, for a moment, his gaze dropped. Then he fixed McBride with a despairing stare. 'You're hardly the person to be giving lectures on relationships with women.'

McBride didn't need to be a clairvoyant to appreciate that this topic was going nowhere. 'Take it easy, old mate – just extracting the urine. More to the point, where are the decent places to eat in Dundee these days? I've barely had an edible meal since I arrived.' He knew he could not have chosen safer ground. Next to haranguing politicians, Richardson's favourite subject was food. He could spend almost as long discussing it as he did devouring it.

For five minutes McBride was given an unwanted rundown on every new restaurant and hotel that had opened in the city in the preceding twenty years. It was a price worth paying for the mood of conviviality to return.

Having worked his way through the deficiencies in most of their menus, Richardson suddenly chose to drop the matter before reaching his ultimate in haute cuisine conversation, desserts. 'So, Campbell, what's this I hear about you and Adam Gilzean? My spies tell me you have business with him. True or false?'

It was one of the oldest tricks in the reporter's handbook. Change the subject without warning and watch for the spontaneous response of the person you've just wrong-footed.

McBride was just as accomplished. 'Been keeping your ear to the ground, eh?' he replied with what he hoped passed for nonchalance. 'Business would be too strong a word. He dropped me a line about my book, telling me his son is an innocent man. That's it really. Don't suppose that comes as any news because I gather he was a regular in the letters column on the same subject.'

'Correct. He became a bit of a pain in the behind after a while. Don't know who he thought he was kidding with all his protestations that his murderous son was some kind of saint. I wouldn't waste any time on him – he's just one of the regulars that everyone avoids.'

The dismissal of Adam Gilzean as a newspaper-office crank prompted long-forgotten memories for McBride. Every local paper attracts the oddballs with axes – most of them exceedingly blunt – to grind and when their letters are no longer published, they turn up in person at reception. Then they start phoning, usually at the times when normal people are asleep. Reporters would rather have their eyes poked out by red-hot needles than permit the number of their direct line or e-mail address to fall into the hands of such individuals.

McBride reflected that, although his bookstore conversation with Adam Gilzean had been hostile and one-sided, it had also been brief – a concept utterly unknown to the eccentrics who inhabit newspaper-office reception areas. Whatever Gilzean was, McBride told himself, he was no crank.

'You're probably right.' He shrugged, having no desire to contradict Richardson. 'I'd forgotten people like that existed.'

Richardson tapped the bottom of his empty glass on the bar and coughed theatrically. 'Going without a cigarette is bad enough. Didn't know I was also in a desert with no oasis.'

McBride held two fingers up to John Black, who was at the end of the bar struggling to cope with a group of loud women who appeared to have no idea what they wanted to drink or who might be paying for them. The man who owned

The Fort grimaced and gestured back with two fingers of his own but started to pull a couple of pints anyway.

'How long do we have the pleasure of your company for, then?' Richardson suddenly asked. 'What's next on your high-flying agenda?'

McBride hesitated, genuinely uncertain but unwilling to open the subject up. 'How long is a piece of string?' he replied easily. 'There's not a lot going on at the moment so I'll probably hang around for a day or two taking in the sights then head back down for Christmas. Depends if they want me to sign any more books in the area.'

They drank together for another hour then shared a taxi back into Dundee. McBride was dropped at the Apex Hotel before the cab headed north up Lochee Road and turned into a cul-de-sac on the slopes of the Law, the hill which dominates the city's skyline and which had given McBride the title for his best-selling book. Richardson got out of the taxi and entered the newly built block of flats where he occupied a top-floor apartment.

From its main window, he could see out over the river to Fife, the pinprick lights of the late night traffic on the Tay Road Bridge and the Apex sitting on the waterfront. He gazed at the architecturally challenged hotel and wondered how long McBride would remain in the city and whether they would become friends again.

9

Snow was still falling when McBride arrived outside the home of Adam Gilzean.

In central Dundee, seven miles away, the early morning traffic had turned it into the kind of grey slush that made you wish you'd never got out of bed but, there, in the countryside, he was in the middle of a scene on one of the Christmas cards that filled the shops. Fields that were usually postage stamps stretched endlessly white and only the telegraph poles marked where they finished and the hidden hedgerows began.

Tyre tracks told him he hadn't been the first to use the road that day but, after turning off the main highway and heading up the hill towards the cottage, he hadn't passed another vehicle. Evidently the locals had more sense than he did. He didn't care. Fresh, out-of-town snow and the silence that accompanied it always made him feel like one of the last people on earth, which wasn't a bad experience if you had to spend most of your life in London.

Adam Gilzean had probably chosen the location of his new home for different reasons, he thought. If your son had been banged up for the murder of a young woman who'd never done anyone any harm, your neighbours weren't all that likely to be offering a cup of sugar. Moving away seemed a sensible option.

He had selected well. The cottage was thirty yards off the road and the nearest house was quarter of a mile away. Nothing stood between it and the main route down into Monifieth and McBride realised that Adam Gilzean, if he was at home, had probably seen him coming for the last five minutes as he fought with the snow all the way up the hill. The swiftness with which he answered McBride's single press of the doorbell confirmed the theory.

But whoever Gilzean had been expecting to see, it was not the man facing him. His gasp of surprise practically burst from him and he seemed to momentarily lose his ability to speak.

McBride broke the silence. 'Mr Gilzean – I thought it would be best if we had a chat. I hope you don't mind me turning up like this but it seemed the thing to do.'

'How did you know where I lived?' Gilzean stumbled out. It was an automatic question and he didn't trouble to wait for any kind of answer, even an evasive one, before drawing himself quickly together. 'Yes, yes, come in.' He pulled the door wider, gesturing McBride in out of the snow that was starting to fall heavier than ever.

For a few moments, they pointlessly discussed the weather, the way awkward strangers do, even those with important topics in mind. The fact that the outdoor conditions might, for once, have made the climate a legitimate conversation piece was still an irrelevance between the two men standing eyeing each other in the short hallway.

Gilzean pushed open the fifteen-panel glass door leading into the main room of his home.

'Let me have your coat. Take a seat. Coffee or tea?'

'Coffee, thanks – just a drop of milk and touch of sugar,' McBride responded, pulling off the faded-red all-weather jacket he'd transported halfway round the world with him and dropping into a two-seater sofa.

Gilzean disappeared back into the hall, taking the coat with him, and McBride looked around the room.

It was unexpectedly modern and had been the subject of much recent renovation since ceasing to be home to several generations of farm workers. The walls, which should have bulged unevenly after a century of settlement, were as flat as a billiard table, tastefully decorated in shades of cream and adorned with a dozen paintings, most of them originals and all of them in fashionable frames. The two armchairs, like the sofa McBride occupied, were taupe and placed either side of an efficient wood-burning stove. It was not the residence of someone lacking taste or money.

When Gilzean returned, he carried before him a silver tray bearing two cups of coffee, four scones, fresh butter and a small pot of jam – more style. Adam Gilzean was even less like the photo-fit of a newspaper-office's reception area nutter.

He spoke quietly. 'Did you get the note I left at Waterstone's?'

McBride nodded.

'I'm glad. Sorry again about that business when you were doing the signings. It just gets on top of me. Thanks for taking the trouble to drop round. But I'm not really sure why you came. You wanted a chat?'

McBride gave up trying to spread the unyielding butter on to his scone. 'Yes, though I'm not all that certain either about why I'm here. It just seemed necessary, in a way, to go through things with you.'

'I think you're right. So, what can I tell you?'

McBride pushed a hand into the inside pocket of his jacket and produced a micro-cassette recorder with its innards held in place by yellow tape. He moved his coffee cup and placed the device on the table between them. 'Do you mind if I switch this on? Force of habit. Saves taking notes and, anyway, the old shorthand isn't what it once was.'

'Be my guest.'

McBride depressed the red record button. 'Can I start by asking a couple of silly questions?'

Gilzean arched both eyebrows and motioned his head in agreement. 'What do you want to know?'

'OK. First, did you also send me a letter via my publishers in Edinburgh?'

Gilzean appeared puzzled. He shook his head several times. 'Absolutely not. What kind of letter?'

McBride ignored the question. 'Right. This may sound strange but did you go into the Central Library in Dundee and cut something out of a copy of *The Courier*.'

His host looked even more baffled. 'I haven't the faintest idea what you're speaking about. Cut what? Why would I?'

'It doesn't matter. I just needed to know these things. Sorry to seem so mysterious but, for reasons I won't go into, it was important to ask. More to the point – would you like to tell me why your son is innocent?'

McBride's words had the same effect as producing the combination to a locked vault. The perplexed look on the face of the man in the armchair opposite vanished, he leaned forward almost in disbelief and eagerly started to speak, retrieving the sentences he had grown weary of uttering three years earlier.

'He's innocent because he didn't do it! And if you want to

know why I know that, it's because he was with me, sitting in my home, when he was supposed to be killing Alison. He was by my side for more than four hours. We chatted and watched television and had supper together. There was no way he could have done it. He was miles away!'

'That's what you told the court when you gave evidence. But the jury didn't believe you. Why should I?'

'Because it's true.'

'Prove it.'

'I've tried to do that from the minute he was arrested. But how am I supposed to prove something like my son visiting me when no one else was there? I know folk – the jury as well – think I was just covering up for him, the way a father would.'

He raised his hand and pointed at a bookcase on the wall behind the sofa where McBride sat. It contained several photographs of the same young man, obviously his son, and numerous books, the most prominent of which was a Bible. 'As God is my witness, Bryan is not guilty.'

McBride nodded understandingly but thought that, in any other context, the gesture might have seemed overdramatic. 'Why did he come round that night?' he asked. 'Not many sons would spend four hours chatting with their dad when they could be in the pub or with a girlfriend instead. It's not exactly what young folk do, is it?'

'No. But that night was special. He's a good son, very good. It was two years to the day since my wife – his mother – had died. He knew how I'd be feeling and came to help me along. We helped each other, as it turned out, just the way we did exactly a year before. I don't know if you've ever suffered the bereavement of someone close to you, Mr McBride, but it doesn't go away quickly. It doesn't go away at all, if you must know.' He was on the edge of tears.

McBride looked gently into the eyes of the figure facing him.

'It doesn't. But what you do is hang on to the good memories and, bit by bit, it gets a little easier as time passes.' There was no need for McBride to explain how he knew this. *How could he tell him that the only way, in the early years, is to hit the 'off' switch in your head so that you blot out the thought of the child you loved because of the pain that comes with knowing he has vanished from your life forever? How can you make someone understand the paradoxes that the death of a small boy throws up? There's the rage at your God for letting it happen so you reject him as cruel or non-existent. But the only way through it is to be glad for every day the two of you shared. So you thank the God you deserted for the gift he gave you. And you pray to the omnipotent being who probably isn't there that he'll take better care of your child in heaven than he did on earth and will keep him safe until the day he reunites you.*

McBride became aware that Adam Gilzean was watching him closely, trying to work out what was in his mind. He said firmly, 'As I see it, there's one – or rather two – things that get in the way of what you've told me. If Bryan wasn't there, how did one of his hairs get on to the tie that choked Alison? Then there were his fingerprints on the wine glass – and the intercourse. You can hardly blame the jury for not quite believing you, can you?'

Adam Gilzean looked down into his half-empty coffee cup, saying nothing for so long that McBride was on the point of repeating his questions.

'Do you think I haven't asked myself that a thousand times, Mr McBride?' He shook his head wearily. 'Look, he lived in the flat half the time. Of course some of his hairs were bobbing about. And it's not too surprising that his fingerprints were on a lot of the stuff there. Anybody's house would be the same. It's hardly enough to imprison someone for life, is it?'

McBride did not answer. 'What about the sex?' he asked.

Gilzean was dismissive. 'The two of them having intercourse was hardly unique. Of course there would be traces.'

'That wasn't the way the court saw it, Mr Gilzean.' McBride was trying hard to reconcile sympathy with realism. 'Looked at from their point of view, one and one makes two and two makes guilty.'

Gilzean slowly shook his head. 'I'm not stupid. I can put myself in their place but they were wrong. If you don't believe Bryan is innocent, what are you doing here?

It was the best question of them all. McBride did not respond and the silence was broken only by the soft whirring of the recorder. Eventually, he switched it off, smiled and said, 'Fair point. But I have been known to be wrong.' He rose from his seat. 'I'd best head back before I get snowed in.'

Gilzean seemed reluctant to break off the conversation. He pushed himself slowly to his feet, starting to speak but hesitatingly. 'Of course – I'll get your coat.' He took a step towards the door into the hall but turned to face McBride again. He spoke haltingly. 'Will you go to see Bryan? I can easily arrange it. Maybe he'll convince you. He'd be extremely happy to see you – extremely.'

He looked eagerly at his visitor. 'It would mean a lot to him – me too.'

McBride reached out and put a soft hand on Adam Gilzean's arm. 'I'd be delighted,' he said quietly. 'In fact, I was going to suggest it. Just fix it up and give me a ring with the details.' He wrote in his notebook and tore a page out, handing it to the pleased man by his side. 'That's my mobile. It's never switched off.'

They shook hands as they parted and Gilzean held his grip. 'I'm very glad you came, Mr McBride. You're making me feel hopeful for the first time in more than three years.'

The snow had gone off, the heavy sky giving way to a sharpness of light that world-traveller McBride only ever experienced in Scotland – and the further north he went, the brighter it seemed to become. He stood by the car door and sucked in the panorama extending before him. At the bottom of the hill, beyond the white roofs of Monifieth, the River Tay sparkled as it joined the North Sea. Behind their seamless junction, the sands of Kinshaldy Beach, where he used to run, lay untouched by snow.

He took in the scene for several minutes and, for the first time since arriving back from London, asked himself why he had left the area. His fingers curled round the tape recorder in his pocket, the way a child clutches a security blanket. It didn't really matter that he knew the reasons. It wasn't an occasion for logic.

He at last got into his car and thought that, like his arrival, Adam Gilzean had probably watched his departure performance with curiosity. He thought about that too for a few moments and came to the conclusion that the man whose son was languishing in Perth Prison had undoubtedly also gazed out over the vista in contemplation many times.

10

It was only when he arrived back into the centre of Dundee that McBride remembered what he had been trying to forget, that it was Christmas Eve.

In City Square, the town's official tree blazed with light in the falling darkness, doing its best, but not quite succeeding, to overcome the handicap of being positioned behind a pavilion of fairground dodgem cars that no one was using. Last-minute shoppers scurried between stores, their hands full of panic-purchase presents and their feet sodden by the slush banked up on the pavements.

He looked at their tight, impatient faces and smiled to himself, knowing it would be the same in every city in the country at that moment – it was the part of the one day of the year when the last thing on anyone's mind was peace on earth and goodwill to men. That altruism only started to kick in later the same night when the shopping was finally over and the living-room curtains had been pulled shut to wrap families together in a warm glow of seasonal togetherness.

McBride once adored the time and the promise it held. Now all he hoped for was its swift passing and, with it, the memories of the last day on earth of Simon, the most magical little boy who had ever been born.

After the accident, neither he nor Caroline could find the courage to open or dispose of the early Christmas presents they had bought for their son. They lay unopened under the tree at home for six weeks before they took the tree down. The presents, still in their shiny Santa Claus wrappings, were put away in the attic, to be dealt with at some future time that never came. As far he knew, they were still in the same state in Caroline's new attic.

When McBride made his way to the Apex Hotel, the office Christmas lunch parties were in full swing though it was now closer to teatime. He watched the procession of inebriated women weaving back and forth through reception and, not for the first time, he wondered why the opposite sex appeared to think they could really only dress up if they removed as many clothes as possible. He decided the same principle probably applied at The Fort on Christmas Eve and resolved to go there that evening. With luck, he would find distracting company.

His instincts didn't let him down. The bar had been jammed since lunchtime and, whenever a group departed, the same number were admitted from the queue outside. Most of the women, indoors and out, were semi-naked and most of the little they did wear was black. That was another thing about celebrating ladies – they always wanted to dress up in the same colour they used for funerals. The species created a lot of discrepancies in logic but that was what made them interesting – that and their other differences.

John Black was too busy making money to chat so McBride searched for a face that might be even remotely familiar. One spotted him first. 'Campbell, Campbell . . .' a voice called out from a column of bodies blocking his way to the bar. A hand lifted up at the second shout of his name and McBride detected who was trying to attract his attention.

It was not someone he recognised at first. He squinted through the mob at the smiling man beckoning at him and tried to imagine more hair of a different colour on the balding head and fewer double chins on the purple face. Even then, it took him several moments to identify Daniel Ford, a court reporter on the *Evening Telegraph* and the undisputed bore of the journalistic community twenty years earlier. At that time, Ford was universally shunned by every reporter in town, except those in search of a cure for insomnia. He was teetotal but had an overwhelming addiction – to himself. He hung around bars for no other reason than to discuss Daniel Ford and to offer his views on the topics on which he was an expert, which was every subject in the universe. The passage of time had not changed matters.

He squeezed through the rows of revellers to arrive at McBride's side. 'On your own?' he said by way of welcome, adding, unsurprisingly, 'Me too.'

McBride resisted the temptation to pretend he was someone else. 'Didn't recognise you at first, Dan,' he said. 'How's business?'

The figure moved closer, his halitosis forcing McBride to edge backwards. 'Good, good,' he replied. 'What about you? Just written a book, I see. Selling well?'

Before McBride could offer a reply, the man, who did not understand humility, launched into an instant follow-up. 'Funny you should have done a book. I've been contemplating one for years. Folk keep telling me that with all my experience of life in the courts – and in general, of course – that I'm capable of a best-seller. What do you think? They're probably right, actually. As a journo yourself, you know we get around a bit – maybe me and you more than most others. Do you think I should give it a go? The more I think about it, the more I'm beginning to realise it's the thing to do.'

McBride had glazed over. Even the forest of hair sprouting from both of Ford's nostrils had ceased to transfix him. He knew all that was required was an occasional appreciative nod. His mind turned to the time he'd been in The Fort with Richard Richardson and he interrupted Ford's incessant flow. 'Do you see anything of Double Dick these days? I met up with him the other night but he seemed a bit subdued. Are things OK with him?'

Ford shrugged a shoulder. 'Women problems. Fell out badly with one, I believe. God knows why. But it seems to have set him back. That's one of the reasons I don't get involved with them – in the end they just give you grief. Me? I prefer male company – not that I'm queer or anything, you understand. It's just that you get more conversation out of a guy. We have more to say to each other.'

He droned on, impervious to McBride's total disinterest in his self-obsessed monologue. After half an hour and at the point where McBride was about to remember a pressing appointment elsewhere, the *Evening Telegraph* reporter spotted another target across the bar. He interrupted himself in mid flow to call out the newcomer's name. 'Andy,' he shouted over the heads of the two rows of drinkers between them. Andy was too late in trying to make himself look invisible. Before he could vanish into the throng, Ford had begun pushing his way towards him.

'Sorry, Campbell,' he said as he departed, 'must go – haven't seen Andy in ages. Been great getting all your news. We'll need to meet up again and I'll give you an update on what's been happening in my world. Give me a ring at the office sometime soon and we can fix up to eat together.'

McBride barely nodded, knowing his lack of enthusiasm would not register with Daniel Ford and that he could never be hungry enough to want to share a table with the hairy-nosed journo.

He was contemplating his next move when a woman's voice broke in at his elbow. 'Excuse me,' it said, 'are you Campbell McBride? Did you write that book?'

McBride turned to find a small blonde smiling up at him. She held a drink in one hand and a half-eaten sandwich in the other. She was early thirties and over-rounded but attractive if you liked women with too much make-up. Her perfume was unspectacular and revived distant memories of an interesting, if unemotional, encounter with a hotel receptionist in Barcelona but at least she'd made the effort.

'The very same,' he replied, fixing her with a worked-at admiring gaze. 'If we've met before it had to be in heaven.' He was almost ashamed at dredging that one up but it was Christmas, the mood was easy and there wasn't a female alive who didn't like a bit of flattery, even when it was from the Stone Age.

She yawned mockingly, giggling at the same time. 'No. It was in Waterstone's. I saw you signing books. Actually, I bought one a few days later as a Christmas present for my dad. If I'd known I was going to bump into you, I'd have brought it with me for a signature.'

They spoke for another hour and that was as serious as the conversation got. Her friends in black dresses called her a groupie and she laughed. Then she took McBride back to the flat in Craigiebank where she lived by herself.

He didn't ask why she was also alone on Christmas Eve

or why her tidy, anonymous apartment contained so little evidence that it was the festive season. He didn't care. The last thing he wanted to do was to open up her particular can of worms when he had demons of his own.

His selfishness extended to his performance in bed. He took what he wanted and, after claiming his moment of satisfaction, his instinct was to go as swiftly as politeness would allow. However, he stayed – not out of consideration but because the soulless room in the Apex was a worse alternative. So he made a weak joke about it not being quite the time of the year for a second coming, embraced her briefly, then turned on to his side, trying to convince both of them that he had fallen asleep.

The next morning the strangers observed the ritual of a breakfast that consisted of coffee without milk or meaningful conversation. McBride, feigning the need to deal with some urgent business back at his hotel, declined the offer of a shower and dressed quickly. At the door on the way out, he held the woman whose name he was struggling to remember in his arms and squeezed her gently.

'That was a great night,' he said with as much sincerity as he could muster. 'Thanks for everything – really. Give me your number and I'll ring you before I leave town.'

She scribbled quickly on a scrap of paper on the table in the hallway. 'My pleasure – any time. Hope the book goes well. The name's Carol, by the way.'

Then they remembered at the same time what day it was. 'Merry Christmas!' they said in unison.

McBride was halfway down the garden path before the significance of his bed-mate's name hit him and he wondered whether she was being serious or had more wit than he gave her credit for – not that it made any difference either way.

11

It took McBride less than an hour to realise that the only thing worse than spending Christmas Day with the wrong person was to celebrate it alone.

He'd given up trying to find an available cab and, as he made his way on foot back to the Apex, every house he passed seemed to be packed with happy families. The only people out walking were couples in their party clothes, arms linked and carrying bags heavy with parcels, as they made their way to share company with those behind the brightly decorated windows.

McBride turned off the main road and crossed into the dock area where the only pedestrians he would be likely to encounter would be far-from-home seamen, who did not celebrate Christmas, making their way to and from ships. It lengthened his journey but shortened the time he had to kill.

Back in his hotel room, he changed out of the clothing of the night before, conscious of how strongly it smelled of mediocre perfume. Then he showered, dressed again and called reception to ask for his evening meal to be sent to his room in a few hours' time. There was not the kind of money on earth that would have persuaded him to sit at a solitary table surrounded by laughing hordes in party hats pulling Christmas crackers.

He left the hotel immediately afterwards and drove purposefully away from the empty city centre, taking a route that was familiar but which he hadn't followed for a handful of years. He journeyed for thirty minutes before pulling up at the gates to a park. McBride sat in contemplation for a moment then walked inside. After a hundred yards, he halted at a deserted children's play area. He gazed vacantly at the frost-covered roundabout and climbing apparatus. Then he sat on a swing, pushing himself gently back and forward, his eyes still directed at his surroundings but seeing the past.

It was where he and Caroline had taken Simon and where their son had always laughed loudest in games with young playmates. It was also the spot where they had gone with his ashes after driving north with them from Kent. The choice of location hadn't been difficult to make. All three of them had experienced happiness there and it was a place where there would always be other children to keep him company, even if they went home afterwards and he remained behind.

McBride tried to imagine how Caroline might be spending Christmas, but couldn't.

He stayed on the swing until his hands and feet had lost all feeling and darkness dropped over him.

12

The next morning, while the cleaners and chambermaids were still doing their best to remove the debris of the night before, McBride checked out of the Apex. He drove the short distance along the shore to the airport, dropped off his hired car and bought a seat on the London flight that departed twenty minutes later. He was one of only three passengers on the plane. The other two were obviously together but had apparently fallen out. They did not speak to each other or to McBride, which suited him – he had things to occupy his mind.

He had to decide, for instance, how he would explain to the news desks of at least three national papers why he would not be accepting any assignments for the foreseeable future and that he would be moving out of London to live in Dundee again. Whatever explanation he gave, he knew it would not be the truth, which was that he had become convinced an innocent man was languishing in prison for a murder he did not commit, though he had absolutely no evidence for that belief.

And nor could he tell them that he had examined the details of the case many months earlier when he was doing the research for a book and yet had found none of the circumstances exceptional. It would be safer, if he wanted to be offered well-paid employment in the future, to find a more acceptable excuse.

He would tell them he was taking a short sabbatical. Some would see that as a euphemism for laziness, of course, but at least it sounded semi-professional. Besides, if the best possible scenario – reporter springs convicted killer – came to pass, he would have one helluva story to sell them. McBride smiled wryly at the thought.

When he arrived back at the Maida Vale flat, which he had never considered home, he exhaled with relief. Nothing seemed to have been smashed and a quick inspection of his wardrobe revealed that no sleeves had been cut off his jackets. More importantly, the Trek still hung gleaming and unmarked on its hook in the small room that doubled as an office and bike shed. Sarah had evidently moved on to pastures new, taking her promise of destructive reprisals with her.

He was still checking for damage in the more obscure parts of the apartment when his mobile sounded 'Strangers in the Night', the song he shared with Caroline.

McBride did not recognise the caller's number but the voice on the line was instantly familiar. Adam Gilzean was apologetic. 'Mr McBride? Sorry to trouble you on Boxing Day, while you're probably still recovering from a riotous Christmas, but it's about the visit to Bryan. I went to see him yesterday and he can't believe you might be prepared to speak to him. Actually, he's ecstatic at the thought and said I couldn't have taken him a better Christmas present. Will you go?'

It was a plea, not a question. McBride could sense Adam Gilzean's anxiety as he silently awaited a response. He replied with matching gentleness. 'Yes, of course, Mr Gilzean. I meant what I said. Can you give me a few days to sort things out? I'm back in London – I've got some stuff I need to do – after that, I'll be heading back up as quickly as I can. We can get everything organised then.'

'That's wonderful. Thank you, thank you.' Gilzean rang quickly off, as though any delay might bring a change of mind from McBride.

It did not take McBride more than forty-eight hours to temporarily close down his life in Maida Vale. In fact, it surprised him just how loose the connections were. Everything he required to transfer his existence to another country fitted easily into the back of his estate car. Reporters do not travel with bulky paraphernalia. What cannot be fitted into jacket and trouser pockets goes into the bag with the laptop. He loaded the car with more than he thought he needed and it was still half empty – even with the Trek carefully protected by a heavy-duty winter duvet.

McBride did not relish the 400-mile journey north. Although he never acknowledged it, he was not a good driver and his short fuse burned at its brightest when he was behind the wheel. His impatience had led to more roadside confrontations that he would admit to. The only reason he possessed a vehicle the size of a Ford Mondeo Estate was to transport his cycle without having to first dismantle it – a simple task which he found difficult.

The trip to Scotland was relatively uneventful, thanks mainly to the absence of heavy lorries, most of whose drivers were still on holiday. McBride had sworn at no more than twenty other road-users all the way north and congratulated himself on his unaccustomed restraint. His most practised motion had been to repeatedly switch off the radio at the sound of seasonal music.

He returned to the Apex on his first night back in Dundee. The following day, he took up the tenancy of a furnished flat. The choice of its location had been straightforward. It was on the Esplanade at Broughty Ferry, three minutes' walk from The Fort and overlooking the River Tay, the banks of which presented the finest running routes in the entire city. Even without a story to chase, he knew he would be content.

13

If it's possible to imagine a smell that combines anticipation with uncertainty and anger with sex, then that's what rises to meet you in The Tank at Perth Prison. It hits you full on the first time you meet it and you know you'll never forget it.

The officers who patrol The Tank stopped noticing it long ago, as they did the rest of the aromas that make every penal institution smell the same. They experience it three times daily, every time a group of inmates are brought there to wait before moving through the system to meet their visitors for sixty minutes in the big room half a dozen locks away.

The faces of the prisoners who sit expectantly in the brown seats round the walls of The Tank tell different stories. Mostly it's excitement at the prospect of the brief reunion with the woman they spend all of their waking time thinking about. Sometimes it's anxiety about the kind of minor matter you'd shrug off on the outside but which makes your head want to explode when you're banged up.

The worst thing that can happen in The Tank is to be told your visitor hasn't turned up and you're left alone on a plastic seat after everyone else has moved out. Society demands most of what you have when it locks you away. Remove the last link with the real world and you'd be as well dead.

The last thing Bryan Gilzean was feeling was any resemblance to a corpse. The scent he was giving off was hope. He rested his head against the cream-painted wall in The Tank, gazed into the middle distance of the afternoon and began to dream.

As the man serving the life sentence permitted himself to contemplate freedom, McBride was being subjected to the drawn-out security measures at the Gate Complex, the visitors' section, which fronted the prison. He had remembered previous visits to Her Majesty's penal establishments and travelled light. It cut down on the rigmarole. The less you had with you, the less chance there was to conceal drugs. Life was easier for everyone if you left the bulky clothing and mobile in the car.

It wasn't difficult to recognise those who had also been previous visitors to a jail. Without being asked, they dumped their travelling paraphernalia into the lockers, walked through the metal detectors and raised their arms for the pat-down searches. The real pros opened their mouths and effortlessly rolled their tongues around to prove there was nothing there but spit.

Like Bryan Gilzean, McBride sat back but not to think about liberty – nobody does until it's removed. Just as he had done each time he visited the institutions where you automatically stop at every door because you know it's locked, he reflected on how wretched the existence was for those who entered the Gate Complex.

Apart from two neatly dressed males who he knew would be solicitors, the rest of those on the benches in the waiting room were women, most of whom had spent the previous half hour trying – but failing – to look glamorous. Those who had forgotten the visiting routine could have saved themselves the trouble of tying their hair up. It would just be shaken out under the scrutiny of an officer who knew a ponytail could conceal a wrap.

The ladies who had come to visit evidently shared the same brand of hair dye and bought their ubiquitous denims and flimsy crop-tops in identical budget shops. Poor diets and drug habits ensured that those waiting to greet them would not have much to cling to in their urgent embrace.

As always, McBride experienced a surge of sympathy. He knew that, without exception, these miserable souls would have been forced to use public transport to travel to the prison. Even for those who lived closest, an hour with their man meant an entire day of waiting on railway station platforms and at bus stops. No wonder they looked defeated. They were as much prisoners as their menfolk and the only crime they'd committed was hitching up with the wrong guy.

McBride was among the first to pass through the search tables and, at the last door into the visiting hall, he found his progress halted once more. 'Hold out your left hand, please, palm down.' An officer, who might just as easily have been sitting behind a post-office counter, stamped an invisible mark on the back of his proffered hand. It was a new one on McBride. He raised an eyebrow.

'This way we know who we should be keeping in or letting out,' the officer, who had said the words a thousand times before, explained.

McBride nodded but silently he thought it would have made better sense if you'd been able to see the stamp mark.

He took his place at the numbered table he'd been allocated and, as he waited for all the other visitors to be branded, he ran an eye round the long room. Times were changing. Nothing was ever going to make a prison visiting hall look like anything else but someone with imagination had tried. At one end, there was the usual raised dais with its table and chairs for some of the supervising officers while, incongruously, at the other end, a wall blazed with colour. Its bright Disney characters marked a play-area for children where there was a blackboard and more toys than most of the kids who would use it had ever seen.

Trying hard and nearly succeeding to disguise the heavy steel bars of the only outside wall were a dozen paintings completed by inmates. The most impressive – and depressing – of the bunch was a large canvas depicting a group of prisoners who gazed unsmiling and flat-eyed back at McBride.

After the last visitor was seated, the door at the far end opened and the occupants of The Tank filed in, every one of them eagerly scanning the row of faces seated at the tables.

When Bryan Gilzean walked uncertainly across the room, McBride did not recognise him at first. The photographs filling Adam Gilzean's house showed a young man with a round face, eyes that danced and more rich, dark hair than any male deserved. Taking the seat opposite and extending a hesitant hand was a figure who might have been Adam Gilzean himself. His cheeks had the hollowness of a marathon runner and the close-cropped hair showed spikes of steel that mirrored the pallor of his skin.

For five minutes they spoke pointlessly about the miserable weather as McBride tried to put his companion at ease.

'All I could think of on the way up here was the warm weather, the freedom of the open road and me on my bike,' he said, with all the sensitivity of a charging rhino.

But the tactlessness of his remark was lost on Gilzean, whose thoughts were elsewhere. 'I didn't do it, Mr McBride,' he said, polite conversation gone and emotion suddenly filling his face. 'Honest to God, it wasn't me. I'm rotting away and nobody believes me except my dad. You do believe me, don't you?' His eyes begged for reassurance.

McBride was uncertain how to respond. 'It doesn't really work that way, Bryan,' he said, doing his best to sound reassuring. 'I'm just interested. The only thing I'm sure about is that your dad believes you. He's the one who got me here. Maybe you're kidding him. Are you going to kid me?'

This brought an unexpected but encouraging flash of something approaching anger from the haunted man opposite. 'Christ! Are you another one of them? I've spent more than three years listening to that bilge. I haven't kidded anybody. They're the ones you should be interrogating.' He slapped the palm of a hand on the surface between them and his voice rose loudly above the quiet hum of conversation filling the visiting hall.

One of the half-dozen officers who strolled the room, apparently watching nothing but seeing everything, moved swiftly to the side of the table. 'Take it easy, Bryan,' he said. 'You don't want this cut short, do you?'

The rebuke was unnecessary. The grey-faced man in the blue sweatshirt had recovered his composure as rapidly as he had lost it. He pulled slowly on his nose with heavily stained nicotine fingers. 'Sorry, boss, just got a wee bit excited – no problem.'

McBride nodded in affirmation and the officer retreated, speaking softly into the microphone on his left shoulder. McBride knew that, for the rest of the visit, the person monitoring the bank of screens in the concealed room adjoining the visiting room would fix one of the six ceiling cameras on their table.

He smiled reassuringly across at Gilzean. 'Look, if I didn't think there was at least a chance you're telling the truth, I wouldn't be here. For that matter, I wouldn't even be in Scotland. Keep calm. All I'm saying is that I've been getting vibes about this since your dad buttonholed me in Waterstone's bookstore. I don't even know why I feel this way. Convince me this isn't a waste of everybody's time.'

McBride was aware of the absurdity of the remark. If Gilzean couldn't convince a jury, he could hardly be expected to completely win over a hard-nosed journalist inside an hour. Besides, how do you prove a negative? McBride appreciated he wasn't going to get anything to take to a court of appeal – all he wanted was something to keep his gut feeling happy.

'Why don't you start at the beginning?' He rested back in his seat and glanced up at the black-eyed cameras in their cages, wondering which of them was trained on the table and curious if it would home in for a close-up on Gilzean as he started to recount his version of the night that had brought the meaningful part of his life to an end.

It was an uncomplicated story. He had not been there. In fact, he had not seen Alison for three days previously. On the day which had been her last, they had spoken on the phone and he had told her he would not see her that night either because he needed to visit his father. She had not been particularly happy but had indicated she would pass the evening at the gym they usually attended together.

When Gilzean had finished, McBride asked him the obvious questions. How was it possible that his semen had been found inside her? How did his fingerprints find their way on to a wine glass? And how could one of his hairs be on the tie used to murder her?

The man with the pale, strained face sitting opposite seemed helpless. He looked desperately at McBride. 'I ask myself that every night,' he said. 'We'd had sex three days earlier. Maybe the traces stay that long?'

McBride raised an eyebrow. 'Not unless she hadn't got off her back. What about the wine, the tie?'

'I never drink white wine,' Gilzean said sharply. 'Can't stand it. I'm a beer man and, if forced into wine, I'll only take red. Besides, I'd never seen the glass in my life before.'

'You're about to tell me you never wear a tie either, right?' McBride said.

'Only for special occasions. I am – was – an architect, Mr McBride, working in a small practice. It was very informal. Nobody dressed up.'

'What about all the rows the two of you had? Pretty frequent, by all accounts?'

Gilzean slowly nodded his head. 'I know . . .' He looked over McBride's shoulder. Into the past – remembering. 'They were never as bad as they might have sounded,' he said quietly. 'We were passionate about things . . . just about everything. We got over the arguments quickly – usually in a good way.' He was speaking more to himself than his visitor.

McBride eyed him steadily, lifted his voice to bring him back to the present. 'OK. Two last questions. Did you have any other girlfriends and did she have boyfriends?'

For the first time since they'd met, Bryan Gilzean could not meet McBride's gaze. He hesitated. Stared at the floor. 'No – don't think that was her style.'

'You?'

Gilzean paused again. 'Not really.'

'What does that mean?'

'Nothing serious. Nothing steady. Just the occasional one-nighter. You know how it is . . .' He looked away, embarrassed.

McBride knew exactly how it was but saw no point in enlightening Gilzean about his own sexual habits. He said nothing, just shrugged his shoulders non-committally.

'Right, finish up,' an officer's voice called out from the dais. It signalled the end of visiting hour. The mothers shouted their offspring back from beneath the pictures of Goofy and the Seven Dwarfs and, at the tables, the women reached thin-fingered hands out to grasp those opposite, the need to make physical contact even more desperate. Some of those on both sides of the table struggled with tears.

McBride rose slowly, unsure how to end the meeting. 'I'm glad I came, Bryan,' was the best he could do. 'I'll kick it all around and get back to you.'

The pleading face looked up at him, a mixture of eagerness and uncertainty.

McBride said the word first. 'Promise.'

'Thanks, Mr McBride, thanks.'

On the way towards the door, McBride noticed for the first time that behind the barred windows and disturbing paintings there was an open-air, triangle-shaped visitors' section with picnic benches and a play-area whose centrepiece was a climbing frame. It was standard height but, even if it had been close enough to a wall, it wasn't going to help anyone over. The cold stone surrounding the unexpected oasis rose for fifteen feet and there was another five feet of razor wire on top of that. As play parks went, you were never going to have to worry about your children wandering off.

McBride reached the end of the room and turned, knowing that Bryan Gilzean, who would be kept at his table until the last visitor had left the hall, would have watched his every step. From a distance, the twenty-seven-year-old looked even more like someone approaching middle age. Oddly, when he raised an arm, the wave that came from it resembled the kind you got when you left a child in the school playground for the first time. It reminded him of how Simon had once bade him anxious farewells.

McBride held out his left hand for the ultraviolet lamp to reassure an officer he wasn't an escaping inmate and waved back with the other one. Instinctively, he put his thumb up.

All the way back to Dundee, he wondered how appropriate the gesture had been.

14

McBride had turned off the coastal path that led from the river and was running towards the series of rises that would test his stamina when an unseen hand flicked a switch. Floodlights flashed inside his head and with the light came the blinding certainty that he had been headed in the wrong direction – not in the route he had taken that morning but in the course of his mind ever since he had left the frozen file room of *The Courier*.

The riddle of the missing section of the Bryan Gilzean murder trial report that had taken him up a succession of mental blind alleys and culs-de-sac was finally making some sort of sense. The sentences that had been excised had not been removed by a warped souvenir hunter – they were making a statement. 'The bastard!' he suddenly spat out, oblivious to the astonished looks from a pair of dog walkers. 'He didn't take something away from the library – he left something behind.'

The realisation that he might have cracked the problem that had swirled almost ceaselessly round his head for days took McBride completely by surprise. He had not even been aware that he had been wrestling with it at that moment. With the dawning came physical release. He subconsciously lifted his pace, lengthened his stride and pushed hard up the first, and steepest, of the short hills, feeling the urgency to somehow make use of the new information.

As he ran, McBride inwardly repeated the words that had become etched into his brain, *though this is not unique. These activities happen from time to time and can be confusing. Care has to be taken to ensure a dispassionate analysis and conclusion. It wouldn't be the first time someone got it wrong and it won't be the last.* McBride became convinced that whoever had taken the passage away from the filed newspaper in the Central Library was giving out a message. The more he contemplated its meaning, the more he began to wonder if the most important part wasn't the opening five words – the ones which did not even form a sentence. He cursed himself for not having come to that conclusion the second he laid eyes on them. Unless they had deep significance, why leave them standing alone, sentence-less and otherwise meaningless? 'Christ,' he muttered, 'they should have been in capital letters!'

McBride covered the remaining four miles back to his new flat faster than he would have believed possible. By the time he arrived, the volume of sweat that usually only poured from his body on warm, heavy days was dripping on to the off-white carpet of his bedroom, leaving a trail of damp stains. Instead of following his usual routine of stretching then showering, he hurriedly towelled his face and armpits while simultaneously lifting his mobile with his free hand.

He rang the offices of *The Courier* but did not ask for Richard Richardson. Instead, he requested to be put through to

Cuttings, the department that every newspaper office cannot exist without. As he waited to be connected, he offered a prayer that Gwen Kissock was on duty. Long before the paper had invested in an electronic retrieval system for recovering selected news items, she had performed the same function as fast as any computer, especially when the story being sought related to crime. She was a human encyclopaedia and could have enjoyed a prosperous existence if she had been interested in television quiz shows on the subject. At the very least, she should have become a police officer. Happily, she had done neither and had remained as one of the paper's most valuable but underappreciated assets.

She answered the phone and recognised McBride's voice instantly for she had also been born with a 'photographic' ear. It had been more than a year since they had spoken – back when he had called her from London for assistance with research for his book. 'Hello, Campbell,' she said confidently, before he had a chance to announce himself, 'what do you want this time?' She could also be direct.

'I just wanted to hear your dulcet tones once again,' he replied with what he hoped was humorous charm. 'It's been more than a year and I've been pining.' McBride could almost visualise her raising her eyebrows in feigned exasperation.

She replied, 'Me too but not for you – just for some of the cash you've made from the book I wrote for you.'

'That's part of the reason I'm calling – to arrange a dinner date in the near future. But, just while I'm on, can you do me a quick favour?'

'Keep speaking.'

'Can you dig into that unique mind of yours and tell me if you recall any murders in the area where someone was strangled?'

'Oh, is that all?' she retorted. 'Be more specific. Male or female victim? Solved or unsolved? Timescale?' Gwen was already pressing her memory buttons.

'Probably female. Maybe solved, maybe not. Say, in the last five or six years.' It did not occur to him that what he was asking might just be a touch unreasonable.

'Thanks for the assistance!' She stopped speaking to McBride for more than two minutes but broke the silence with occasional brief discussions with herself. 'Let me think . . . no . . . yes . . . right . . . OK.'

Suddenly she returned to share her deliberations. 'Don't know if this helps but off the top of my head I can think of a half a dozen, maybe eight. Nine if you count a hanging of sorts that was probably suicide.'

She ran through her list. 'There were three in Dundee, one in Perth, one in St Andrews and another one in either Montrose or Brechin, can't remember which but it was in Angus somewhere.'

McBride was grateful but not satisfied. 'Great – but do you have any more details?'

Gwen sighed. 'The best I can do is tell you that I think most of them, but not all, were solved. I'm fairly sure there was no one in the frame for the Fife one and at least one of the Dundee ones.'

'You're a marvel. Can I ask one more thing?'

Before he could expand, Gwen broke in. 'Yes, I know. You want me to look them up and supply you with copies of the cuttings.'

'Christ, Gwen, on top of everything else you're a bloody clairvoyant. What a woman!'

'Yes, and I also have total recall of every conversation we've ever had and I've heard all that crap before. But you can keep saying it. I'll dig the stuff out later today and leave it down at reception for you, OK?'

'Brilliant. You're a gem. Oh, just one other thing – last one, promise – if you happen to bump into Richard Richardson, don't tell him I rang or what I was after. Will you do that for me?'

'Okey-dokey. Why all the mystery? What's all this about?' She hesitated for all of a second before adding, 'Why did I say that? There's not a chance you're going to tell me, is there?'

'Of course I will . . . but not right now. When I take you to dinner, I'll give you complete chapter and verse – well, more or less. Anyway, you'll be first to know.'

Both of them laughed as they hung up.

15

He promised himself he would give the magnificent Gwen two hours to fulfil her promise to have the cuttings waiting for him. But an hour later McBride was behind the wheel of his car doing his best to impersonate Michael Schumacher as he cut through the heavy afternoon traffic that was pouring in and out of the city centre.

At the crowded roundabout where the Kingsway city bypass converged with half a dozen other roads, he gunned the silver Mondeo through the junction, ignoring the fury of other drivers.

Moments later, he arrived at the imposing red-brick home of *The Courier*. Few strangers to the town would have recognised it as the print headquarters of one of Britain's most successful publishing empires. There were no illuminated signs or boastful banners. Just discreet lettering above the main entrance announcing the company name – DC Thomson & Co Ltd – only just enough to let the postman know where to drop the mail. McBride smiled as he suddenly remembered the name it had been given by a forgotten former colleague – 'the Red Lubyanka', a reference to its position on the outskirts of the city which, the cynic said, 'made prisoners' of the reporters who might otherwise have been interrogating 'contacts' in the city centre bars. There was nobody as economical with the truth as a journalist in search of a drink.

McBride screeched to a halt, taking up two parking spaces in his thoughtless haste. He strode swiftly into the building and looked at once to see if one of the large buff envelopes always used by Cuttings had been placed on the desk at reception. The memory woman of Kingsway had not let him down. Gwen's precise handwriting in her hallmark heavy black ink jumped out at him from a bulging packet – 'To Await Mr Campbell McBride'.

Bloody marvel, he thought as he identified himself to the receptionist, picked it up and walked just as quickly back to the car park, hoping none of the reporters inside had spotted him from their 'cell' windows. He resisted the temptation to rip the envelope open as soon as he was back in his car, knowing his search of the thick bundle of newspaper clippings would not be brief or easy to conduct from the confines of the Mondeo.

His journey back through the city was no less impatient. He drove on the brakes and horn, wondering, as he always did, why his fellow motorists seemed to resent his presence. McBride had an uncomplicated view of other road-users – those who drove slowly in front impeding his progress were idiots; those who overtook were morons; and those who sat behind at precisely the same speed as himself were a combination of the two. It seemed a reasonable enough appraisal of all those inconsiderate enough to want to make a journey at the same time as himself.

When he at last reached the privacy of his new flat, McBride paused only long enough to throw off his jacket and shoes. Then he sat on the floor, slid an impatient finger along the seal of the packet and tipped the contents out in front of him. There was much to scrutinise. More than a hundred cuttings had tumbled from the envelope, each of them carefully dated and bearing the name of the paper it had been snipped from and a special file reference number. Gwen had taught her assistants well.

Journalists spend much of their life browsing clippings and, very early in their careers, they acquire the art of rapidly recognising and dispensing with those they know will be of no value. McBride employed his talent and, in very little time, he had divided the old news articles into two groups. The largest pile was swiftly eliminated and he pushed it out of the way. He studied the remainder for the best part of an hour before discarding all but three of them. What was left were the accounts of how a trio of women, apparently unknown but with a number of things in common, had met their maker in circumstances that were not dissimilar.

One, a twenty-five-year-old call-centre worker, had been discovered in an upstairs bedroom of her semi-detached home on the outskirts of Dundee some six years earlier. Nicola Cassidy had lived there alone after parting from her husband the previous year. She had not been known to have formed any other relationship and had apparently led a quiet, uneventful life until her murder. She had been choked to death, probably manually, and had apparently lain in the house for some four days before concerned colleagues alerted police to her non-appearance at work. The husband, who would inevitably have been the initial prime suspect, had been able to prove he was 300 miles away in Birmingham at the time of her death.

The few leads that had appeared promising petered out after a couple of months and her killer had never been traced. Police had announced that several items of modest value were missing and hinted that intercourse had taken place around the time of her death. McBride knew that attempts to find a match on the national DNA database must have drawn a blank – otherwise there would have been an arrest, even if it hadn't led to a conviction.

'That's another bastard who'll spend the rest of his life shitting himself in case he has to get his mouth swabbed for some minor misdemeanour,' McBride muttered. He finally laid the clippings down, all of the relevant details subconsciously stored away.

He turned to another, smaller bundle of yellowing cuttings, opening them out again from the deep creases that had formed during their life in the buff envelope. The tale they told was of an attractive young mother found dead in her bed by a neighbour who lived in the same block of flats in Brechin, a small country town only twenty miles from Dundee. The two communities, however, were a million miles apart in terms of lifestyle. This victim had also experienced her last moments on earth fighting for breath, before expiring as a result of sustained strangulation. Reading between the lines, there seemed to be an absence of a ligature, meaning it had been a pair of powerful hands that had brought her short existence to a brutally premature conclusion. Her name was Roberta Kerr and she had apparently enjoyed a night out with a group of female friends before making her way home alone, slightly the worse for drink, some time after midnight. That evening, her two small children had been cared for by her parents in nearby Montrose and it seemed she had returned by herself to an empty apartment.

However, she had evidently encountered a man at some stage because the clippings quoted the senior investigating officer as saying, 'We know she must have been in the company of a male at some stage during the evening,' police-speak for evidence of sex having taken place. Her purse and some other items of limited value had been stolen. Like the unfortunate Nicola Cassidy, her murderer had not been traced in the five years that had elapsed. It was another cold trail awaiting the kick-start of a DNA match that could happen tomorrow or maybe never.

McBride scanned the clippings for several more minutes until he was satisfied he had missed nothing of importance. Then he placed them on top of the impersonal, clinical particulars recounting the sad life and death of the quiet call-centre employee.

Almost two hours had passed since McBride had started to examine the results of Gwen Kissock's meticulous research and he became aware of a growing stiffness in his lower back – the kind of warning sign he usually experienced when he had spent too long in the saddle of his Trek. He rose from the floor and executed a short series of stretching exercises, which were the closest he ever allowed himself to come to performing yoga. The pain slowly subsided and he crossed the room to change the three CDs which had played repeatedly since he had settled in the room. The replacements were almost an exact replica of the genre of those being removed. He slid Rod Stewart, Elton John and Simply Red into the waiting trays, eager for the room to be filled again with music. McBride was aware that his musical tastes might be ridiculed so he would never admit to them in public but, for reasons he never fully understood, he always wrote – and thought – best when some dated middle-of-the-roader was singing invisibly in the background. Not that he could ever recall much of what he had heard – unless it was Don McLean's rendition of 'Vincent', the lyrics of which always managed to move him.

He returned to sit on the floor and removed the paperclip holding the final batch of cuttings together, once more beginning to read how life had ended cruelly for someone who was entitled to believe her best days were still ahead of her.

Ginny Williams had come to Scotland from New Zealand to live in the midst of academia. She also died there, about a year after the murder of Alison Brown. The young lawyer's journey from the other side of the world had taken her to St Andrews where she was midway through a postgraduate course at the famous university. Tall, blonde and striking, she had taken occupancy of a furnished ground-floor house at Clay Braes, an easy ten-minute walk down Largo Road and along South Street to her place of study.

She apparently adored good books, fine food and even better wine. Ginny did not appear to have much in common with her sister corpses, those of Nicola Cassidy and Roberta Kerr. She was neither separated from her husband nor a mother living in a small town. The trio had shared the same ultimate fate, however, for the stunning Kiwi had also been throttled into perpetual silence in her home – although, in her case, the precise nature of the ligature that had been used was not disclosed.

McBride reread the news reports of her murder several times, aware that the absence of precise detail was a deliberate act by the police who invariably withheld the kind of information that only the killer could be aware of. It helped eliminate the nutters who couldn't wait to confess to murders they had never committed.

You did not require to be any kind of genius, however, to appreciate that the killer had obviously left traces of himself behind. After weeks of going nowhere, the inquiry had attracted world headlines when Fife Police announced there had been some sexual element to the killing and declared their intention to seek DNA samples from every male under the age of fifty who lived in and around St Andrews. It was specifically directed at the significant male student population but not particularly at the ancient university's most famous undergraduate of all, Prince William.

The student prince had joined his peers in having his DNA taken. His discreetly conducted test meant he did not have to queue up with the general population but that did not stop the headlines from proclaiming 'Prince William Leads the Way'. McBride shook his head in wonder at the feeble attempt to pass off the prince's public duty as some kind of act of benevolence. 'Christ sake,' he sighed, 'he could hardly have done otherwise.' He imagined the field day the media would have had if he'd declined the test – 'Future King Refuses to Co-operate with Murder Cops'.

Not all that unexpectedly, the sample taken from the heir to the throne was not a match. At any rate, he had not been arrested. Surprisingly, no headline along the lines of 'Prince Cleared of Murder Rap' had appeared anywhere. The tabloids must be losing their touch, McBride mused.

The prince, who shared a cottage on the edge of town with a select handful of friends, was not the only one to have been ruled out of the exhaustive inquiry. Hundreds of others had also had the inside of their mouths painstakingly swabbed, without the remotest sign of a lead emerging. Like the murder hunts that had so hopefully been launched after the untimely deaths of Nicola Cassidy and Roberta Kerr, the inquiries had trailed off before grinding to a halt. Officially the investigations remained 'open' but the dedicated teams had been stood down and the frustrated officers had redeployed to normal duties.

McBride returned the clippings to their envelope and finally rose from his awkward position on the floor. Rod Stewart was on a 'Downtown Train' for the fourth time, darkness had descended outside and the central heating had infuriatingly switched itself off. But McBride barely noticed any of this – he was starting to sift what he had learned and replaying in his head the anchor points of all the text he'd studied that afternoon. He searched for the similarities and differences that might exist between the trio of murders and that of Alison Brown.

What it amounted to was this – over a six-year period, three women in their twenties had died after some form of strangulation, all of them in their own home. There was evidence of sexual activity in each case. All of them had probably been drinking to varying degrees. No one had been arrested for any of the killings and all had occurred within a twenty-mile radius of Dundee. In two of the cases, robbery had taken place – though it may not have been the motive. Although a few thousand pounds' worth of household items had been stolen from the home of Nicola Cassidy, it would not have warranted her murder.

Apart from the lack of arrests, the death of Alison Brown might have fitted very neatly into the pattern that had emerged.

OK, he admitted to himself, women being strangled wasn't exactly unique and maybe there were more differences than similarities but there was enough there to make him want to dig deeper.

McBride felt satisfied with his afternoon's work. He mentally noted that Gwen should be encouraged to have the most expensive dessert on the menu when he eventually took her to dinner.

16

The doors of the Central Library had been unlocked and open to the public for all of two minutes when McBride strode briskly through them and headed, once more, for the local studies section.

Elaine with the breasts was nowhere to be seen. In her place behind the counter was a male in a badly ironed shirt and tie that was too tight. His hair was greasy and needing cut and, although he appeared to be in his mid thirties, his pockmarked face still bore traces of acne. An unpleasant mix of body odour and cheap deodorant rose from him.

McBride was the only other person in the room but he might as well have been invisible while he waited for the assistant to acknowledge his presence by raising his head from the computer printout he was apparently studying. Nothing happened for at least twenty seconds. McBride shuffled his feet and cleared his throat. Still nothing. He was seriously contemplating making the slimeball's tie even tighter when there was a flicker that his existence had been recognised.

An expressionless face with dead eyes looked up at him. Although the heating system in the library had still some work to do to warm the place, sweat glistened on the forehead of the man gazing sullenly at him. The badge on the crumpled shirt identified him as 'Brad'. McBride found himself transfixed by the word and the inappropriateness of it. *Christ sake – nobody was ever going to mistake him for Brad Pitt.* He controlled an urge to laugh. 'Brad', as though reading his thoughts, stared defiantly back.

McBride knew things were not going to go well. He resolved to be polite . . . and for ten seconds he succeeded. 'Can you help me find some back editions of *The Courier*, please? I need to go back eight years. Are they beside the more recent ones?'

'Over there.' The limp hair nodded vaguely in the direction of the other side of the room.

'Where?'

'There.' Another inclination of the greasy head, this time barely discernible and towards no particular part of the premises.

McBride's jaw tightened and he was aware that the fingers of his left hand were drumming on the countertop while his right fist was starting to clench. He marvelled at his own restraint. 'I don't know where you mean. Take me there, please. And, if you don't, "Brad", I'm going to write down your name and complain about you all the way to Number Ten Downing Street. I'm also going to squeeze you by the neck until your eyes bulge.' McBride instantly regretted the remark. He knew instinctively that Brad would have learned the book on employees' rights off by heart, particularly the chapter about being intimidated by customers. He waited for the outraged response. At the very least he would be asked to leave, more probably he would be threatened with the police.

Neither happened. The hunched figure of the surly assistant rose from his seat and walked slowly from behind the counter. If he had dropped his pace by a fraction, he would have ground to a halt. But he was moving and in the direction of a rank of bound files. He motioned McBride to follow. The journey across the room took an eternity but finally they arrived at a section covering a ten-year period.

'The more recent ones are round the corner. You'll have to get them down yourself.' Then, as he sniffed and turned away, the man whose smell was now almost one hundred per cent body sweat, added over his shoulder, 'No cutting anything out.'

'Thanks, you've been extremely helpful.'

McBride had no idea if the sarcasm had been noted. Nothing seemed to penetrate Brad's air of implacability and he shuffled off without giving any sign that he had even heard the remark. Moments later, he was back at his desk, crouched, once more, over the computer printouts.

After locating the files of six years earlier, McBride hastily turned the pages of the old newspapers until he found the one chronicling the death of Nicola Cassidy. He was not looking for additional information – he wanted less than was already contained in the cuttings dug out for him by Gwen. He hoped the report of the call-centre worker's untimely death would be at least a sentence short of what had originally been there. He needed it to be telling him something, even if he could not understand what it was. He wanted a 'message' like the one left behind after the trial of Adam Gilzean.

He did not receive it. Every word detailing the murder of the twenty-five-year-old was as intact as the moment it had been printed. He repeated his search another two times to be certain but the file was as complete as the day it had been stored away. He doubted if anyone had even read it, far less approached it with a razor. McBride knew he should be glad but a rush of disappointment spread through him.

He replaced the file, aware that Brad had lifted his gaze from his printouts and was watching his every move from the other end of the room. He resisted the urge to fix him with a stare in return and instead pulled down the bound volume of newspapers for the year when Roberta Kerr had perished and left her two little girls motherless.

The only thing a close examination of the contents produced was a burst of sneezing from McBride, brought on by the release of an excessive number of dust particles that had triggered a near-forgotten allergy. Apart from the grime, the news reports of Roberta's strangulation were pure and untouched.

McBride blew his nose – loudly, in the hope that it might irritate Brad. He moved from the main file area, round the corner to the section containing the more recent newspapers, and dragged the one he wanted from its place on the shelf. Feverishly, he pulled back the pages.

The story of Virginia Williams' demise in douce St Andrews was instantly rewarding. A neat square hole under the headlines was obviously where a photograph of the Kiwi lawyer had once been positioned. In the last column of the report, five paragraphs from the end, there was a much smaller aperture where two sentences appeared to have been removed. McBride fought off an overwhelming desire to punch the air but permitted himself a soft, 'Yessss.'

Like the other larger extraction, the missing words had been excised with infinite precision, by a sharp blade. He flicked the page over and whistled in admiration. There was no trace anywhere of a carry-through cut. Whoever had performed the surgery had also come equipped with some kind of protective pad to prevent damage to other parts of the file. 'Impressive . . . and interesting!' he exclaimed inwardly.

McBride was still marvelling at his discovery when a whining voice sounded from twenty feet away. 'Are you nearly finished here?' It was the slimeball walking towards him, a set of keys in his hand, his moist forehead glistening under the bright ceiling light. McBride snapped the file shut, anxious that he should not see where it had been opened.

The sweating librarian seemed suddenly uninterested in the activities of his visitor. He paid no attention to the file McBride had now lifted up into his arms.

'I have to go out and I'm not allowed to leave anyone alone if no staff are on duty.' He noted McBride's questioning look and added, hurriedly, 'We're short of bodies – flu – so I'll have to ask you to leave.'

'Give me a couple of minutes more and I'll be gone for good. OK?'

Brad hesitated. 'OK, two minutes, no more.' He rattled his keys officiously and walked reluctantly away. 'Remember, two minutes – I'll be waiting at the door,' he called out as he disappeared back round the corner of the aisle.

McBride replaced the file on the table, reopened it at the cut pages and wrote swiftly in the pad he had pulled from a pocket, noting the precise spot where the extracted words had been.

Brad kept his promise and was standing with his arms folded at the door of the library, one foot gently tapping on the scuffed vinyl floor covering. His truculence remained to the end. He did not meet McBride's eye as he ushered him through the entrance and nor did he acknowledge the short 'Thanks' McBride grudgingly uttered as he filed past.

It was only when he was in the street outside that it occurred to McBride that Brad had not followed him out. Instead, he had remained inside the file room, locking himself in after McBride had left. McBride shook his head at the unpleasant assistant's odd behaviour but, somehow, it did not surprise him.

He did not waste time reflecting on it. All he wanted was to return to his car as fast as humanly possible to read Gwen's copied article about the killing of Virginia Williams – the same one as the one in the library, only without the missing sentences.

He resisted the urge to run to the car park, knowing he would have looked like a shoplifter or someone with bladder problems, and contented himself with as fast a walk as seemed decent. Once inside his car, all control deserted him and he ripped at the packet of cuttings bearing Gwen's distinctive handwriting like a child tearing opening a Christmas parcel. His eyes raced to identify the mystery absent passage. At first, he skimmed over them. They seemed so inconsequential that he believed he had mistaken their location. He rechecked his notebook only to discover there had been no error.

The words that had been so painstakingly removed were part of a statement given at a press conference by one of the murder team in answer to a reporter's facetious question about the possible reasons for Ginny's murder. The complete text of the affected sentences ran:

Your suggestion of a royal crime of passion is just one more on the list. Another much further away from reality is that Prince William is also a descendant of Jack the Ripper!

The parts removed were:

> just one more on the list. Another much further
> away

McBride repeated them over and over.

'Jesus!' McBride exclaimed. He slammed his hand hard into the steering wheel, hitting he horn and sending a deafening blast round the echo chamber of the multi-storey. Conveniently, it blotted out the sound of McBride's voice, which was roaring, 'If you want to tell me something, just lift the phone! Bastard . . . bastard . . .'

17

McBride lay wide awake in the darkness and tried again to empty his mind. He did not succeed. Instead, he reached out and pressed the button to illuminate the clock beside his bed. It dimly pronounced 1.40 a.m. – seventeen minutes since his previous time-check.

He stared at the ceiling and thought about Ginny Williams and why she had died. He thought also of what had been written about her death. But most of all he thought about what someone had wanted him to learn by apparently keeping it from him. He had deliberated on almost nothing but the excised sentences since leaving the library.

McBride pulled himself from the bed, crossed the room and thrust a Coldplay disc into the CD player. He turned the rod of the window blind until the slats were open enough for the light from the moon to reveal the incoming tide rushing up the beach towards him and again he appreciated the gentleness of the whispers the river brought with it as it washed over the sand. At any other time, he would have lingered at his good fortune to be living where he was but all that crowded his mind was a picture of a New Zealand lawyer lying perfectly

91

attired but even more perfectly dead in her apartment in St Andrews, ten miles away as the seagull flies.

At least he was now fairly certain he did not need to concern himself with the deaths of Nicola Cassidy and Roberta Kerr, disturbing though they were. Deeper reflection suggested greater differences between their murders and those of Alison Brown and Ginny Williams than he had first imagined. Apart from the longer timescale since Nicola and Roberta had died, both had literally perished 'at the hands' of their killer, signifying more impulsive, unpremeditated acts than the ones where ligatures had been used. In the case of the call-centre worker, a petty theft had also occurred. A discrepancy with the other victim was the timing – she had arrived home drunk in the early hours after a night on the town with her friends. *They really didn't fit very well at all*, he told himself. *Besides, no 'message' had been sent about either of them.*

The music stopped and McBride hit the replay button on the remote. Briefly, incongruously, he wondered how anyone with the talent of Coldplay's frontman could also be so inconsiderate as to name his children Apple and Moses. It made almost as little sense as the message someone was so painstakingly trying to deliver.

Whatever way he viewed it, he ran into the same brick wall. How could the person who had taken such trouble to so deftly wield the razor be certain anyone would come across the results of their efforts? Was there really any connection between the murders of Ginny Williams and Alison Brown or was a warped mind simply setting up a tormenting game for him to play? And were there any other participants?

He wanted a drink but even he couldn't contemplate the cold sharpness of a beer after getting out of bed at that hour.

He poured an inch of Metaxa brandy into a straight glass and filled it to the top with Coca-Cola. For the next ten minutes, he sipped easily at it and watched as the tide carried two empty detergent bottles back and forth on to the beach.

Then he returned to bed to gaze at the ceiling again – only now he was thinking of Caroline and his beloved bike. Christ, he'd always lectured her about her grasshopper mind and her inability to switch off. At least the new images were preferable to the two dead women who had come uninvited into his life.

The woman who used to share his bed was still in his head when sleep overtook him. It was 3.20 a.m.

18

When he jerked back to life less than four hours later, sunshine was flooding the room. It was the kind of morning that folk who ran prayed for – bright, cool and windless and with a rising winter sun for company. But McBride resisted the desire to put on his trainers and head for the beach. Miraculously, what had passed for sleep had cleared his head and so there was no need to sort out his mind with the consumption of several miles by his legs.

He knew exactly what he must do. He needed to consult the police but it had to be someone familiar and not necessarily someone still serving. What he required was contact with an officer with enough seniority to have been informed of the background of the Alison Brown case, even if they had not worked on it, and who was prepared to speak off the record. Such a man, he believed, was David Novak.

He could not remember when they had last spoken but thought it had been when the then detective inspector had thoughtfully called him in London to express his sadness at Simon's death. There were few officers in Dundee who were tougher or more demanding. There were also few more compassionate or caring. If DI Novak had arrested you, there was little prospect of an acquittal but, if the evidence was not there, the lanky Novak would not indulge in dishonest investigative techniques to create it. It was always a fair cop by a fair cop. Strangely, his approach was often appreciated more by those he endeavoured to arrest than by some of those who served with him.

McBride felt genuine fondness for the man. It was an emotion that had been reciprocated when they had used each other's services all those years ago. He was unsure of Novak's whereabouts. *Please God he wasn't dead.* An easy find in the phone book erased that concern. The fact that there was a directory entry for him also told him that Novak was probably retired – for obvious reasons, few serving officers were ever listed.

McBride noted his address, breakfasted on toast and coffee and absently reread the previous day's newspaper as he waited for sufficient time to pass before it would not seem indecent to turn up unannounced on someone's doorstep. His impatience overtook him and, shortly after 9 a.m., he turned his car into a small estate of 1980's private houses on the western perimeter of the city just before it met Invergowrie.

The house was at the end of a cul-de-sac and McBride smiled softly, wondering if its location was accidental. Probably not, he decided. The detective inspector, he remembered, left very little to chance and the smart bungalow would likely have been chosen for its secure position more than its price.

Although milk bottles were still sitting on the doorsteps of the houses on either side, Novak's home bristled with wakefulness. The windows of what appeared to be the main bedroom were open, the front door was ajar and a wheelbarrow full of garden debris occupied the middle of the drive which led to a garage.

McBride drew to a halt at the same moment as a lean figure carrying perished plants appeared from the rear of the house. The man stopped, knowing instinctively that the visitor was for him. But he did not move in McBride's direction. He remained standing at the corner of the house, as though deciding whether the caller should be welcomed.

McBride's uncertainty about whether it would be necessary to introduce himself vanished within ten seconds of stepping from his car. The face of the man staring intently at him from thirty feet away slowly changed into a spreading smile and he called out, 'Campbell McBride, if I'm not mistaken!' And, with that welcome, he walked briskly down the drive, throwing the long-dead plants into the barrow and extending a hand that looked as though it had been used to excavate a ditch. McBride grasped it warmly, pleased he had been remembered and oddly glad to have been reunited with the policeman.

'Hello, David, good to see you again,' McBride said inadequately. It was the kind of remark that might have been appropriate had they been reintroduced at some official function but, as an opener from someone who had appeared on your doorstep out of the blue at nine o'clock on a winter's morning, it had a decidedly artificial ring.

Novak dallied only long enough to politely respond, 'You too.' Then he got down to business. 'So, to what do I owe this dubious pleasure? I have a feeling you are not here to enquire about my looks. Tell me I'm wrong. Tell me you're not seeking information.'

McBride flushed and laughed at the same time. 'So cynical for one so young. But why are you not more direct? You must be losing your touch.'

It was Novak's turn to chuckle. 'OK. Come inside and tell me all about it. I could do with a cup of tea anyway,' he said.

For half an hour, McBride did not tell him anything about it. They used the time to identify the milestones in the lives of each of them since they had last faced each other.

Novak, still a year away from his bus pass, had eventually risen to the rank of detective chief superintendent and had commanded the Tayside Police crime management department, which was the new but meaningless title for what had been the CID – the name most folk still used for it. He had retired four years earlier but cruelly his wife had passed away three months after he had become a civvy. They had not even had time to take the cruise every retiring police officer seemed to deem an essential part of the leaving ritual.

In the time since he had handed in his warrant card and walked out of police HQ in West Bell Street for good, Novak had devoted himself to his garden. Unexpectedly, he had also rediscovered a suppressed talent for art. He combined the two and numerous paintings of flowers lined a wall of the room where they sat. They weren't good and they weren't bad. They were just watercolours of flowers – the end product of someone with time on his hands.

The ex-chief superintendent professed a contentment in his new existence but McBride didn't swallow it any more than Novak did. A cop with his skills would never feel fulfilled just painting pansies, even if they had been masterpieces.

'OK, Campbell, what is it you want?'

McBride sensed that the former policeman had become desperate to move away from the small talk. That he was eager to reconnect with the old days, and anxious to learn what had caused the reporter to track him down.

'Has it anything to do with this book you've written?' Novak gestured to a shelf of books over his visitor's shoulder.

McBride turned to see the spine of *The Law Town Killers* sandwiched between a thick manual on painting techniques and Charlie Dimmock's latest offering on garden water features.

'I'm flattered, Dave. Is it a rare unsigned copy you have? Glad to see you haven't lost your deductive powers, though. Then again, maybe you don't have to be the world's greatest mathematician to put two and two together. What can you tell me about Alison Brown? Or, more precisely, what do you know about the background to it all?'

Novak spread his hands, turning the palms upwards. 'What's to know? She argued with her boyfriend, he strangled her and now he's up in the pokey at Perth where he belongs. By all accounts, the case didn't take much solving.'

McBride looked questioning. 'What do you mean "by all accounts"? Weren't you involved?' he asked.

'No. I was back at Tulliallan doing another stint in the classroom.'

McBride had forgotten. David Novak's gift for catching the bad guys made him a natural for teaching duty at the Scottish Police College. Half his career had been spent in and out of the classrooms at the college.

'Yes, but she was a policeman's daughter. That made it a bit special, didn't it?'

'Of course it did. Frankie Brown, God rest his soul, was a popular bloke. Nobody likes to see a young lassie ending up that way but it's ten times worse when it's the bairn of someone you know.'

McBride moved his head in agreement. 'That would make it all the more important to get a result,' he said.

'Sure – we're all human. You'd be the same if it was the child of a reporter you worked with.'

McBride nodded again. 'So, all the lads would have tried extra hard on it?'

'Yeah. But what are you saying?' Novak was becoming agitated. 'Are you heading where I think you are, Campbell? If you're trying to say the boyfriend was fitted up just because of who her father was, forget it. He left a trail a mile wide.'

McBride soothed him. 'No, no, nothing like that,' he replied, not entirely convincingly. 'But it didn't take long to bang him up, did it?'

'That's the way it goes sometimes. You know as well as I do that murder is usually either the easiest or hardest crime to solve. Most of the killers are known to their victims, so you get them quick. It's the bastards who strike out of the blue that you have all the problems with. They're the ones you sometimes never catch.' Novak was becoming impatient. 'Look, Campbell, what's this all about? Why the big interest?'

McBride was amazed he hadn't put the questions much earlier. 'Now you've got me, Dave. Gut feeling – can't explain it. Just doesn't ring true.' He struggled to find a credible explanation for his belief. 'I've spoken to Bryan Gilzean up the road in Perth. He did a good job of convincing me it wasn't him. So did his father, come to that.'

'His father? Adam Gilzean has told everyone his son is innocent. Apart from the fact that he's a bit of a religious maniac, he isn't exactly unbiased, is he? You'd say the same if it was your son.'

Novak suddenly remembered that McBride no longer had a son. 'I'm sorry, Campbell.' He reddened with embarrassment.

'I didn't mean it to come out like that. I was going to ask. How have you been?'

McBride paused, searching for the kind of response that would make his host feel better. Before he could reply, the heavy silence was broken by the melodious chime of a doorbell, followed immediately by the sound of a door closing at the back of the house. There were light footsteps. Then a female voice called out. 'Hi, Dad. It's me. Where are you?'

The door of the sitting room swung open. The woman who entered was startled to find someone with her father. McBride was equally taken aback by the attractiveness of Novak's visitor. She was aged about thirty with limbs like a gazelle. Her face shone with perspiration and her dark hair was tied back in a ponytail by a crimson ribbon. She wore a navy-blue sweatshirt, matching bottoms and discoloured trainers. A pair of almond eyes stared back at him from above two sculpted cheekbones. She lifted a hand to her mouth. 'Oh, sorry, Dad, I didn't know you had company.' She recovered quickly, looking questioningly at her father.

'Petra, you remember Campbell, don't you? The reporter . . . the author . . .'

The eyes smiled at McBride. So did the soft mouth that opened to reveal two rows of perfectly even teeth. She moved towards him, reaching out a slender hand. Then she remembered she had been running and that it was covered with sweat. She wiped it over a buttock and extended it again.

McBride took it willingly and felt its moistness. Unnecessarily, he cleared his throat. But, before he could speak, Novak intervened. 'Campbell, this is Petra – my daughter. You've probably forgotten, but you came to her assistance many moons ago.'

McBride hesitated momentarily. 'How could I forget?' It wasn't a lie but it wasn't the truth either.

Threads of faraway memories started to creep back. It had been down in London, just a few years after he had gone there to live and work, and she had come to visit him in the newsroom of the *Daily Express*, an awkward teenager moving away from childhood but not quite an adult, in spite of the carefully applied make-up and high-heeled shoes.

He trawled deeper. It hadn't entirely been a social call – the schoolgirl, who was in the capital with classmates for an educational visit to the Houses of Parliament, was starting to make her career and examination choices. Top of her list was journalism and she needed advice from someone like McBride. Images of her sitting beside him at his desk flashed into his head. He smiled at the memory. For ten minutes, she had hardly taken in a word he said. Her eyes had darted round the room and she'd watched in wonder as one of the world's greatest newspapers came together out of the professional chaos. He remembered how she had blushed when trying to put some intelligent questions together. The recollection of her juvenile innocence touched him again.

'So, are you a reporter, then?'

Her cheeks turned pink but this time she was composed and in charge of her mouth. 'Not exactly – I really wanted to but, well, I went off to university and, you know how it is, you change.' The flush had rapidly vanished from her face but she seemed embarrassed, as though she'd let him down.

'So, what *did* you do at uni?'

'Law.'

'A lawyer, eh? Oh, well,' he said mockingly, 'at least you'll have pots of money.'

'No – not that either.' She paused, searching for her next words.

Her father, who had listened to the exchanges in silence but with a broadening grin, laughed out loud. 'She's a cop, Campbell!' Novak took delight at his revelation.

'What?' McBride was genuinely taken aback, practically to the point of speechlessness. 'A cop – Jesus, that's a bit of a turn-up. Christ sake!' He wasn't sure why he was so surprised.

The very grown-up woman standing two feet away started to laugh as well. His amazement had allowed her to take charge of the conversation. She glowed with pride at his astonishment, suddenly brimming with confidence. 'There's a lot of us around, you know,' she told him. 'We don't all have two heads.'

McBride had recovered. 'No – or law degrees.'

Novak, the most modest of men, as McBride recalled, couldn't conceal his pride. 'Or first-class degrees at that,' he beamed.

McBride's lips mouthed a silent whistle. 'My admiration knows no bounds.'

Novak moved into full flow. 'She went straight from university into Tayside Police as an accelerated promotion candidate, one of the few to be accepted.'

McBride understood his satisfaction. Scores of unemployed graduates turned to the police as a career, confidently imagining a degree would guarantee rapid promotion. They didn't seem to realise that every force required far more foot soldiers than high-flying brainboxes. There was no point in recruiting folk whose ambitions surpassed their realistic opportunities for advancement so accelerated promotion entrants were selected sparingly and with care.

He nodded at father and daughter. 'Good on you.' He knew the fast track practically guaranteed her promotion to the rank of inspector after seven years.

'So, what are you? Professional Standards?' He used the name of the internal affairs department, where cop investigates cop. It seemed a reasonable assumption. Law degree, smart, female, probably resented by male plods anyway.

Novak smiled once more. It was becoming irritating. 'Tell him, Petra.'

'Dad! OK – I'm a detective inspector, Campbell, recently made up and enjoying it. Now, can I have cold drink? And do you two want more tea?'

McBride watched every step as she disappeared in the direction of the kitchen.

19

Richard Richardson was quietly insistent when he phoned his old colleague. He wanted to have dinner with McBride and he wanted to pay for it. They would dine at 8 p.m. in Broughty Ferry and afterwards seek drink or women, more probably both.

He suggested they meet in the restaurant at the hotel situated where Queen Street meets Claypotts Road.

McBride asked the name of the hotel.

'That's all it's called,' Richardson explained. 'Its official title is "The Hotel" – capital T capital H. Nothing else. Bloody stupid, I know, but that's the label they saddled it with.' It did not occur to him that there was an element of 'pot' and 'black' in his dismissal of the strange name.

McBride wondered aloud why he was being treated. 'It's not my birthday. Is it yours?' he asked. 'Have you come into money?'

Richardson tried to sound exasperated. 'I haven't come into anything – at least not for some time. Maybe later tonight . . . This is just a typically generous act on my behalf. Besides, I'll fiddle it on expenses.'

When McBride arrived precisely on time at The Hotel, his benefactor was already there, seated at a corner table in the busy upstairs restaurant. A bottle of white wine that looked expensive was open and the glass at Double Dick's right hand had only a mouthful left in it. McBride sensed it would not be the only bottle they would consume that evening.

'You shouldn't have bothered waiting,' he said sarcastically. 'Have you ordered? Maybe you've eaten as well . . .'

'Now, now, old son, no need to be offensive.' Richardson was in exuberant mood. 'Plenty more left in the bottle,' he continued, filling the empty glass on the opposite side of the table. 'Drink up and let's talk.'

McBride lifted his glass, held it theatrically up to the light and then sniffed the contents. He took a mouthful and made exaggerated swilling motions. 'French, a Chardonnay, and probably early this century, unless I'm very much mistaken,' he said, finally, after swallowing the wine.

Richardson's eyes narrowed in disbelief. Then he realised that the label of the bottle faced his companion. 'Very funny. You'd struggle to know the difference between gnat's piss and champagne. Everything doesn't have to come in a pint glass.'

McBride drained his glass in two quick movements and pushed it across for a refill. 'OK, what do you want?' he asked. 'Has to be more than my company.'

Richardson tried to look hurt. 'Do people never do anything nice for you, McBride? I just thought it was time we touched base again.' He toyed with his drink. 'Bring me up to speed. How's this feature you're supposed to be "working up"? Must be some size if it's made you move back up from Pooftown.'

McBride raised an eyebrow. 'You heard?'

'You should know better. My spies are everywhere. Nothing moves in this town without Richard Richardson being aware of it. My sensitive finger is constantly on the grubby pulse of the city.'

The verbal sparring lasted until the food arrived. Then Double Dick appeared to lose interest in the man seated opposite. His concentration on his plate was awesome. He dissected and arranged, discarded and rearranged. Every mouthful was savoured.

It was only when his three courses had been consumed and a fresh bottle of wine was in place that normal exchanges were resumed. McBride concluded that, whatever his former colleague wanted from him, he also wanted a hunting companion that night.

It was only when they were ensconced in The Fort some time later that he fully appreciated Richardson's need for female company. The wine had given way to lager and the combination of copious amounts of both seemed to open a verbal tap inside Double Dick's mouth.

'When did you last have a shag, then, Mr McRide?' he asked abruptly, his face twisting to a leer. 'Do you know that's what they used to call you – Campbell McRide, the fastest prick in the west . . . and the south, north and east. The scourge of every housing scheme round the back of Kingsway.' Richardson became conspiratorial. 'Do you remember the days when we went hoorin' together?' he asked, nostalgia overtaking him. 'We did OK, didn't we? Except you always seemed to get the best-looking one. Still, that wasn't always the one with the biggest tits. Suited me. Sometimes the ugliest were the most rewarding – and the most grateful.'

It was a philosophy Richardson had comforted himself with at the time. McBride would lay money he still adhered to it. Not that he was alone in the practice. McBride had even heard Omar Sharif admit to the same kind of selection process on a TV show interview. He reflected on this for a few moments and concluded that not in his wildest dreams would he have imagined himself ever finding a close similarity between Double Dick and a suave movie actor.

'Never mind twenty years ago. Are you still getting your share now, Richard?' McBride asked.

The man who was never lost for words when he penned his paper's finest news articles struggled to respond. He rolled his head slowly from side to side, making up his mind what to say. Finally, he said, 'A bit here, bit there – you know the way it goes. Not as much as I'd like. Same as everybody else, I suppose. Except you, maybe.'

McBride changed the subject – or tried to. 'I ran into Dave Novak, the other day,' he said lightly. 'Met his daughter too. Petra. Didn't recognise her. Hasn't half grown up. Couldn't believe she's a cop.'

Richardson said nothing at first. Then he managed to combine another leer with a laugh. 'No chance,' he rasped. 'You don't have a snowball's chance in hell, McBride. She wouldn't touch you with a bargepole. I don't care how often you get lucky with women. The girl has class – and sense. Forget it.' He chortled, taking delight at the thought of McBride being rejected by the divine Petra.

Before McBride could retaliate, Richardson began to gesture across the bar towards two females. They had entered ten minutes earlier but he had not been aware of their presence. McBride had. Richardson pointed at them and made drinking motions. They nodded. He shouted to John Black behind the bar to give them what they wanted and handed him the money.

'An investment,' he explained to McBride, unnecessarily lowering his voice. 'That's Kate from the office with one of her mates. Good lass. You can have her. I'll see what I can make of her pal.'

After they collected their drinks, he waved again, this time beckoning them over. The two women hesitated only long enough to take a sip from their glasses before joining the predators.

The quartet observed the ritual of witty conversation, which was polite but unnecessary. All four understood the protocols required of those who sought the company of the opposite sex in The Fort.

20

Kate Nightingale – it was a great name for a byline.

Campbell McBride had no idea if she could write. He did not care. That night she was exactly what he wanted. She was late thirties, medium height, brown curls and eyes that flashed. Looked foreign – southern European. She wore a soft green blouse, two buttons undone, a black bra peeking at him. The trousers were black as well – tight as the top. A white jacket hung off a tanned shoulder. She was in control and when she laughed it sounded like an invitation to take her to bed – except it wasn't.

When John Black threw them out at closing time, McBride offered to walk her up the hill to where she lived and she accepted. When they arrived at the house, which was in darkness, they went inside. They did not go to bed but they lay on it. They spoke and drank the coffee she made.

She told him when her marriage had ended and why. That it hadn't been all his fault.

He didn't tell her about his break-up or whose fault it had been. That was private stuff. He never spoke of Caroline to other women in the same way he never spoke of his women to other men. Everybody was entitled to their secrets.

They chatted about newspapers and she said she had admired his work from afar.

He didn't tell her he had never seen any of hers.

She asked about the five awards he'd received for his work and he brushed her off – not out of false modesty but because the prizes were for big stories, the kind that wrote themselves. You just had to be in the right spot on the right day for them. The ones that gave him most satisfaction were the down-the-page pieces that needed most digging. So what if they didn't have any international or national significance if they made life better for someone? But no one gave you trophies for them and no one else was really that interested, even on the day the stories appeared.

Then they spoke about Richard Richardson and she said Double Dick had told her he knew McBride was sniffing out a story. He'd even strongly implied he knew what the story was, she said. She wondered if that could be true and then, point blank, she asked what the story was.

McBride laughed. He did not answer either of her questions. Instead, he asked some of his own – like why Double Dick seemed to be troubled about something.

She said she didn't know for sure but there was a rumour in the newsroom that he'd had a bad experience with a woman he'd met on the internet.

An hour later, McBride told Kate he should leave and waited for her to suggest he should stay and extend an invitation for breakfast. She did neither. Instead she put her arms round his neck and kissed him softly but briefly on the lips. Then she swung herself off the bed and took his hand, leading him towards the door.

When they reached the hallway, he turned both her shoulders until she faced him and asked simply, 'Yes?'

'Yes,' she replied, lowering herself to the floor.

After they had removed each other's clothing, it did not take long but what occurred did not depend on time, just compatibility. Then they said 'Yes' again but in perfect unison.

Not much later, as he walked back down the hill, McBride had no feeling of triumph, just the faintest suspicion that the conquest had been all hers.

21

The midday conference of *Courier* senior editorial staff had been brief. As the paper's chief reporter, Richard Richardson might have been expected to give a full account of what could fill the next day's paper but, beyond a swift rundown of the usual certainties of major court cases and other predictable events of the day, he did not elaborate. He had other things on his mind and had no desire to linger with the others in the editor's room.

Back at his desk, he looked again at the clock on the wall facing him. Then he checked what he saw with his wristwatch, which he always removed and placed to one side of his desk on the opposite side from his computer mouse. The times matched identically, as they had five minutes earlier. Kate Nightingale was rostered for a 2 p.m. start. It was 1.45 p.m. and she had not yet arrived. It did not occur to Richardson that none of the other two o'clock starts were in the building either – or that there was no need for them to be.

When she walked into the room eight minutes later, Richardson was momentarily diverted from the task in hand by her appearance. She was no longer the glamorous pub-goer of the evening before. The curls had been stretched straight and the hair was tied back. In place of the tight top and trousers, she wore a masculine, bottle-green business suit with white blouse and olive-coloured tie. She was still a looker but the outfit had lesbian overtones. Not that he entertained any serious thoughts in that direction. He'd never had the pleasure himself but her heterosexual credentials were, by all accounts, impeccable.

Perhaps McBride would confirm their authenticity – more likely, he wouldn't. The bastard had always been infuriatingly selfish about revealing precisely what he did with his women. Richardson did not believe for one minute that his silence had anything to do with protecting the reputations of his conquests. Knowing McBride, it was almost certainly because he didn't want to ruin his chances of being welcomed back for a second helping.

The businesslike Kate was still booting up her computer when Richardson appeared, unheard, beside her L-shaped desk. She turned, startled, as he burst out, 'Well, did McBride have his filthy way with you?'

'Christ, Richard! Why pick your words so carefully? You should just blurt things out.' She noted without surprise that he still wore the same shirt and tie from the night before. The only thing different was the amount of cigarette ash obliterating the pattern on his neckwear. 'He's a nice man, with a bit more sensitivity than some folk I could mention,' she continued.

Richardson was dismissive. 'How very charming for you. Another lamb to the slaughter, more like. Did he give you the spiel about only wanting to have sex with women who connect intellectually with him?'

A red flush appeared on Kate's neck. 'Piss off, Richard. What is it you want?'

'Payback. Remember our little arrangement? I would introduce you to the great Campbell McBride if you would pump him for information. I need a return on my investment. You don't think I bought you all that liquor just because I like the way you smell, do you? I need to know what you found out from your new boyfriend. I need to know what story he gave you about why he is back staying in town. I need to know if he's still raking over the Alison Brown murder case. And I need to know if he's following up any new information. You must have had some time to speak before or after – perhaps even during – your shag-fest. I will refrain from the obvious crudities about your mouth being too full to speak. What did he tell you?'

Kate shook her head in despair at Richardson's vulgarity – as well as his interrogative techniques – but also to indicate a negative response. 'No luck, I'm afraid.' She didn't sound sorry. 'Whenever I touched on his professional activities, he just smiled and said precisely nothing. I think it's called discretion – a word you may not be familiar with – but I can tell you from what he *didn't* say that he believes there's something big out there.'

Richardson said nothing. He did not question her final remark. He nodded several times. Finally, he spoke softly, more to himself than to his female colleague. 'I bet he does – I bet he does.'

22

McBride felt like a stalker – or a pervert. He sat in his car wearing running shorts and a T-shirt that was torn at the shoulder. At his right hand was a pair of binoculars which he raised to his eyes every time he detected a distant new arrival at the Monifieth end of the Esplanade.

It was the second successive morning he had sat waiting for Petra Novak to appear. He did not know if she would show that day either but every athletic instinct in his body told him she would not be able to resist routing at least some of her training runs along the river's edge where her only companions would be seagulls and dog walkers. She would be attracted to the solitude just as he was, especially on fresh mornings which were so clear that the only thing in the sapphire sky was the high vapour trail of a jet airliner bound for North America.

His conviction that she would pass that way was not entirely intuitive. From the moment he had driven away from her father's house, he had resolved to be reunited with her as quickly as he could. There was the attraction he felt for her, of course – half the men in Dundee probably felt that way

– but he also needed her police mind and her access to the information available only to police officers.

Once he learned where she lived, it had been easy to work out where she might run. His people-tracer website revealed that she lived in Monifieth, the upmarket suburb that ran along the coastline from the east end of Broughty Ferry. Her home was 200 yards from the high-tide mark and, when she ran, she had a choice of three directions: east, on the cycle path skirting the perimeter of the army camp, which was safe but uninteresting; north, which was more appealing but hilly; and west, which would take her over the soft sand of the beach where there were the kinds of views they put on picture postcards. He reckoned it was odds-on she'd be running over the scenic route. So he waited. And, whenever a running figure came out of the distance, he watched with raised glasses, like someone awaiting the arrival on the shore of a rare seabird.

When she appeared as a distant speck, he could not distinguish her features but he knew instantly that it was her. Two slender legs stretched easily across the sand where it appeared from the river's edge and she moved gracefully, making good progress over the firm surface. There was no hint of effort and her relaxed shoulders swung lightly whenever she turned her head to take in the vista of the waves breaking gently ahead of her on her left side. The occasional flash of crimson showed she was wearing the same ribbon that had held her hair back on the day she appeared at her father's home.

McBride watched longer than necessary to establish her identity. He refocused for a sharper image and, when her face filled the eyeglasses, he noted that, although she was moving at an impressive pace, her breathing appeared to be perfectly normal. It was more than might have been said about his own.

After a last lingering look, he started up the Mondeo, turned it and drove away from her. Half a mile down the Esplanade, he drew to a halt in a car park. He left the vehicle, crossed over a bank of sand dunes on to the beach and started to run towards the advancing figure of Petra Novak. Their paths crossed less than a minute later.

McBride had mentally rehearsed his performance. He would raise a friendly, fellow-jogger hand but show no recognition – at first. He would allow her to pass then belatedly and uncertainly call her name with a question in his voice. But his doubtful acting abilities were not required – when he was over fifty feet away, the lithe legs he had observed a short time earlier through a pair of binoculars suddenly changed direction and came straight at him. Their owner started to wave a delicate hand.

'Campbell, hi, it's me – Petra. What a small world.' She seemed excited at the coincidence. She drew to a halt in front of him. 'I'd heard you were a runner – a bit of a regular by the look of it.'

McBride felt a surge of guilt at his deception. Her enthusiasm reminded him of her visit to his newspaper office in London. He cleared his throat and wondered why she always produced that reaction from him. 'Hi, small world indeed.' He tried to sound casual. 'Been doing it for years but it never feels like it. You look pretty useful yourself. Going far? Been far?'

She lifted a hand and pointed past McBride's shoulder. 'I'll go to the castle and then retrace my steps back to Monifieth. That's where I stay. What about you. Are you out for long?'

117

'Just started. I'll probably do about five miles.' He appeared to have a sudden thought. 'Actually, if I go to the castle then head out your way, that would give me my distance. Do you mind if I join you? A bit of company always helps when your fitness is as dodgy as mine.'

She beamed. 'Great. But I'll be too slow for you. You'll have to do all the speaking if I'm to have any hope of keeping up.'

McBride protested modestly. 'From what I've seen it will be the other way round. Anyway, you'll be the one talking. I want to hear all about this police career of yours.'

He turned and moved slowly off and, together, they strode out along the shoreline, McBride allowing her to set the pace.

She may have been one of the most feminine women he had encountered since returning to Dundee but she was deceptively fast, better than most men he'd run with. She was also infuriatingly relaxed.

'So, how's life as a detective inspector?' he asked, doing his best to appear to breathe easily. 'Do the guys give you a tough time? What are you working on? Any good murders on the go?'

She laughed quickly. 'You'd never know you were a reporter. Which question would you like answered first?' She laughed again.

McBride felt foolish. 'Sorry – old habits . . . OK, in your own time. Tell me about being a woman cop.'

For the next five minutes, Detective Inspector Petra Novak spoke confidently and informatively about her current career. It was a Pavlovian response. McBride rapidly came to the conclusion she was delivering a practised spiel she'd used a dozen times at women's groups and addressing equal opportunities seminars at the police college.

When she finished, he broke in, 'OK, now tell me what it's really like.'

Once again, gentle laughter rose from her throat. 'Was it that obvious?' Her mood abruptly changed. 'If you really want to know, it can be hard. She hesitated, then swore to emphasise just how hard.'

McBride was taken aback at her sudden descent into male-speak. 'With the guys?' he asked.

She nodded. 'Yeah – some of them. When I was a detective sergeant, I was one of the boys. Everything changed when I was made up and took over a shift. A few of them had to work very hard at coping.' She gave a dismissive shake of her head. 'You know male cops – biggest bunch of chauvinist bastards in the country. But I'm getting there.'

She glanced up, apparently realising that the castle was only 200 yards ahead. Without warning, she increased her pace and accelerated away. Caught unawares, McBride was slow to respond. She had ten yards on him before he reached her. He did not reduce speed after arriving at her side. Instead, he pressed harder until he was running as fast as he could. He did not look back but, over the next fifty yards, he was conscious of her footsteps thudding into the sand closely behind. Then their sound faded and he knew she had dropped away. He stopped sprinting only when he reached the castle wall.

In the space of a minute, McBride had learned three things about Petra Novak. She had a healthy understanding of her male colleagues, she could run at speed and she was competitive.

He liked all of that.

23

The return journey along the beach was more sedate. She had tested him. He had responded and had triumphed. They were both competitors but he had the edge – just. It was good to understand the position.

They spoke almost continually – mainly small talk about the awkwardness of her shifts, his return to his home town, their shared need to exercise.

It was Petra who raised the subject McBride had been struggling to introduce. 'I meant to ask what was it you wanted from Dad?' she said, as though she had been contemplating the question for some time. 'He said it had something to do with the murder of Alison Brown, one of the chapters in your book. Congratulations, by the way, the book was excellent. Couldn't pick any holes in it – well, not many.'

McBride nodded his thanks but said nothing about his literary achievement. He did not want to move away from the subject that had prompted his furtive activities with the binoculars for the last two mornings. He slowed his pace, anxious that nothing like rapid breathing should inhibit their conversation. He gulped a mouthful of air.

'OK, I'll give it to you with both barrels. I think you lot screwed up. I think you banged up the wrong bloke and Alison Brown's real killer is still out there. That's all – nothing too serious.'

McBride turned to look into the face of his running mate. She did not return his gaze but continued to fix her eyes ahead of her.

Finally she spoke. 'Proof?' she replied simply. 'Where's your proof?' Now she looked back at him. 'Anybody can make these kind of remarks about any case. Show me the money. How do you know these things?'

McBride had waited for her to say that. He wished he had been better prepared to provide the right kind of answer. 'If I had proof, he wouldn't still be banged up – just call it intuition.' He braced himself for the expected response.

She did not disappoint him. 'Intuition?' She practically spat the word. 'Oh, that's good. Intuition. Just pop through to the Court of Appeal and tell them that. They'll set Bryan Gilzean free the same day.' She stopped in her tracks, forcing him to do the same. She faced him, the warm brown eyes suddenly chilly. 'You're going to have to do better, Campbell – a lot better. You're accusing several police officers of lying or being totally incompetent. Either way, you're going to have to come up with something better than some kind of journalist's hunch.'

McBride dropped down on to the sand beside a low dune and leaned back. He patted a soft area beside him, inviting Petra to join him. She sat next to him but there was no kind of relaxation in her posture. She held her knees below her chin. The body language said defensive.

McBride attempted to soothe her. 'Every wrongly convicted man has had to battle to find good enough proof to walk free. It's never easy but you have to start somewhere,' he said, in an effort to be placatory. 'What about this? If we accept the scenario that Bryan Gilzean visits his girlfriend, they have a drink and sex, in whatever order, then they argue and he strangles her.'

Petra nodded, cautious in her agreement.

'Three things,' McBride continued. 'They all seemed to have only consumed one glass of wine each. Fine, except Gilzean doesn't like white wine. If he'd wanted something to drink, it would have been a beer. Since he practically lived there, there would probably be some in the house. Next – why was Alison Brown wearing one of her best dresses and still in high-heeled shoes when she was found dead? Why dress up for your long-term boyfriend unless you were going out somewhere, which they weren't? And why was she in high heels in her own flat? She would have kicked them off the minute she sat on her sofa . . . if she'd ever worn them in the first place when all she was expecting was him. Would you still be trotting about in high heels for any regular boyfriend of yours? It's just not what you do, is it? You get comfortable in your own home, unless you're expecting somebody special, that is. At the very least, they would have been taken off or come off if they were having a bit of rumpy pumpy. Don't tell me she would have put them back on afterwards.'

He had DI Novak's full, if grudging, attention. She said nothing for a few moments, then asked, 'OK, my three things. How do you explain the presence of his semen? What about his fingerprints on the wine glass? And how did his hair get on the tie used to kill her? Basic stuff, really, and that's before we even start on the fact there was absolutely no sign of any other man having been in the flat.'

McBride had anticipated the questions but it did not make answering them any easier. He replied slowly, tentatively.

'Don't know. He says he hadn't seen her for three days and that's when they'd last had sex. Maybe some of the semen stayed in place?'

She gave him a disbelieving look. 'You can't even convince yourself of that, can you?'

Ignoring her truth, he moved on but he still felt sheepish doing so. 'His fingerprints on the wine glass – that's no big deal. He said he'd never seen the glass before but who remembers wine glasses? He was just about a lodger in the flat for spells. Of course he would have handled some of the glassware. Same with the hair on the tie – that could have been picked up off a sofa or something.'

McBride did not need another derisive look from Petra to make him aware of the weakness of his case. 'All right, maybe it isn't the strongest defence you'll ever hear. If it was, the jury wouldn't have convicted him. You convince me he's guilty.'

'Don't have to. The law says he is and everyone, except you and his father, thinks so too.'

He changed the subject. 'Did you work on the case at all?'

Petra shook her head. 'Not in any way,' she said. 'I was still a uniformed sergeant behind a desk at headquarters. Besides, it was all signed, sealed and delivered in no time. There was no need to rope in the uniforms to do any donkey work like knocking on doors and crawling about looking for witnesses.'

McBride hesitated, wondering how he would phrase his next question. Put the wrong way, she would back off faster than a retreating Italian army. 'Look, just to satisfy me, can you do me a small favour?'

Her eyes, filled with reluctance, widened, but she said nothing.

'Can you find out about the beer? If there was any. And can you get more information on the tie? Was it a young man's style or what? And, if there's any chance, whether the wine was cheap plonk or something better? Oh, and can you tell me what sort of music she might have been playing that night?' He waited for her reaction, wondering if she would come over all official.

She took so long to reply that McBride was on the point of rephrasing his request.

'If you're asking me to reopen the case, forget it,' she said bluntly. 'I've just made DI and that's the kind of trick that would put me back on the beat in the housing estates. Nobody likes a smart-ass trying to prove how clever they are, especially when it's an accelerated promotion female. There are at least half a dozen tossers just waiting for me to do something like that. But, because you were good to me when I was a daft schoolgirl in London – and because you have a nice bum when you run – I'll make a couple of enquiries. Tell anyone what I've done and I'll hack your balls off with a blunt knife.'

She rose from the sand and bent over in front of him, reaching down to touch her toes. As she slid her fingertips down the endless legs her sweatshirt rode up, revealing an expanse of soft, unblemished flesh. She stopped stretching as unexpectedly as she had begun and looked at him with the kind of smile that made him think she had read his mind. Then she started to run away from him. Her last words over her shoulder before she crossed the beach and on to the track back to Monifieth were, 'By the way, the bit about your bum – that's why I let you stay in front of me on the race to the castle.'

24

The last remnants of the afternoon sunshine had disappeared and, in the gathering darkness, street lights splashed pools of yellow along the Esplanade. McBride watched as a Royal Navy frigate slid soundlessly across the window in front of him, commanding the centre of the river and being pursued on the outgoing tide by a dozen seagulls.

He wondered where the warship was bound. Probably back to Portsmouth. Maybe round the coast to the Forth where the crew would be anticipating a run ashore in Edinburgh. Better if it was heading across the North Sea to Sweden where the women were sure to be more exotic, he mused.

McBride had occupied the seat at the window for an hour. It had been a time of relaxed contemplation, a pastime he excelled at. Next to running, cycling and sex – their order of priority variable – he liked to do nothing, if you called thinking nothing.

That afternoon he had considered many things, but mostly Alison Brown and Ginny Williams – and the supple, soft back of Petra Novak. Although he knew why he had not told his running partner of the morning about Ginny Williams and his unsupported belief that she had shared the same killer as Alison, he still felt strangely guilty. The flexible detective inspector had acquired the indefinable edge of all police officers but she had somehow retained the trusting purity of the schoolgirl who had come calling at his newspaper office in London. His conscience did not trouble him long. He knew he would tell her sometime, probably soon.

McBride finally removed his feet from the window ledge and rose from the high-backed seat where he occasionally also slept. Other things entered his mind. Whether he would dine at home, which was distinctly unlikely since he had only ever mastered the preparation of three different dishes – chilli, fried steak and pasta, all of which he had consumed in the last week – or visit the upstairs restaurant of the Ship Inn half a mile away. That option would give him the excuse of dropping in to The Fort on the way back. He might even find company there – perhaps not as appetising as the delightful Petra but also not the kind who would be looking for a lifetime commitment.

His whimsical deliberations were interrupted abruptly by a sound he did not immediately recognise. It was only when he heard it for the second time that he identified it as the doorbell. It was the first time it had rung since he had moved into the Esplanade flat. Although it had not sounded previously, he knew instinctively that the caller was female. It was not an aggressive or impatient ring. The touch was light, polite, almost apologetic.

His instincts did not let him down. When he pulled the door open, he looked into the face of DI Petra Novak and a smile that was simultaneously innocent and sensual. The sweatshirt of the morning had been replaced by an outfit that exuded chic. She stood before him in a short, simply cut black jacket and matching skirt that stopped two inches above the knee. She looked taller because her black leather shoes had three-inch heels. Her white blouse had an upturned collar and her legs were sheathed in black opaque nylon that, on anybody else, would have looked prudish. On her, they made him wonder about the colour and nature of her underwear.

He cleared his blocked throat as he cursed the discomfort he felt at being caught wearing the same shorts he'd had on that morning. But despite this, he couldn't hide his pleasure at her unexpected arrival. He did not even think to ask how she knew where he lived.

She was first to speak. 'Sorry to burst in on you,' she said, foolishly believing an apology was necessary. 'It's just that I was on my way past and I thought I'd update you on our conversation this morning.'

McBride threw the door wide, extending a welcoming arm and gesticulating towards the stairs. 'Please, come in, please. I was just thinking about you.'

She continued to explain her unannounced arrival. 'I'm on my way home. It's better than using the phone.'

McBride nodded. Inwardly he smiled. All police officers are pathologically suspicious, especially about the use of phones – hardly surprising since most calls in and out of headquarters are routinely recorded. Petra might have been being disarmingly open but she was also healthily cautious. By the time she gained another pip on her shoulder, she would be satisfactorily cynical as well.

They climbed the stairs to the sitting room where McBride had been exercising his mind. He began picking up discarded clothing and magazines and tried to put her at ease, forgetting that the room was in almost complete darkness.

'Grab a seat,' he said, waving into the gloom.

Her lips parted in a girlish grin. She stretched a hand over her eyebrows, theatrically peering towards the black recesses of the room. 'OK – just give me a clue about direction.'

They both laughed.

'Sorry, sorry.' McBride dashed around, switching on every lamp and stumbling into the corner of a low table. He swore silently again at her ability to make him clumsy.

She dropped on to a sofa and went straight to the point. 'Right. Answers to your questions – though God knows why I'm providing them. I need my head examined. First, there was beer in Alison Brown's flat – four cans, two lager, two export – in the fridge. The tie she was strangled with was black, and fairly well worn. The wine was white and, according to the photographs taken of the interiors at the time, the label on the bottle indicated it was a Chardonnay. I checked and it would have cost around six or seven quid a bottle. Don't know about you but that makes it expensive in my book. Last, and probably least, there didn't seem to be any music that night. The CD player was switched on but no one had bothered to put a disc in.' She watched his face, waiting for a reaction to her revelations.

McBride rose quickly from his seat opposite. He did not shout, 'Yesssss!' but clapped his hands once. In his excitement, he neglected to say anything by way of thanks.

'What did I tell you? I *knew* there would be beer in the flat. A black tie – why black? Morbid bastard . . .' McBride was no longer addressing his visitor but conversing with himself.

He rushed a question and without waiting for a reply followed it with another. 'The photograph – where was the wine bottle? Was it on the table beside Alison Brown's or her killer's glass?'

Petra closed her eyes, conjuring up a memory of the photograph. After five seconds, she said, 'The bottle was at the far end of the table beside the other glass – not Alison's. What's the difference?' She looked baffled.

'Plenty. If it was down the table, he did the pouring. And, if he did the pouring, the odds are that he brought the wine with him. Just imagine for a moment that Bryan Gilzean was *not* the killer. Alison Brown is expecting a visitor and is dolled up in high heels and flashy dress. Her caller arrives, bringing wine. Because he brought it, he pours. You're hardly likely to help yourself in someone else's house. And the bastard brought something else along as well – a black tie to throttle her with. If Bryan Gilzean had done the strangling and wanted to use a tie, he would have taken off the one he might have been wearing or another one that had been in the house. Either way, there's little chance it would be a black one – Christ, nobody wears a black tie unless they're at a funeral. That night it was Alison's. And whoever attended it was warped enough to bring along the appropriate neckwear. A right sicko.'

Petra had listened in silence, nodding two or three times but waiting for him to finish. 'Before you ask, the wine bottle had been wiped clean,' she said finally. 'No fingerprints, no sweat to take DNA from.'

McBride did not speak for a few moments. Then, almost as much to himself as Petra, he said softly, 'No music . . . the CD player on . . .' He paused again. 'Clever guy.'

Petra looked at him expectantly, waiting for him to expand. 'So?' she said.

'So, he brought his own disc,' McBride said. 'And it didn't contain music. I'll give you top odds it was something he'd recorded himself. Off one of the TV soaps.'

She still looked baffled.

'He needed the neighbours to think Alison and Bryan Gilzean had argued so he invented it. All he had to do was wait for a soap couple to fall out – which they do all the time – then record it. Played back at the right volume, it would sound exactly like the occupants of a nearby flat having a row. Neighbours never hear the actual words in these situations – just the angry voices.'

Petra looked impressed. 'OK, it all fits,' she said, 'except for his semen, hair and prints . . .'

'Jesus, Petra, we've been there. You know there could be an explanation for all that,' he protested, ignoring that he could not satisfactorily provide it.

She shrugged. 'The theory's not bad – I'll give you that – but that's all it is. Find the proof.' She stood up. 'I'll leave you to work on it.'

McBride remembered his manners at last. 'I'm sorry.' He spread his hands, seeking forgiveness. 'I haven't even thanked you for all that. You've been fantastic.' He hesitated. 'Look, I was thinking about eating. Can I buy you a meal to show my appreciation?' He looked at her expectantly.

'I'd love to but not tonight, I'm afraid – I'm due back on duty in just over an hour.'

She moved towards the door leading to the stairs. It was her turn to hesitate. 'If you really want to show your gratitude, you can give me a few running tips sometime. I'm running a half marathon in twelve weeks and need all the help I can get. They tell me you're an expert. True?'

McBride smirked in satisfaction. 'You're addressing a sub-three-hour marathon man,' he responded too quickly. It was one of his proudest achievements.

'So, any chance?' She looked at him hopefully.

'You're on,' he said, knowing it would not be a chore.

On reaching downstairs, he walked with her to her car. McBride did not know what she drove but headed towards a silver Volkswagen parked on the opposite side of the road. It just fitted – stylish, dependable, classy. Petra stopped beside it.

When she opened the driver's door, she did not immediately enter the vehicle but paused, turning towards him with an expression that said she was not sure how she would phrase what she was about to say. 'Look, Campbell,' she began, picking her words, 'I can't be seen to be getting involved in any reinvestigation of the Brown case. Without any kind of evidence, it's a non-starter as far as we're concerned. Any interference from me would go down like a lead balloon so you're on your own. But, for what it's worth, one of our guys heard a bit later, after the trial, that Alison Brown might not have been the Mother Teresa some folk made her out to be.'

McBride raised his eyebrows but said nothing, waiting for her to expand.

Petra hesitated again. 'I'm not saying she was a tart but, from what I gather, she was said to discreetly put it about a little bit. Nothing too regular – but, by all accounts, she was happy enough to have a touch of variety from time to time. That doesn't make her Public Enemy Number One but it might help explain a couple of things.'

McBride nodded. 'Such as?'

'Such as the reason she and Bryan Gilzean had argued before she died.'

'Sure, but it might explain something else as well,' McBride said.

'Yes.'

'Yes. That she had one of her "discreet" friends to visit that night. And that "friend" was the one who choked the life out of her.'

Petra slowly moved her head up and down. 'I know. It's a possibility. It's also a possibility that it gave Bryan Gilzean the motive to do what they convicted him of.'

McBride looked at her intently. 'You don't sound too convinced.'

She did not reply but sat in the car and turned the key in the ignition. The engine of the Volkswagen burst softly to life, waiting to be kicked to a louder response. The attractive woman behind the wheel obliged, stabbing the accelerator pedal twice and moving the gear stick into first. But she did not complete the procedure to engage the engine. Instead, she slid the stick back to neutral.

She looked up at McBride. Once more she spoke with something approaching reluctance. 'OK, naturally we checked out the "other man" theory before the trial and it didn't produce any kind of lead. But – and I'm not a hundred per cent on this – I get the distinct impression we may not have been quite as energetic on that aspect of the investigation as we could have been. Minds were probably closed because we thought we had the bloke responsible locked up.' Her expression was apologetic, as though the oversight had been hers. 'There's something else,' she continued.

McBride waited.

'Adam Gilzean was aware of Alison Brown's occasional infidelities.'

'What?'

'He seemed pretty clued-up according to a statement he gave us. He came to see us to say he'd learned that there had been at least one other man in Alison Brown's life at some unknown time and wanted us to reopen the case.'

'What happened?'

'Nothing. His son had been found guilty and there wasn't a shred of evidence putting someone else in the frame. We had better things to do.'

McBride's mind weighed the new information. 'Why wouldn't he have told me that?' he said. It wasn't a question to Petra but himself.

She shrugged.

He spoke again to himself. 'Why not tell me?'

She pulled the car door shut and drove slowly away from the kerb. The Volkswagen was 100 yards away before McBride was aware it had moved off. Belatedly he raised a hand in farewell. Petra watched his embarrassment in her driving mirror. She allowed herself a smile. Without turning she lifted an answering hand.

But McBride did not see it. Inwardly he seethed. Why on earth had the man chosen to stifle information that might have helped eliminate his son as a murderer? Just what was Gilzean up to?

25

Adam Gilzean enjoyed the darkness. He liked to observe without being observed.

He placed a stool beside the object which shared his secret activity and tried to decide what would interest him that night. He moved the telescope several inches to his right, sat on the stool, leaned forward and began to survey the distant, eastern suburbs of Dundee. For a few moments he browsed the diamonds of light spreading white and orange along the lower slopes of the Law. They shone in a broad line, house lights and street lights coming together to form a sparkling necklace round the bottom of the dark hill.

The unseen spectator eased the telescope minimally to either side, each movement opening up a new vista of flickering jewels. After a few moments, he raised the end of the eyepiece an inch, focusing on a panorama of house lights lower on the hill and nearer to him. He adjusted the magnification of the powerful lens again until only a few blocks of flats filled the circle of disclosure which was pressed close to his right eye. He turned the brass ring on the telescope once more so that only a single turret of apartments was in view.

Adam Gilzean knew the scene intimately. He gazed on it, becoming transfixed again by the sight of the flat where Alison Brown had perished.

Campbell McBride absorbed the same display of far-off lights as he drove closer to the home of Adam Gilzean, marvelling at the magnificent spectacle Dundee presented in the darkness. He envied the choice of house of the man he was about to visit. The further up the hill he progressed towards it, the greater his admiration became.

It was only in the dusk that he appreciated the full extent of the land- and seascape that opened up in front of the long bay window of Gilzean's cottage. Clusters of brightness punctuated the twilight in every direction. Out over the Tay, the glow from St Andrews cast a warm halo over the far edge of the firth. He realised the man he was about to visit would be able to view the ancient town directly, with nothing coming between him and the spires of its university buildings.

The thought of the place reminded McBride that, at some time in her now-expired life, Ginny Williams had probably looked in the opposite direction over towards Dundee and its surrounding countryside. He wondered idly if she had spent much time in the city or if she had visited it at all.

If Adam Gilzean had been startled by McBride's sudden appearance, he did not show it. He opened the door almost before the sound of the bell had faded, smiled a welcome and invited McBride inside. His politeness continued beyond the point when most other people would have blurted out a request to know why someone had come calling in mid evening unannounced. McBride reflected again that the man beckoning him towards a seat possessed the kind of composure usually found only in a priest or someone incapable of any sort of spontaneous act. He would have been a good witness in a courtroom – or a difficult one if he was on the other side.

Before McBride could explain his presence, Adam Gilzean provided an explanation of his own. 'You caught me star-gazing,' he said, gesturing in the direction of the telescope and stool at the window. 'It's a fascinating pastime, Mr McBride. Have you ever done it? It transports you to another world. An hour can pass before you are aware of it.'

His visitor gave a mumbled response along the lines of, 'A couple of times, a long time ago.' McBride was aware that Gilzean invariably took control of conversations. He seemed to be in control of most things. Especially himself – except when he was addressing authors in bookstores.

McBride struggled to claim the initiative he thought his unheralded arrival should have given him. 'Sorry to drop in out of the blue,' he said, trying to sound friendly but detached. 'It's just that something came up that I needed to ask you about.' McBride neglected to add that he could have telephoned except he wanted to look into Gilzean's face when he got his answer.

'Is there some news?' His host had become animated.

'No, nothing new. This is old ground.'

Gilzean said nothing but looked back at him expectantly.

'It's about Alison – I need to know about her boyfriends.'

McBride's decision to be direct wrong-footed the figure seated in front of him. 'Boyfriends?' he replied awkwardly. 'What do you mean?'

'Just that. What can you tell me about them? I gather Bryan wasn't her only male acquaintance.'

Gilzean rose from his seat and went to the large window,

pulling the curtains and killing the panorama of sparkling lights. It was as though he did not want the outside world to eavesdrop on what he was about to say. 'I'm not sure I can help all that much, Mr McBride. I don't know who you've been speaking to but, yes, I believe Alison might have had an occasional friend, male, at some time.'

'You didn't mention that before.' McBride made no effort to conceal his irritation. 'Didn't you think it might be helpful?' He was struggling to keep himself in check.

Gilzean looked embarrassed. 'Perhaps I should have referred to it but there wasn't really much to say. I didn't know anything about him – them – or even if there was more than one,' Gilzean said.

McBride was still irritated. 'How did you find out about it?'

'A few weeks after the trial, I received a phone call from a man who wouldn't identify himself but said he was a police officer. He said he was just passing on some information to be helpful – it was more than his fellow officers were. I took it up with them but they didn't want to know. As far as they were concerned, Bryan had done it. They saw no need to waste time on what they obviously considered a wild goose chase,' Gilzean explained.

'What about Bryan? Couldn't he help?'

Gilzean did not respond immediately. He picked his words. 'I didn't tell him – not then or since. It's one of the reasons I didn't inform you. Life is hellish enough for him in there. It would be a thousand times worse if he thought the woman he loved had been unfaithful. What's the point? It isn't going to change anything. It would just make his existence even more intolerable.'

The thought of his son's incarceration cast an air of

dejection over Gilzean. He sat down and practically slumped in despair.

McBride furrowed his brow. 'Have you any idea where she might have met someone else?' he asked.

Gilzean shrugged. 'At work? She was a nurse – Ninewells Hospital is a big place. I don't know if you've seen any photographs of Alison but she was a beautiful young woman. She had eyes as black as her hair. Attracting men would not have been difficult. Maybe she met him on the internet?'

McBride interrupted. 'Internet? Surely you checked her computer?'

Gilzean shook his head. 'She didn't have one – at least, not as far as we knew. She could have used one at work, I suppose, but the police apparently went through the motions of checking that out. They didn't come up with anything.'

The conversation between the two men stuttered to a halt – Adam Gilzean being a less than enthusiastic participant. But McBride was not prepared to ease the embarrassment caused by his son's cuckolding. 'Didn't it occur to you that Bryan might have known there was someone else and that he might have had more than enough of Alison's behaviour?' he said pointedly. 'That would make it fairly understandable if he suddenly lost his temper and killed her.'

Gilzean did not reply.

McBride pressed on, deliberately trying to provoke the man opposite him. 'She'd made a fool of him – maybe once too often? She got what was coming?'

Once again Adam Gilzean rose from his chair but now he stood taut and erect. His jaw tightened. A look of anger flashed over his face. 'Yes, maybe she did. She made fools of all of us. And we'd been nothing but good to her.' His cheeks had turned white. 'But Bryan didn't kill her. I've told you that. Nothing you've said changes that fact.'

This pronouncement seemed to signal an end to Gilzean's willingness to discuss the matter any further. Calmness spread over him and once more he took command of the exchanges. 'Perhaps I can offer you a cup of tea, Mr McBride?' It was not so much an invitation, more a polite change of subject and indication that their meeting was coming to an end.

McBride responded appropriately. 'That's very kind. Thanks but no thanks. I'd best head home.'

Gilzean extended his hand, which McBride grasped. 'Don't give up on us, Mr McBride. Perhaps I should have been more open before but nothing has really changed.'

Two minutes later McBride was outside in the darkness, pointing his car towards the lights of Monifieth.

As his unexpected visitor drove down the hill Adam Gilzean slid the end of his telescope through a gap in the closed curtains of the sitting room. He perched on the stool on the other side of the drapes, lowered his head to the viewing end of the eyepiece and adjusted the focus until the back of McBride's car was sharply defined. He watched the progress of the Mondeo until it finally disappeared.

26

Becoming an author had created a sense of order in the normally erratic life of Campbell McBride. It also imposed a discipline that had been lacking. His publisher had required 80,000 words to be delivered within nine months. So, the formula that dictated his existence for the pregnancy period of his unborn book was straightforward. He would produce 10,000 carefully crafted words every four weeks, a mathematical equation which permitted a comfortable safety net to allow for any slippage. It was a satisfactory, if unimaginative, routine but it created a welcome simplicity.

To dissect his waking hours further, McBride divided the day into three parts – the morning, when he exercised his body by running, cycling or visiting a gym; the afternoon and early evening, when he exercised his mind by writing what he had thought of in the morning; and the mid to late evening, when he socialised or, if fortune smiled upon him, he enjoyed other forms of exercise. He embraced the new orderliness, especially the first and last segments of the day. Now, even though *The Law Town Killers* had long been completed, he maintained the benefits of the structure.

That morning, he had cycled twenty-five miles over a route that took him away from the river's edge into the countryside. He had chosen the circuit for its combination of testing climbs and flat, fast sections and where the wind was not always in his face or backside.

By the time he had swept down the final descent from the village of Wellbank into the outer suburbs of the city, he was exhausted but elated. The time on the mini-computer fixed to the handlebars of his beloved Trek showed he was well ahead of his usual schedule. The number of consecutive mornings spent in the saddle or running was paying deserved dividends.

Although it was not yet 9 a.m., two callers had been to the flat on the Esplanade during his absence – the paperboy and the postman. The former had delivered *The Courier*, the *Daily Mail* and the *Daily Telegraph*, a spread of titles that covered most of the bases. The postman had apparently left nothing more interesting than invitations to sign up to credit card or insurance deals. It was only when he retrieved the pile of deliveries that McBride noted that one of the envelopes did not bear the usual frank mark indicating that disposable business material was inside. It had a real stamp in the corner and the name and address looked as though it had been produced by a human being and not churned out from a database.

The rectangular, white envelope also had a strangely familiar appearance, which was surprising since only a very small handful of people were aware of his new address and none of them were letter-writers.

He tore it open. The single sheet of white paper he removed bore only three sentences, all of which were word and punctuation perfect. They read:

141

Is the investigative journalist still baffled? All you know for sure is that Prince William is innocent! My new message to you is that the police have much to answer for. You will need to pay attention to the news.

McBride felt a hand reach inside his gut and pull tight. It might just as well have been his testicles which were being squeezed. He was being slowly castrated by an expert. What was worse, he didn't have the remotest idea how to protect himself.

27

The journey to St Andrews did not take long. In distance terms it is separated from Dundee by just a dozen miles. Culturally, and in practically every other way, the two towns could be on different planets. The home of golf and Scotland's most ancient university is everything the city on the opposite side of the River Tay isn't. Life is gentle and genteel. Women still use bicycles to go shopping, filling baskets on their handlebars with small pots of expensive marmalade and baguettes. Their menfolk potter in neat gardens, cutting hedges that are already too short and trimming lawns where weeds dare not grow. Sometimes man and wife come together in the family conservatory to struggle with the crossword puzzle in a quality newspaper. It is not the kind of town that ticks any of the deprivation boxes or is ever likely to have one of Britain's largest bingo parlours.

Campbell McBride had not visited the place for over a decade but he marvelled at how little had changed. The office of the *St Andrews Citizen* was still in Greyfriars Gardens, in the middle of a mixed row of houses and other properties, squeezed between a coffee house and a charity shop. Only the window full of photographs marked it out as the headquarters of the town's news organ and not another estate agent.

McBride knew without checking that at least one of their reporters would have been on the staff at the time of Ginny Williams' murder. Two kinds of journalists work on small-town weeklies, ambitious trainees starting out and long-serving veterans who have settled for a secure, if poorly paid, existence in a place where they like to live. It was one of the latter who came from the back shop to the counter to answer the bell that rung above the door when McBride entered.

The journo was mid-forties and was dressed in a checked shirt with the sleeves turned back and dark-coloured chinos. His muscular arms were mahogany brown and McBride remembered the *Citizen* also attracted people who took the job because cheap golf on one of the world's finest courses was a perk.

Douglas Wilson was undoubtedly such a man and, judging by the depth of his tan, he was probably a single handicapper. He bade his caller a cautious welcome. 'Morning,' he said, managing to make the word sound helpful and hostile at the same time. It was the traditional greeting of all newsmen, who start out by assuming that every stranger either wants a favour or is there to complain. Few people seek out reporters to be of assistance, unless they also desire money in return.

McBride knew the quickest way to remove the suspicion was to immediately identify himself as a fellow scribe. It opened doors at once. The *Citizen*'s deputy editor visibly relaxed, pushed the door to the back room and nodded for McBride to go through. Inside the cluttered office, the four desks were unoccupied, which explained why the paper's second-top man was answering the bell.

They exchanged the usual routine small-talk pleasantries for a few minutes until McBride decided it was time to lie. 'Actually, I'm having a bit of a sabbatical up here but, to help keep the wolf from the door, I'm knocking off the odd travel feature and the like,' he said, almost convincing himself. 'I recall hearing about a female from Australia – or maybe it was New Zealand – who was killed a little while back and was thinking I could do a potboiler on it for one of the Sundays Down Under. You know what they're like out there – anything to do with Prince William and the home of golf goes down a treat, especially if you work it in with a murder. They're all ex-convicts after all!'

Wilson appeared to accept McBride's reason for calling. He gave something that passed for a laugh. 'Tell me about it!' he replied. 'We've been flogging the story off and on since it happened. We're just keeping our fingers crossed they don't get the bastard responsible so we can keep churning it out.'

McBride laughed sardonically in return. 'So, what can you tell me about it all? I'm looking for the stuff you couldn't print. Was there any kind of suspect, for instance?'

For the next twenty minutes, the man with the strong brown arms gave chapter and verse on the life and death of Ginny Williams. He was so familiar with the circumstances of both that he never once referred to the files or clippings.

When he had finished, McBride said simply, 'So, who killed her?'

'That's the sixty-four-thousand-dollar question,' Wilson replied. 'The general reckoning is that she had a boyfriend of some kind who had called round, shagged her and then strangled her. But God knows why. There doesn't seem to have been any kind of motive, unless they'd fallen out about something. It certainly seems to have been someone she knew.

The sex was consensual – you know, no sign of a forced entry – and nothing seemed to have been stolen from her house.'

McBride finally asked the question that had been on his lips since their conversation began. 'What did he strangle her with? The police kept that back as usual,' he asked, trying to sound only partially interested in the answer.

Wilson shrugged. 'I don't know for sure but, from what we heard on the grapevine, it seems he used a belt. Christ knows if it was the one off his trousers. That would have made it a bit tricky if he'd had to do a runner!' This time Wilson laughed from his belly.

McBride barely took the joke in. The revelation that the Kiwi had died with a belt round her throat and not a tie took him aback. It was not what he had expected to hear.

'A belt? Funny thing to use,' he said, as much to himself as Wilson.

'Why?' Wilson responded at once. 'By all accounts, she was a bit of a belter!' He was enjoying himself now.

McBride ploughed on. 'What about the DNA? Anything ever come back on that apart from it not being Prince William's?'

Wilson chortled again. 'That was a cracking turn up, eh? "Heir to Throne Tested in Murder Inquiry" and all that. Great stuff. But no, they tested half of the male population. Even a lot of the cops came forward to donate their samples but there wasn't a single lead that we heard of. Not too surprising, I suppose. She was an upper-crust kind of bird and, if her murderous friend was the same, it's not too likely that he'll have found his way on to a database. No doubt he's crapping himself that one day he might.'

They spoke for another ten minutes or so. When it was clear Wilson had run out of theories and gags, McBride, profusely offering his thanks, made to leave.

They went back through to the front counter and shook hands. 'Be careful what you write, though,' Douglas Wilson said absently. 'Ginny Williams' old man is – or was – a cop in New Zealand. He'll shit on you from a great height if you make her out to be some kind of tart.'

From the *Citizen* office, McBride headed the Mondeo away from the town centre, steering an anxious course between the endless procession of golfers and tourists who pack St Andrews for most of the year. There were even some students, foreign ones mainly, who had stayed on rather than gone home for the holiday. Miraculously avoiding hitting any of them and only having to sound his horn at a dithering motorist once, he arrived, less than five minutes later, outside the house Ginny Williams had occupied at Clay Braes. He was not sure what he had expected to find – it had just seemed important to view the place where she had spent her last moments on earth.

As a murder scene, it was about as sinister as a kindergarten. He could just imagine the small garden in summertime, when it would be filled with brightly coloured bedding plants. The centrepiece on the postage-stamp lawn was a wooden bird table where two chaffinches were taking turns to extract nuts from a string bag. A stone path led from the street to the white-painted door. At the rear of the house, a privet hedge enclosed another garden about the same size as the one at the front. It was just as meticulously cared for and looked like it would be very productive in the vegetable department. McBride surveyed the bare earth and wondered what crop had been harvested from it in the summer and autumn months. It was a fruitless train of thought – with his limited knowledge of gardening, he was never going to cause Alan Titchmarsh to lose much sleep.

As he peered over the hedge towards what he imagined was the bedroom of the house, McBride became aware of a movement at the window of the house immediately next door, on the right. A middle-aged woman, who looked like she was one of those with a shopping bike, gazed unashamedly back at him. He smiled and did his best to nod in a friendly fashion. She gave no indication that she had seen either of his greetings but continued to stare back at him. McBride reasoned that there was probably very little she would not have known about the movements of Ginny Williams while she had lived in the neighbouring house. He entered the garden of the woman, pointlessly ringing her bell as she was already opening the door.

McBride smiled once more, this time endeavouring to appear relaxed but purposeful. 'Good morning,' he said in his best official voice. 'My name's McBride – I wonder if you can be of assistance to us.' He used the plural pronoun to indicate he was on a joint mission. 'It's about Ginny Williams. Terrible business – but we're still making enquiries.' He hoped the scowling woman defensively holding the door open by only a foot would assume the 'we' meant the police.

She looked steadily back at him, her face expressionless. 'You're not the police,' she said flatly. 'Policemen wear ties. Who are you? What do you want?'

He tried to sound reassuring. 'No, no – press.' He pulled his National Union of Journalists card, with the photograph that made him look like a mortuary attendant, from his wallet and held it up towards her. 'We haven't given up on it either. Like everybody else we want to see someone caught for this. Maybe you can help?'

She said nothing but the door eased open by another six inches.

'Were you at home when this awful business happened?'

The woman nodded.

'Did you know any of her friends?'

She nodded again.

'Were any of them there that night?'

This time she shook her head but also spoke, all suspicion leaving her. 'She had quite a few friends. Nice people, like her – not yobs. They always waved to me or spoke if I was in the garden. None of *them* would have harmed her in any way.'

McBride inclined his head in agreement. 'No, of course not. But was there anyone . . . not her sort . . . who was hanging around or looking suspicious?'

'Not that I noticed. I didn't see anyone arriving but, when I was in bed, I heard the back door closing late on. By the time I got to the window, whoever it was had vanished. It was dark anyway and late.'

'How late?'

'Eight minutes before midnight.'

'Did you hear anything before that – shouting or loud noises of any kind?'

'Not a cheep – Ginny was very nice, very quiet. She read a lot and used her computer all the time. She studied hard but always had time to speak to me. There was never any trouble.'

McBride chose his next words carefully. 'Would anyone have got into her house without you seeing – you know, if you happened to be in the garden or at the window?'

She did not take any offence at indirectly being accused of being a busybody. 'No – unless I was at the front and they came in the back way. If it was after dark and they used the rear path, practically no one would see a person arriving – or leaving.'

McBride had one other thing to ask. 'Did Ginny have a boyfriend?'

The woman seemed surprised at the question. 'Not in that way.' She was almost indignant. 'Well, not that I knew of – and she would have told me, I'm sure.'

McBride tried to soothe her as he departed. 'Of course,' he said gently. 'You've been extremely helpful. Thank you so much.'

As he turned to leave, she suddenly became anxious. 'I hope you're not going to put any of this in the paper,' she said, her voice brimming with apprehension. 'We're very private here. We mind our own business, keep ourselves to ourselves. You understand?'

'Yes, yes. Don't worry, nothing will appear. This was just between you and me.'

His fellow conspirator gave a relieved smile and retreated into the house. As he walked back down the short garden path, he knew without turning that she would be standing at the window watching.

Like most car journeys, McBride's return trip through Fife was an opportunity for contemplation and he used the time to idly replay the two conversations he'd had in the tranquil university town. They hadn't been the most productive, he reflected, but they had reopened a window on a serene way of life that he had almost forgotten existed. He smiled at his memory of the next-door neighbour in Clay Braes. She counted herself as someone who 'kept herself to herself' but still had a perfect mental chronicle of every movement Ginny Williams ever made. Douglas Wilson, the chunky golfing journalist, would have been astounded to learn that he probably represented the dream of half the scribes in London – only one deadline a week and the biggest problem in life being whether to go home for lunch or spend the time on the golf practice ground.

McBride remembered Wilson's parting words to him and smiled once more at the warning he'd been given – 'He'll shit on you from a great height . . .' Then he recalled what was said to be the occupation of the man who might carry out the arterial defecation – 'a cop in New Zealand'. A cop? Just like the father of Alison Brown? McBride swore quietly. How did he miss that first time round? Much more importantly, was that coincidence or an essential part of the selection process?

28

Detective Inspector Petra Novak answered her mobile at once. McBride, caught off guard by her speed, was still wondering what ring tone she would have chosen when she spoke. 'Novak.' The voice was brusque, clipped, businesslike. It did not sound like her.

'Petra? Didn't think that was you.' He neglected to introduce himself, unreasonably assuming that he always sounded like himself.

'Hello, Campbell.' Her voice softened. 'Sorry – thought that was one of the guys from work. You must want something?' She wondered if he would detect the sarcasm.

He didn't. His mind was too full of what he needed to discuss for irony to be on the agenda. 'More questions,' he said. 'I'm hoping you'll provide more answers.'

She sighed in mock impatience. 'Unlikely – you probably know more about Alison Brown's death than I do.'

'It's not about her.'

'Who then?'

'Ginny Williams.'

'Who? Never heard of her. She sounds like a tennis player. Is she?'

'No. She's a murder victim.'

Silence. Her long delay made McBride uncomfortable.

Finally, she responded. 'Sorry. Was negotiating a roundabout. And thinking. OK. I know who you mean now. She's not one of ours. She was the student over at St Andrews, wasn't she?'

'You're driving?' It hadn't occurred to McBride.

'Yes. Hands-free.'

'Oh, and what do other parts of you cost?'

'My, Campbell, you are a card. They'll be putting you on television next – *An Evening with Campbell McBride*, the sensational new humorist!'

'Why not? They've been after me for years to act as George Clooney's stand-in! They can tie that in with me being a replacement for Billy Connolly as well – I'd go down a bomb.'

She failed in her attempt to suppress a laugh. 'OK, I give up. Wish I'd never started it. Look, I know even less about Ginny Williams than I do about Alison Brown. There's no way I can be of assistance. That's a Fife case. Ask a friendly cop over there. Now, can you let me make my way to the gym in peace?'

'Sure. No problem,' McBride said, preparing to drop his bombshell. 'You're right, Alison and Ginny have nothing in common – except that they were probably killed by the same person.' It was like rolling a hand grenade slowly towards her feet.

'What?' It was not a question but an expression of anguish. He enjoyed her discomfort.

After several moments, he spoke. 'Sorry about that,' he said insincerely. 'Thought that would get your attention. Hope you didn't hit a tree. Can we speak about this off the phone? I need your full attention.'

'Bastard,' she replied. 'Since you've been such a shit, you can buy me a coffee and something to eat. You can do both at my gym.' She gave him directions and told him not to appear for an hour, by which time she would have completed her workout.

The Next Generation health and fitness centre, just off the highway behind Monifieth, is a squat, functional building made of yellow and grey concrete blocks. It is surrounded by a car park that looks too big but every evening it is full to overflowing. No more strategic spot could have been chosen when the owners looked for a site for their new club in the Dundee area. They built it on the edge of one of the most prosperous, developing townships in the district, where the young incomers had money to spend and prematurely bloated bodies to reshape. The thousands who joined paid the highest gym fees for miles around but, for their money, they received unrivalled facilities. McBride knew from the moment he walked through the door that he would take out a membership – not just for the use of the swimming pools and one of the largest gymnasiums he'd ever seen but also as a launch pad for new relationships with athletic women. He watched an endless procession of them pass by as he waited for Petra to appear.

When she strode across the restaurant floor to greet him precisely an hour after they had spoken, she was in another new persona. Her hair was still wet, her cheeks glowed and her teeth shone brighter than ever. She wore a close-fitting white, polo-neck jumper and designer denims than looked as though they'd come out of a gun in a paint-shop. To his surprise, she embraced him briefly, turning one of the radiant cheeks to him to be kissed. He complied willingly.

In sympathy with the surroundings, they ordered sensible food. He added a white coffee and she asked for half a pint of Guinness. McBride's jaw must have dropped because the request was swiftly accompanied by an explanation that it was required to replace nutrients lost in the workout session. He nodded, unconvinced, but made a mental note to use the excuse the next time he wanted to get pissed.

Their small talk lasted at least ninety seconds before Petra cut to the chase. 'OK, give it to me,' she demanded.

Although he had prepared what he would say to her while he sat waiting for her, McBride was still uncertain how to start. He began at the end. 'A year after Alison Brown was murdered in her home, the body of Ginny Williams was found in her house a dozen or so miles away. Both of them were about the same age and both had been strangled.' He paused and looked across the table at his surprised companion.

'Is that it?' the wet-haired detective inspector asked, incredulity spreading across her face. 'That adds up to a serial killer, does it? Let's get real, Campbell.'

It was the response he had anticipated. 'Relax,' McBride soothed, 'that's the easy bit.'

For the next few minutes, he recounted in detail the series of events that had prompted his move back to Dundee and the growing conviction that a double killer was at large.

His summary of his initial bookshop meeting with Adam Gilzean, followed by the prison visit to son Bryan, was received with interest but not much else.

It was only when he slowly narrated the sequence of communications that had come into his possession that he knew he had her undivided attention. He told her of the letter sent to him via his publisher, leading to the discovery of the missing words cut from the court report of Bryan Gilzean's trial. Then he described how he had unearthed similar extractions in the library about the death of Ginny Williams and the subsequent arrival of another letter, apparently from the same source.

She did not interrupt him until he finally stopped speaking. 'My God, Campbell – this is straight out of a John Grisham novel,' she said, shaking her head in something approaching disbelief. 'Who else have you told about this?'

It was his turn to shake his head. 'Just you – and I won't be spreading it around any more either. I want the same promise from you,' he told her.

She raised a questioning eyebrow.

'In case you've forgotten, I'm a reporter,' he explained. 'Mention it in the wrong place and there will be a big splash in the tabloids about a mad strangler on the loose. The fact that it's my story is only the half of it. If I'm right that Alison and Ginny shared the same killer, then the murderer and the message-sender would have to be the same person. Who else would know? Who would be able to make the link? But start to make that public and he could take fright and vanish as quickly as he seems to have come to the surface. My guess is that this has some way still to run. This isn't a guy who is in hiding and keeping quiet about what he's done. He wants us – me – to know about his murderous activities. God alone knows why. But he can't tell me straight out. He's some kind of fruitcake getting a kick out of spinning me out. He has to drop clues for me to follow up. What sort of psychotic is that? Whatever else he is, he's a control freak. So far, the only way we've any chance of finding out who he is, is by keeping him interested. He's still in charge of the game and that's the way he likes it. Scare him off and he'll drop right out of sight, probably for good.'

Petra absorbed every word, nodding occasionally. When McBride stopped speaking, she remained silent for some time, looking deeply into her nearly full glass of Guinness.

It was only after two hyper children had shrieked their way to the games room that she finally spoke. 'You know you're putting me on the spot, don't you? If there *is* someone out there who's killed two people, I have to do something about it. I can't pretend it hasn't happened.' She looked concerned.

McBride was prepared for her conclusion. 'In your own words – show me the money,' he said. 'Where's the proof? All we have is some madman sending me notes. He could be stringing me along, just making the whole thing up. Having a quiet laugh. What's to pass on to your superiors? They already have someone banged up for one of the killings.' He smiled at her, delighting in playing her at her own earlier game.

Petra did not return his smile. 'You don't believe a word of that.'

'No – but that's not really the point, is it? That's how it stands. You're the one who dismisses hunches and wants evidence. And meantime, there's very little of that.' McBride wanted to put an arm round her. She looked confused and unexpectedly defenceless. She was no longer the confident, high-flying police officer on accelerated promotion. She was the uncertain teenager visiting London for the first time. 'Look,' he went on, 'if I'm right, this isn't going to go away unless something chases it. Let's play it out my way and see what happens. No need for the cavalry just yet.'

She gazed back at him, anxious for reassurance.

He provided it. 'OK, think about this. The messages are

being sent to me. There's nothing that says I have to pass any of this on to the police, for the reasons I've just given you. It's my ball and, unless we play by my rules, I can just go away and play by myself. Then where would the police be?' McBride knew the logic of what he had just said was undeniable.

It was also the clincher she desired. Her expression changed to relief. 'Makes sense,' she said thoughtfully. 'So, where do we go from here?'

'We look for what links the two victims, that's where,' he responded. And we look for what links them to the last person they ever saw on this earth.'

29

McBride toyed with the remnants of his coffee. He stirred the last half inch in the cup for the third time and pondered over his next move. It was still early evening, Petra's hair had dried and the scent of her perfume drifted over him. He wondered what her plans were for the rest of the night and whether he should become part of them.

It wasn't the first time he had entertained such thoughts and the dilemma was the same. If he blundered in without finesse, he would probably be dismissed as some kind of prick-in-hand merchant – a sexual opportunist with testosterone for brains. Although it might have been a fair description of his approach in other liaisons, it didn't altogether fit with the way he viewed the detective inspector – not that he was entirely certain of the exact shape of that. What he was convinced of was that he wanted to do nothing to jeopardise the relationship – personal and professional – that was developing between them. The truth was that he was also growing afraid of getting too close.

Life after Caroline had been complicated but simple. Lots of women attracted him but he pursued the ones who shared his needs. Some company. Some conversation. And sex, always sex. But no commitment, never commitment. Easy come, easy go. The guys who marked him down as having a high success rate didn't understand the game. The trick was to know when a woman was interested. That way you didn't waste time. Funny thing was that some of the women who wanted the same didn't know it or wouldn't admit it to themselves. It was easier for them to pretend their desires were less basic.

McBride was not required to wrestle with his thoughts for long. As he lifted his cup to drain the dregs, a voice sounded behind him. It was quiet, feminine and warm and the accent was neutral. It made a statement and asked a question at the same time. 'You're here – and with company,' it said, the last three words an enquiry.

He turned to look into the face of a blonde who was speaking to Petra but gazing directly back at him. She was about the same age as the policewoman but taller. Her hair was not wet but blow-dried and carefully brushed back. She was wearing an Adidas stretch top and expensively cut casual bottoms that did everything for her athletic figure. If she wasn't one of the club's tennis pros, she worked out and regularly, McBride thought. Either way, he was impressed. He was invariably drawn to women who looked after their bodies – for what they achieved as well as what the discipline said about them. When they also possessed neat noses with nostrils that flared, McBride liked them even better.

Anneke Meyer did not play tennis but she most certainly worked out. Two evenings a week, after thirty minutes on a treadmill and a session with loose weights, she attended body combat sessions. Petra was among her classmates but that was not their only contact. Anneke Meyer's day job was in the laboratory of Tayside Police where she was a senior forensic scientist. Beauty, a little brawn and brains – like a moth being pulled towards the flame, McBride found himself irresistibly drawn.

He was pleased when she accepted Petra's invitation to join them, sitting on his other side in the curved dining booth and ordering mineral water and a smoked salmon sandwich. *A sandwich* – McBride repeated the word to himself and smiled inwardly. That was how he felt. In his occasional dreams, he'd imagine himself as the filling in an American sandwich, when he would be placed in bed between two outstanding examples of the female form. It had happened only once, in Northern Ireland, but that didn't count because the amount of drink the three of them had consumed to get them there had produced only incompetence, impotence and somnolence. Now, seated between two perfect specimens, he pondered on how differently he would react if given a second opportunity – in his dreams.

The conversation he had with the two of them was light, impersonal and sporting. They spoke of a forthcoming 10k women's road race and the closest they came to mentioning a threesome was when Petra and Anneke discussed the viability of them joining with a third runner to form a team. When more water was ordered, he knew it was time to depart with his fantasies intact.

He took his leave with the promise to Petra that he would follow up on their earlier dialogue and hoped she would do the same, trying to sound vague enough not to prompt interest from Anneke.

McBride was barely past the reception desk on his way out when the exchange between the two women swiftly altered direction.

'Nice.' The body combat instructor nodded her head in approval as she watched his retreating figure.

'Him or his bum?' Petra asked, light-hearted but curious.

'Both.'

Petra smiled but made no reply.

'So, what's the state of play between you? Sorry if I broke something up by gatecrashing your meal.'

'No – nothing like that. Just a kind of friend,' Petra said by way of explanation. 'I've known him since I was at school – sort of.'

'And?'

'And nothing. That's it. He's come back to town and we've met up a couple of times. No more – zero, zilch.'

'Whose idea is that?'

Petra felt her cheeks flush once more, this time without the assistance of a gym workout. 'Mine . . . his . . . both of us, probably. He's just a friend. Besides, he's a serial shagger.' She surprised both of them with the strength of her comment.

'Oh, like that, is it?' Anneke laughed, loudly enough to attract glances from a group of silver-haired aqua-aerobic enthusiasts in the adjoining booth. 'Is that a complaint or a compliment?' She giggled again.

Petra's flush deepened. She struggled to find a suitable response but failed. Her customary poise had disappeared.

'OK, relax. Just wanting to know how interested you are. Wouldn't want to tread on any toes.'

30

The news bulletin washed over McBride. More terrorist activity in Iraq . . . a drive-by drugs shooting in Manchester . . . four dead in a motorway pile-up . . . the usual stuff. Sure, it was serious but who really cared except those involved – and their families? For the rest it was acoustic wallpaper. Two minutes after the car radio got back to playing music, you'd forgotten all about it.

Not that day. The tailpiece item jerked him into full consciousness. *Police in Aberdeen are investigating the death of a thirty-year-old woman who was found dead in her home earlier today. She was said to have been the victim of an assault.* The voice of the female announcer was flat, unemotional. She might have been running off the local fish prices. *It is thought Claire Bowman, a lecturer at Aberdeen University, may have known her killer. A police spokesman said there was no evidence of a break-in to her ground-floor flat and nothing appeared to have been stolen. She may even have shared a drink with the person responsible.*

McBride felt hairs start to straighten on the back of his neck – *shared a drink . . . thirty years old . . .*

The 'message' about the murder of Ginny Williams that had been left in the library for him to find roared into his head – . . . *just one more on the list. Another much further away.* So did the note in the white envelope sent to his flat – *You will need to pay attention to the news.* The writer of the letter could not have been more explicit. He had promised another victim and had just delivered it. McBride did not entertain a single doubt that he was correct.

He pulled the Mondeo into the kerb and waited for the traffic to clear. Then he swung round in a tortuous U-turn and headed back to the apartment he had left ten minutes earlier. Inside, he went straight to the bathroom where he shaved and brushed his teeth once more. He dressed quickly, this time in a shirt and tie and suit that needed pressed.

Before leaving the house, he slipped his tape-recorder, a notebook and ballpoint into his jacket pockets, before checking the battery level on his mobile. Then he hurried downstairs and jumped back into his car. The entire operation had taken four minutes.

McBride drove above the speed limit as he cleared the suburbs. That was his usual practice and he never attempted to justify the fact that he consistently broke the law because he imagined all drivers did the same, except the slow ones who got in his way. But the journey he was embarking on called for haste, he told himself. He turned on to the motorway taking him north to Aberdeen and pressed the accelerator pedal further to the floor. An hour later, he drew into the car park of the headquarters of Grampian Police.

Instead of entering the building, he noted the force's telephone number from an information board outside, rang their switchboard and asked to be put through to their press office. An officious constable informed him curtly that the next press conference about the murder was due to be held a short time later. McBride congratulated himself that his instincts had not let him down. Unless a suspect is detained within the first few hours, the police invariably lean heavily on the media to broadcast appeals for assistance. They saw no irony in the fact that, at other times, they treated reporters like pariahs. That afternoon they would be anxious to make the teatime radio and TV bulletins. Unless Grampian Police were different from their colleagues nationwide, they would seek much but offer little in return.

So it turned out. When the media assembled in the badly ventilated room hurriedly pressed into service for the occasion, they were addressed by a detective chief inspector with the name J. Brewster on a chest badge who looked as though he wished he was anywhere else but there. He was starting to sweat under the white lights of the TV cameras even before he began speaking. After three mouthfuls of water, he read a prepared statement, using the ponderous phrases that only police are capable of. McBride stifled an urge to laugh. Why did police speak in public in a manner they would not contemplate in private?

'At approximately zero nine forty hours today, the body of a female was found in a house at 21a Park Avenue,' the chief inspector intoned. 'She has been identified as the occupier, Claire Inglis Bowman, aged thirty years. Her death is being treated as suspicious. There is no evidence that the house had been entered forcibly. We are interested to hear from anyone who may have seen any person or persons entering or leaving the house at 21a Park Avenue between approximately twenty-one hundred hours last evening and zero eight hundred hours today. We would also be interested to hear from anyone who was aware of any kind of disturbance or noise coming from the house in Park Avenue between these hours.'

The police officer finished reading from the official printout and sat down, clearly relieved to have concluded his message. He drained his glass of water in a single gulp then patted his shining forehead with a handkerchief taken from a trouser pocket. He did not seem to be aware that the cameras were still running.

A chorus of questions rang out from the two rows of reporters seated in front of him. Most of them asked the same thing. How did Claire Bowman die and what did he mean by 'suspicious'?

The detective chief inspector looked uncomfortable. He struggled with his words. 'We are awaiting the result of a post-mortem but her death may have been the result of an assault upon her. That is why it is being treated as suspicious.'

The journo sitting directly opposite the DCI was forced to state the obvious. 'So, if the PM shows the assault killed her, it's murder, isn't it?'

'It would be fair to say that,' the policeman replied, his serious expression unchanging.

The reporter continued to press him. 'What kind of assault was it?'

The sweating cop shook his head. 'We're not prepared to disclose that at this stage.'

And so it went on.

'Was anything stolen?'

'Not that we're aware of.'

'Did she have any enemies?'

'Well, *somebody* obviously didn't like her.'

'Any suspects?'

'No comment.'

'Is an arrest imminent?'

'No comment.'

Verbal jousting going nowhere. The media pack pushing. Brewster resisting.

After twenty minutes the exchanges had become pointless and the reporters began speaking among themselves.

Brewster welcomed the opportunity to wind it up. 'Thank you very much for your attendance and assistance,' he said, convincing no one.

The disgruntled hacks filed out, muttering about the impossibility of getting a front page out of all the evasions.

McBride did not go with them. He had long ago learned that more could be gleaned from a two-minute informal chat on the way out than from the set-piece interviews.

A female journalist with brown hair that was too long and lipstick that was too dark thought so too. She pretended to be completing her notes while the room emptied and hung back for the opportunity of a one-to-one with Brewster. She and the chief inspector obviously had history. She tried the old-pals act and used his first name. 'Jim,' she said sweetly, doing her best to sound conversational, 'would it be fair to say a weapon had been used?'

The officer appeared to soften. He smiled at what he was about to say. 'No joy, Joy!' He chortled at the joke she had heard a thousand times. 'We're not saying anything about any of that. If we change our minds, you'll be the first to hear.' It was difficult to know if he was being charming or sarcastic.

Joy did not care either way. 'Tosser,' she said. She tried again. 'What about sex?'

'OK but not here.' DCI James Brewster laughed uproari-ously – he loved his own humour. 'But, even if you're really good, I still won't tell you!'

'Double tosser! And you've no chance.'

'Only joking. Wouldn't want to be done for Joy-riding, would I?' The chief inspector was practically rolling on the floor. He put a friendly arm round her shoulder and attempted a charming smile. It materialised as a leer.

Joy gave an exaggerated shake of her head. 'You're pathetic, Jim,' she said. 'When you meet your usual brick wall, don't come begging me to use your crappy witness appeals.'

She walked away, leaving only a local TV station team in the room. They persuaded DCI Brewster it would be a good idea to do a short piece to camera on the headquarters steps outside.

McBride was pleased at their persistence. It would give him the chance he wanted to speak to Brewster alone. The camera crew departed with their reporter to set the interview up, leaving McBride and the police officer together.

'That was great stuff, Chief Inspector,' McBride said, hoping to appeal to his vanity.

The officer's face brightened. 'Glad you enjoyed it. Hard as nails is Joy. But she can take a joke – and probably a lot else besides.' He was moving back into comedian mode.

McBride responded in the same vein. 'Just a quickie – sorry, must be infectious – a quick question. I heard on the radio that Claire Bowman might have had a drink with her killer. Any truth in that?'

The detective suddenly became serious again. 'I heard that too. But they didn't get it from me.' He turned and walked from the room.

McBride went with him. 'I thought that – but is it true?' he asked.

'Sorry, can't say. You know the story – evidential and all that. We're not even saying murder until the PM is complete.'

'Do you have any doubts?'

Brewster said nothing but slowly shook his head. His brow had begun to glisten again. TV interviews were evidently more intimidating than female journalists.

There was just one more thing McBride wanted to know. 'Oh, by the way, Chief Inspector,' he began, 'Claire's father – do you happen to know what he worked at?' He tried to make it sound unimportant, an afterthought to help pad out the limited information issued at the press conference.

Brewster scowled but replied quickly. 'A cop – retired chief inspector from the Northern force next door. Poor bugger,' he went on, shaking his head in sympathy, 'he's seen his share of bodies and now his own daughter's one of them.'

McBride nodded in agreement, saying nothing but his mind was moving into top gear.

Back in the car park, McBride was heading for his Mondeo and contemplating his next move when a horn urgently sounded three times. He looked towards the noise and saw a small, black hatchback coming from the entrance and moving towards him at speed. The woman behind the wheel was waving frantically in his direction. When it pulled up, Kate Nightingale got out. She almost ran to his side. In one hand she carried a bulging bag and in the other a small tape-recorder. She was stressed.

'That bastard traffic,' she said by way of explanation. 'The press conference? I've missed it, haven't I?'

McBride nodded. 'By ten minutes. But you can relax. You missed nothing. I'll give you all there was – and it won't take long.'

'One of those, was it?' The tension lifted from her shoulders. 'Christ, I don't know why they bother with them. They're all the bloody same these days. You get a prepared statement that says almost nothing. Then they throw it open to questions but refuse to answer them.'

McBride nodded again, this time vigorously. 'You could have been there!' He lifted his eyebrows. 'Actually, why are you here? It's a long way from Dundee for what looks like a routine murder.'

She stared back at him and attempted a sardonic smile. 'That's a bit rich coming from you, isn't it? I could ask you the same question. In fact, I am asking. What in God's name are you doing in the Granite City? This is pretty small beer for a big-time investigative reporter. Why are *you* slumming it?'

He had been prepared for the interrogation. 'Got to eat, even when I'm in Scotland,' he said easily. 'The corpse is – was – a university lecturer. Nobody in the pokey for it yet. That gives it a bit of legs. A couple of the nationals will take a few pars. Besides, it will help me keep my hand in. That's my reason for being up here. What's yours?'

She seemed happy to accept his explanation. 'Double Dick,' she replied. 'He sent me. Seems to think it could be a bit of a runner as well. That apart, not much is happening in Dundee.'

She asked McBride for a quick take on the press conference, telling him she had been instructed to call Richard Richardson with a rundown before he went into *The Courier*'s evening news conference.

McBride obliged, nodding in approval when she took notes in flowing shorthand. 'I'm impressed,' he praised. 'Good to see they still have some standards at *The Courier*.'

She made a face. 'Nobody gets to work for Double Dick without it.'

McBride listened as she called his old friend and colleague

with what he had just given her. He knew Richardson would not be satisfied. Even by hearing only one side of the conversation, he could sense the outrage of the Dundee newspaper's chief reporter.

She did not make it worse by admitting that she had missed the conference. 'No. That's all the cops are saying,' she replied in response to what seemed like the same questions being repeated at least three times. 'What? Nothing like that. They wouldn't go into any of the details. Yeah, bastards. They'll be back grovelling to us for help in a couple of days if they don't get a quick result. Bastards with two faces right enough.'

She listened intently while Richardson appeared to be passing information and instructing her on what she should do next. She rang off without mentioning McBride's presence in Aberdeen. 'Interesting,' was her only comment as she squeezed the mobile back into her bag.

McBride realised she was deliberately stringing him along – that she had some nuggets to impart but was savouring having the upper hand for a few moments.

'What is?' he asked, knowing he would have to play the game.

'Don't think I can tell you,' she replied solemnly.

'I'll tell Double Dick you were late,' he threatened. 'I'll let him know you had to be bailed out. He'll kick that glorious backside of yours. Your expenses will be chopped.'

She laughed at his light-hearted blackmail. 'OK, you have me over a barrel.'

If only, McBride thought.

She affected the stern look of a schoolmistress. 'Right. Pay attention. Claire Bowman may have been the victim of a brutal sex killer.'

171

McBride was paying attention all right. And there was nothing affected about it. Her carefully chosen words left him stunned. 'Brutal sex killer' wasn't part of the scenario.

'What?'

The force of his question surprised Kate Nightingale.

So did the urgency of his next question. 'How do you know that?'

'Double Dick – he got it from some contact. Says the killer apparently made a bit of a mess of her but he doesn't have full details. Still, not bad to be going on with, is it?' She smiled broadly, enjoying her triumph.

31

They went together to inspect the ground-floor flat at 21a Park Avenue where Claire Bowman's life had expired. McBride had dropped his car at the motel where he'd booked a room and travelled with Kate Nightingale in her over-powered hot hatch. He told her he was hitching a lift because he didn't know the area and because she did since she'd once been based in the city.

His explanation was true but it was a lie. He knew she'd have to drop him back at the motel later and he'd invite her to eat with him and then convince her to stay over.

Their investigative mission to the crime scene was about as fruitful as the press conference. The short street of middle-priced houses leading towards a park was taped off at each end, with bored policemen standing guard to prevent everyone but residents from passing through.

McBride remained in the car. Past experience told him that, in these kinds of situation, it was always more productive if a female reporter tried to charm her way through the tapes. Cops with nothing to do could never resist a pretty face, especially if it was accompanied by a magnificent posterior. Kate Nightingale possessed both but they got her nowhere.

Her conversation with the overweight constable in his mid twenties lasted long enough but it was one-sided. She tilted her head, gazed into his eyes and did her best to smile demurely. McBride could not hear what she said but knew she was being flirtatious and engaging. It was how she was.

The constable was unimpressed. He did not say much. Just shook his head. Didn't smile back.

Further down the street, McBride could see six other officers inspecting the footway on both sides of the entrance to the flat where Claire Bowman had lived and died. Two were on their hands and knees, minutely examining the gutter. A female constable, looking even less interested than the guys manning the tapes, stood by the doorway. She was doing her best to suppress a yawn when a team of scene of crime officers emerged from the entry. They carried metal cases that shone and were still wearing their white paper suits, masks and overshoes. McBride looked again at the search team of cops in their all-black uniforms and idly thought a good cameraman could have secured a neat front-pager out of the scene of contrasting colours.

He was starting to mentally place the human chess-pieces in artistic composition when Kate arrived back at the car. She was no longer smiling.

'Waste of bloody time,' she said with unexpected venom. 'He wouldn't give an inch. Never mind get through the tapes, he wouldn't even give me a couple of scraps off the record. Tight as a bloody nun's backside.'

McBride thought her disgust probably owed more to the fact that her charms had not worked rather than any lack of information. He decided not to press her.

'Nothing strike you as odd?' he asked.

'What do you mean?' She looked blank.

'The search teams and the SOCO squad – eight hours after the body was found and they're still going over the place and in detail. They're usually away home long before now.'

Kate said nothing.

'What about your friend manning the barriers? Don't tell me you didn't get his juices going, even just a little bit. Yet he wouldn't give you as much as a morsel. I don't think you've lost your touch, do you?'

She stared back, still puzzled.

'OK, enlighten me,' she said.

'I wish I could. It just a feels a bit big time, that's all.' McBride shrugged. 'Maybe my imagination,' he said without conviction.

Kate Nightingale did not seem convinced. 'That's the trouble with you London reporters,' she said, her face brightening. 'You think, if you're working on something, it can't be ordinary.' She shook back her brown curls and allowed herself a soft laugh. 'Small things happen, even to big-timers.' She started the car. 'So, are you buying me supper before you attempt to get lucky?' She laughed again, this time because she wanted to let him know that, even if she couldn't charm policemen, she could read minds.

He awoke at 7 a.m., which did not surprise him. She was not beside him, which did. He heard a sound and rolled on to his other side to see what had caused it. She emerged from the bathroom wearing a pink towel and a white smile. She allowed the towel to drop to the floor and stood naked at the bottom of the bed. Tiny drops of water shone on her breasts. She brushed a hand lightly over them.

He watched every movement and tried to decide if he had enough time for what she had in mind. 'I'll make a deal,' he said, still gazing at her moist body. 'You can come back to bed if you put the room on your *Courier* expense account.'

'Bastard,' she replied, stepping up on to the bed and walking towards him. She reached his side and stood over him for a moment, inviting him to admire her dewy body. Then she lowered herself and moved slowly on top of him. 'Double Dick will never know the sacrifices I make on behalf of the paper,' she said softly.

32

McBride took the coast road home. The route followed the very edge of Scotland and swooped and turned like a bird of prey in flight as it hugged the shoreline. It attracted the tourists with time on their hands who didn't want to join the racetrack of the inland motorway. It didn't matter that it would add half an hour to his journey. McBride needed to think. Not about Kate Nightingale, whose scent still lingered, but about Claire Bowman, whose last smell to the world would be the anonymous, undignified mix of disinfectant and chemical preservatives. The softness of her body that, in life, would have pressed gently against a man, just as Kate's had done to him hours before, would, in death, be hard and unyielding. On the pathologist's slab she was no longer a woman – just a carcass to be sliced apart and stitched together again. She was also an enigma.

If he was right, she was the third victim – at least – of the same killer. Yet nothing, apart from how her father earned his living, appeared to connect her to her sisters in death. Nothing to say they'd ever met. Nothing unique but the same. Different cities, different friends, different backgrounds but inextricably bound, he believed, by the greatest similarity of all. Each of them would have gazed in terror into the same set of eyes before taking their unwanted leave of earth.

Maybe he'd got it wrong. If Double Dick's information was accurate, Claire Bowman's exit from life was a significant departure from the kind of fate experienced by Alison Brown and Ginny Williams – 'brutal sex killing' did not seem to be part of the deal. But what was the deal? It was three dead women. Three women who lived alone. Three women of the same approximate age. Women carefully selected by someone who wanted to drink with them before taking away their existence. Nobody said it had to be neat. That each of the pieces had to dovetail smoothly. There was just one small issue that needed resolving. Why?

McBride pulled into a lay-by just south of Stonehaven and used his mobile to call Detective Inspector Petra Novak. He told her where he was and where he'd been but not with whom. He said he thought his killer had moved north to Aberdeen.

She did not react as he had expected. 'Absolutely wrong,' she said as soon as he stopped speaking.

'Why?' he asked, surprised.

'Different modus operandi. Claire Bowman would probably have been very pleased to have been strangled instead of dying the way she did.'

'And how was that?'

'Long story. But you're off beam. This guy was a sadist.'

McBride could barely contain himself. 'Give me chapter and verse.'

'Too busy. There's a three-line whip on it up in Aberdeen and it's about as bad here. There's also a big security clampdown. Very little is being put out.'

know. Can we meet when I get back to
orking hard at keeping urgency out of the

aid again. 'I could be here all night.'
'Don't you want to know why I think
same person for all of them?'

lied, laughing softly. 'If you make time,
would be unable to resist questioning

it for at least a second. 'I'll need to eat
she said, trying to inject resignation into
ay me a cup of coffee.'
gate Centre?' He had chosen the nearest
dquarters in the hope that she would
ence there would run the risk of being
fficers and he knew she would not linger
to say if they went there.
d, considering an alternative. 'Make it
Bell Tree.'
Bride. They rang off. He was delighted.
named was a restaurant next to a Premier
tside of town where he'd eaten several
from London. The food was good but not
urroundings were pleasant, if unoriginal.
was not why Petra had chosen it. The
ts in the Bell Tree were discreet and
ted by enough distance for conversations
te. It was easy to enter and exit and, on a
noon, there would be few locals eating there.
rs would nearly all be businessmen breaking
to or from Aberdeen and other points north.

McBride sat for a few minutes in the l[...]
a rush of North Sea white horses crashed [...]
rocks extending into the water from a sm[...]
Contentment washed over him. He was [...]
Petra had something she wanted to discl[...]

He was not wrong. She arrived pr[...]
barely glanced at the menu before c[...]
without chips.

'OK, you first,' she instructed, 'then I[...]
mistaken.'

McBride gave her a rundown on h[...]
received a coded message hinting that t[...]
could be in Aberdeen. 'His phrasing – [...]
list. Another much further away" – didn[...]
sense at the time but, if you read it as[...]
it hangs together perfectly,' McBride sai[...]
explanation. And tell me why I'm mistak[...]

Petra took a long breath before she an[...]
strangled like the others,' she said, speaking[...]
Bowman was murdered by someone who [...]
the place – a pervert who gets his jolli[...]
women. The place was like an abattoir. I[...]
killed her by what he did, she would hav[...]

It was not what McBride had anticipat[...]
for a few moments while he wrestled with[...]
her revelations conjured up before he fin[...]
did he do?'

Petra pushed away the half-eaten on[...]
another breath. 'He knocked her unconscious[...]
her repeatedly using the same weapon. They'r[...]
count but they reckon he'd thrust it into her va[...]
dozen times – maybe twice that.'

McBride looked stunned.

Before he could reply, Petra spoke again. 'He did the same in her rectum.' She was starting to stumble with her words. 'They're not sure of the exact point at which she would have died – probably halfway through the ordeal.'

The detective inspector's poise was disappearing with every word. Her eyes were starting to mist. She was the schoolgirl who needed protection again. He covered the back of one her hands with his own.

She spoke once more but, this time, so softly that her words were only just audible. 'She wouldn't even have been able to cry out in her agony. The bastard had made sure of her silence by putting a scarf round her mouth first. So, you see, Campbell, strangulation would have been an act of mercy.'

McBride felt her hand tremble. He had no idea how to respond. He was torn between spitting out his disgust and reaching out to take the crestfallen woman opposite in his arms. But he had no opportunity to do either. Before he could speak, the silence was broken by the muted ringing of what sounded like an old-fashioned phone.

Petra reached into the bag at her feet and picked out her mobile. She checked the caller's identity, pressed the talk button and spoke quickly. 'Novak.' The authority in her voice took McBride by surprise. Her composure was back. She listened for several seconds then said, 'There was? What kind? Expensive?' Another pause while she received an answer. 'Any request to send someone up?' Pause. 'OK. I'll be back inside an hour.' She rang off and placed the BlackBerry back into her bag. McBride was impressed – both by her recovery rate and her choice of mobile.

She was first to speak. 'I may have humble pie for dessert,' she said with what seemed like sheepishness.

McBride gave her a questioning look.

'Seems Claire Bowman and her killer probably did share a bottle of wine. My sergeant doesn't know if it was expensive but he says he's never seen it in Tesco so it probably is.'

McBride was on the point of delivering his gem about the occupation of Claire Bowman's father but did not get the chance.

She spoke again. 'I'm going to tell you something which I know you're going to ask me but which you must promise not to write about.' It was a question as well as a statement.

He nodded his acceptance of the condition.

'The weapon – it was a police baton.' She watched his face for reaction.

He did not disappoint her. His mouth opened almost as wide as his eyes. 'Give me that again. A baton? A police baton?'

'Yes, an ASP retractable, the kind practically every force in the country uses.' She was almost apologetic, as though she was personally responsible for the choice of weapon the monster had used.

McBride whistled silently. He remained silent for several seconds then said, 'There's something else – Claire Bowman's father was a police chief inspector. Three dead women, all the daughters of police officers.' Before Petra could speak he added, 'And don't say "coincidence".'

She stared back, shook her head. 'No – I don't think so either.' Bewilderment filled her face.

McBride paused and then, as much to himself as to the watching woman sitting opposite, he said, 'We're into a different ball game. Are we looking for a killer cop? Is that why the bastard always seems to be one jump ahead? Or

are we after someone who just happens to hate them?' They weren't really questions.

Petra didn't try to provide answers. She lifted both shoulders in a shrug. She wasn't indifferent. Just baffled – like him.

33

High above the city, Richard Richardson stood at the long window of his flat and gazed absently down at the early evening traffic heading out of the centre of town. He took in the familiar panorama for several minutes, looking but not seeing as the usual tailback of cars built up on the road bridge stretching over the river. Finally, he turned away.

First he went to his bedroom where he selected a fresh shirt and trousers. He dressed quickly and entered the room at the rear of the apartment which had been converted into an office. Sitting at his laptop, he moved his fingers rapidly across the keys, opening up a familiar internet site and accessing a life that existed only within the walls of the room and boundaries of his mind.

He remained hunched over the keyboard for almost an hour. For much of the time, he breathed normally but, when his fingers were at their most animated, he inhaled sharply and a small hammer beat out a quickening rhythm in his chest. Sometimes the saliva dried in his mouth but he was unaware that such a thing had occurred for he was not required to communicate vocally but with keystrokes. When the strokes became sensual, his breathing, like his desire, was urgent. His composure returned only after he had removed his hands from the scrambled alphabet of plastic letters to place them upon himself. His satisfaction invariably came swiftly.

That evening, the two women who sat at home computers in other towns sharing his silent conversations had no idea who their communicant had been. Like him, they also used assumed names to explore their fantasies.

When he had finished, the occupant of the top-floor flat on the slopes of the Law carefully closed the lid of the electronic box that stored his best and worst dreams and returned to the bedroom. He changed clothes again and walked back to the long window of the sitting room.

Once more Richard Richardson stood looking out over the city without absorbing much of what was before him.

After ten minutes had elapsed, he called Campbell McBride with the casual suggestion that, if he had no better way of spending his evening, they should meet a short time later in The Fort. McBride, who had been contemplating ringing Richardson, agreed with the same pretence of nonchalance.

When they met, their conversation was only briefly light-hearted. Richardson made a few desultory attempts at humour but gave up before he had finished his first drink. It was apparent the topic foremost in his mind was the death of Claire Bowman. McBride felt the same but hoped he was being less obvious.

'How did things go in Aberdeen, then?' Richardson asked, trying to make it sound like an afterthought. 'Kate says you bumped into each other.'

McBride wondered if he was being uncharacteristically euphemistic but immediately dismissed the thought. When it came to discussing sex, Double Dick was never anything less than direct. He appeared not to know where his female reporter had spent the previous night – either that or he did not care.

Before McBride could respond, he launched forth, 'Funny business by the sound of it.'

McBride assumed he meant the murder of Claire Bowman. He nodded in agreement and wondered just how much his drinking companion knew about the precise circumstances of the lecturer's demise. 'You could say that,' he replied non-committally. 'It's anybody's guess what it was all about.'

Richardson drained his glass and called for another round. 'I hear it was pretty messy,' he said, looking directly into McBride's face for a reaction. 'A lot of blood, by all accounts.'

'You're well informed,' McBride replied. 'The cops weren't saying much in Aberdeen. So, how did she die?' He wanted to test the man seated next to him.

'God knows. Stabbed, probably, if it was as bloody as some are making out.' It was impossible to tell if Richardson was being disingenuous.

McBride said nothing but waited for the chief reporter of *The Courier* to continue.

Richardson stayed silent for a few moments before changing direction. 'I was a bit surprised to hear you were up in Aberdeen, actually. Good to see we provincials still have the kind of murders to excite the hotshots from London.' Coming from anyone else, it might have sounded like a compliment – from Richardson it was unquestionably sarcasm.

McBride shrugged it off. 'Always happy to help the local press,' he said.

Richardson did not smile or respond with a smart crack. Instead, he said quickly, 'I'll be happy to take you up on that.

What about keeping me posted with anything decent you turn up? We won't give you a byline but we'll pay you . . . quite well.'

McBride laughed. 'Sure you will. If memory serves, "quite well" is *Courier* code for a pittance. I'll probably just about manage to survive without it.'

Richardson tried again. 'OK, for old times' sake, then?'

McBride made no attempt to keep his face straight. 'Like that, is it? Desperation must be setting in.'

He was wondering how to get off the subject when John Black called out to him from behind the bar. 'A friend of yours was asking for you a few nights ago,' Black said, trying to sound mysterious. 'Said her name was Carol.'

McBride looked blank.

Black paused, enjoying the thought of what he was about to say. 'Well, she described as herself as "Christmas Carol", to be exact.'

The memory of Christmas Eve and the soulless sex he had shared with the woman he met in the bar returned to McBride. It was the first time he had thought about their encounter since walking out of the home of the small blonde who wore too much make-up. Unexpectedly, he felt a small surge of affection for her, more than he had experienced at the time.

Black held up a piece of paper with her phone number on it.

McBride waved it away. 'Give it to Richard,' he said, jerking a thumb in the direction of Double Dick. 'He looks as though he can do with it more than me.'

'Arrogant bastard,' Richardson said without smiling.

McBride deliberately turned his back to the bar so he would not see whether his old friend took the scrap of paper.

34

McBride cursed repeatedly, spitting the words out so loudly he turned his head to be sure he had not been overheard. It was an unnecessary gesture. In his irritation he had forgotten he was still at home, alone and cursing over the sound of an Elton John track playing on the CD player in the corner. He could not believe his stupidity or the slowness of his thought processes.

He moved swiftly from the chair at the window where he had been contemplating, crossed the room in two strides and grabbed his mobile from the table where he had emptied his pockets the night before. He stabbed in DI Petra Novak's number and drummed impatient fingers on the wall as he waited for her to answer. She did so within ten seconds but McBride was already starting to transfer his guilt.

'Christ sake, Petra,' he said testily, 'don't hurry.'

She was taken aback at his ill temper. 'Campbell?' she asked, the curtness of his voice making her unsure it was him.

He did not apologise or explain. 'Yes, who did you think?' he said loudly, without trying to conceal his annoyance. 'Look, we've boobed.' He had convinced himself the mistake was partly hers. 'We haven't staked out the library or put cameras up.'

'What?' She was baffled.

'The Central Library in Dundee – we should have someone down there – NOW.'

'What?' she repeated. 'You're not making any sense. Calm down, speak slowly and explain.'

McBride struggled with his exasperation. He chose his words and delivered them like bullets. 'On the basis that you might actually want to catch this lunatic, you should be at the library waiting for him. If he's true to form, he's going to leave his calling card by cutting out a message for me. That's when you nab him. Simple, isn't it?'

There was a pause, so long that McBride wondered if there had been a loss of signal. When she finally spoke it was to repeat McBride's own expression of self-anger. She swore quietly but with equal vehemence at their blunder. 'I'll get back to you.' She rang off with an abruptness that matched McBride's.

Half an hour later she called back. 'OK, it's done,' she told him. 'Two officers, a male and female, are in place. One was a student until a couple of years ago, still looks the part. The other is from the Drugs Squad. They usually dress worse than the folk they're after so he'll look as if he's there putting off time till his next fix. Both will just be part of the furniture.'

McBride asked softly, 'Cameras?'

'Being installed even as we speak – trained on the files of *The Courier*.' She answered his next question before he could ask it. 'No, we weren't too late. We checked today's paper which has already been filed and it's complete – nothing cut out. Don't worry, we're there for the duration. If he shows up, we'll get him.'

McBride's mind turned to the time of his last visit to the library in downtown Dundee. He thought of the sweating, odious figure of the inappropriately named attendant and his unwillingness to be of assistance. 'Was a creep called Brad on duty?' he asked Petra. 'He's an unhelpful little shit with a chip on his shoulder. Don't count on him for much assistance.'

'Didn't hear his name mentioned,' Petra said. 'From what I'm told, it was a female who was in charge. According to my sergeant, he didn't notice her face because he was too busy looking elsewhere at her anatomy.'

McBride laughed. 'If it's who I think he means, I can understand his fascination.' McBride might have opened the door of a refrigerator as an icy blast ran down the line.

'Why are men so prehistoric? Must women always be judged by the size of their chests?' Petra said. Then, as an afterthought, 'Besides, the ones who want to show them off are usually pretty thick.'

McBride laughed again, taken aback at her sexism. 'How unworthy – or do I detect a note of envy?'

Petra spoke again, changing the subject, becoming businesslike. 'On the subject of messages, I presume you still have the letters which were sent to you by the nutter you think could be behind all this?'

'Of course. Why?'

'They'll have to be checked for prints and DNA. Same as the files in the library. It's probably hoping for too much that we get a match but we'll have to complete the process.'

McBride's muttered response was as much to himself as to DI Novak. 'Fat chance.'

She went on, 'We'll need a fingerprint sample from you, as well as a mouth swab for DNA, for elimination purposes.

Same from anyone else you can think of who may have handled the letters.'

McBride thought back to the morning in the Apex Hotel when he returned from an early morning run and smiled at the recollection of the package Janne had sent to him from his publisher's office. He did not tell Petra of the black, lacy pants she had included but said she was the only person he could think of who might have touched the letters – her and all the postmen involved in sorting and delivering them.

McBride had more urgent matters to discuss. He needed to know the latest developments in the investigation into the savage slaying of Claire Bowman. He needed answers about how she was dressed, what she had to drink. Needed information of sexual contact between her and her killer. Most of all, needed an update on the hunt in Aberdeen for a possible killer cop.

Petra listened without interrupting, then replied. She could have been marking a tick sheet. 'She was well made up, well dressed – smart. She and the killer had apparently drunk wine, quite expensive stuff – both glasses are being checked. The matter of sex is less straightforward. Because of the internal injuries and all the blood, we'll probably never know for sure if intercourse had taken place. But there was some sexual activity.' She hesitated, picking her words. 'Semen was found on her face. By the looks out of it, the killer may have stood over her, masturbating – probably after she was dead.' Petra paused once more. 'Depending on how long he had been with her, it's probably unlikely that he would have had the desire, or ability, to ejaculate twice within a short timescale. That changes the profile of the bastard. It elevates him to the weirdo category. Sex with corpses – not nice.'

McBride had listened in silence. He started to speak but once again Petra anticipated what he was about to say. 'Yes, in addition to checking the usual databases for a DNA match, steps are being taken to get samples from every officer in Grampian Police,' she explained. 'Some of them are already on record, the ones who've been processed before for elimination purposes. Most of the others should volunteer. The politically correct types, who decline on the ground of an infringement of their human rights, will still be checked out – covertly. In fact, the ones who refuse will be given priority. The forensic science squad will follow them round for sweat traces on canteen cups etc. It might be a slow business but it will be completed eventually.'

McBride spoke at last. 'Impressive,' he said. 'What about the baton? Anything on it?'

'You won't be surprised to hear that, Claire Bowman's blood and gore apart, it's as clean as a whistle. Worse, it doesn't carry any numbers linking it to an individual officer.'

'What does that mean?'

'It means it's a needle in a haystack,' Petra said. 'If it had been officially issued, it would have had an identification number. But anyone as bright as our killer appears to be would hardly have left a murder weapon that virtually bore their name.'

'Where does that leave us?'

'Up shit creek – that's where. Maybe the person who used it to such sadistic effect on Claire is a cop. Then again, an ASP baton isn't exactly the most difficult thing to acquire. You'd manage to get one in five minutes off the internet.'

'So, it's back to square one?'

'Worse.'

'Can't be – but tell me anyway,' McBride said.

'When Claire Bowman's father was informed of her death, he couldn't take it in. Not because it was so shocking but because he's doolally – Alzheimer's. He's never going to be able to explain why him having been a policeman might have had something to do with her losing her life.' She paused, then added slowly, 'Come to think of it, for him, that's a blessing . . . definitely.'

35

The detective sergeant did not like McBride. He made it obvious as soon as they looked into each other's eyes. He didn't smile at the reporter. Didn't attempt small talk. Just introduced himself in a voice that froze in his mouth. 'My name's Sergeant Rodger,' he said. 'DI Novak says you have letters I need to collect.' Icicles hung from every word.

McBride looked at the figure standing on his doorstep. He wasn't short, wasn't tall – just somewhere in between. Good shoulders. Intelligent eyes. Nice face. If he learned how to smile, he'd be attractive.

McBride was tempted just to leave him out in the rain while he went for the letters that needed to be examined in the science lab. Instead, he beckoned him in.

'Nice to meet you, Sergeant,' he pretended, offering a hand. 'Come in. Dry off. Cup of coffee?'

Detective Sergeant Rodger even managed to make the handshake cool. He looked as though he would have preferred to remain outside but politeness forced him over the threshold. He declined the coffee and the offer of a seat and made the same excuse for both refusals. 'No thanks – in a bit of a hurry.' Still no smile.

McBride abandoned the struggle. He left the room without speaking and went to collect the letters the frosty cop had called for. When he returned, DS Rodger was holding open a transparent, polythene sample bag and making it clear he expected McBride to drop them into it without his own cold hands having to touch them. McBride silently complied and said nothing until he was showing the sergeant out.

'Give Petra my love and tell her I'll ring this evening,' he said, trying to imply an intimacy.

Rodger said nothing. His nod of agreement was practically imperceptible and, if McBride had blinked, he would have missed it. But the policeman's reaction answered McBride's question to himself. Detective Sergeant Rodger didn't like him because he believed Petra Novak did. McBride felt reassured and unexpectedly possessive.

Two hours later, he called Petra for a progress report on Claire Bowman. But first he asked about her detective sergeant to tease her and because he wanted to be sure he understood the relationship between her and the unfriendly visitor to his home. 'Thanks for sending round the iceman,' McBride said. 'I've received warmer receptions in the mortuary. Joke-a-minute, isn't he?'

She laughed softly. He could imagine her lips parting and her eyes crinkling at the corners. He wondered how her head looked on a pillow.

'Gavin? He's just suspicious of reporters – especially flash gits from London. Tries to protect me from your unscrupulous methods.' She laughed again.

'If he thinks I'm the enemy, he can't be very bright,' McBride said.

'On the contrary,' she countered, 'he's accelerated promotion too. Social and management sciences graduate – first-class honours.'

'Oh, a right clever Dick. Actually, I think that's his problem.'

'What is?'

'His dick. He seems to want to hold it in his hand when he thinks about you.'

This time Petra's giggle told him it was not something she had ever witnessed or even contemplated. 'Hmm – now, that might be interesting.' It was her turn to tease. She laughed again. 'You can be very basic, Campbell. At least Gavin's refined – and not some kind of machine out to shag the entire female population of the world. Just a pity he's so young. I prefer my men with a few more cobwebs. Besides, I outrank him. It would be a right wham, bam and thank you ma'am with him. On the other hand, he might stand to attention all night!'

McBride snorted. But he was satisfied that, whatever the bond was between Detective Sergeant Gavin Rodger and Detective Inspector Petra Novak, it was not physical.

He changed the subject and asked about the progress of the stakeout at the Central Library in the centre of town.

'Still nothing happening,' Petra said. 'The usual regulars have been reading *The Courier* and the other dailies but, so far, no one has shown up with a razor – beginning to think no one will.'

McBride shook his head dismissively. 'He'll turn up. Put money on it. It's part of the little games the bastard is playing with me. He won't be able to stop himself.'

Petra was not convinced. A doubtful look, which he could not see but felt, passed across her face.

'He must know that sooner or later – *later*, as it happened – we'd get round to staking the place out,' she said. 'Whatever else he may be, I don't think an idiot is among them. Why would he walk into a trap he knows is there?'

'Because he'll be driven to it. Same as he is driven to kill young women who are the daughters of policemen. Being intelligent doesn't preclude a person from being unable to resist acting compulsively. There wouldn't be many smokers if that wasn't the case.'

Petra did not reply.

McBride gave up trying to explain the urges which can persuade otherwise rational males to commit irrational, self-damaging acts. He could have used himself as an example but didn't. Instead, he changed the subject again, ironically turning to the theme which had punctuated his own life with episodes of foolishness. He spoke of a woman. 'What of the stunner at the library? Is she still behind the counter?' he asked.

'Seems so – much to the delight of some of my hormonally challenged officers. Your friend Brad is on holiday, apparently.'

McBride tried to imagine the odious library assistant lying in the sun somewhere but was unable to. Sun cream being applied to the sweating little man's face and body was not a vision he could comfortably conjure up.

Petra spoke again – this time to impart information that gave her control of the conversation. 'Forensics have made some progress up in Aberdeen. Amidst the blood and semen, they found a pubic hair on Claire Bowman – on her face. Not her pube but his. It's a perfect DNA match with the semen.'

'Great,' McBride said.

'Yes and no,' she replied. 'We know the source is the same but we've no idea who he is. He isn't on the database.'

'At least we'll know him when we find him,' McBride said.

'Will we? We have three corpses, apparently linked in death. Each of them had sex before they died but, according to the checks we've run, not with the same man. Helpful, isn't it?'

Neither of them spoke for a few moments.

McBride broke the silence. 'You're not going to like this,' he said, 'but a little theory has been pushing its way to the surface with me.'

'And?'

'And think about this – we're not looking for one man but two or three, acting as a small team.'

He could hear the disbelief in the thunderous hush coming down the line.

When, at last, she did reply it was to ridicule him. 'Get real, Campbell! You're starting to grab at straws. A team? For God's sake!' She repeated it in capital letters. 'A TEAM?'

'Why not? And here's something else for nothing – the team is made up of cops.'

McBride did not permit her an opportunity to mock him further. Before she could unleash another shaft of derision, he pressed on. 'You guys always go about in pairs. You have to hold hands in everything you do. Gets to be a habit. Why not extend that to perversions? And don't tell me none of you entertain impure thoughts when it comes to sex and violence. If you accept my scenario, it answers some of the questions.'

'Such as?' The detective inspector was unable to keep a scornful note out of the two words.

'Such as the ease with which the killer seemed to get in and out of the murder scenes. When people are asked if they've seen anybody acting suspiciously, no one thinks of replying, "Oh yes, officer, it was that other nice officer I saw in the area."'

She was not convinced – not nearly. 'What else does it answer?'

'Why they are all the daughters of policemen – that may be a big part of their perversion.'

'What else?' Petra asked, sounding as though she was doing nothing more than going through the motions.

'It helps explain how they could have been admitted to the victims' homes. If a cop comes calling, you're happy to invite them in. You sure as hell don't call the police!'

'Oh, right – and then you ask them to sit down and have an expensive glass of wine with you? You're in fantasy land, Campbell.'

'Cops drink,' McBride said defensively.

'OK, if you're right, we've got them,' Petra said, her voice starting to mock.

'How do you mean?' He was wary.

'All we have to do is take DNA swabs from every policeman in the country. Unless, of course, your team of perverts are just pretending to be cops – then we're back to square one.'

McBride was deflated but not defeated. 'So, smarty-pants Detective Inspector, what's your theory? You're not exactly Sherlock Holmes on this, are you?'

She ignored his petulance. 'Unless you've forgotten, the first person to be swabbed in all of this is you. We need to eliminate you from any traces on the letter and envelopes collected by the warm-hearted Gavin Rodger, the detective sergeant with the impeccable taste in senior officers.'

36

The wind was blowing out of the west so McBride headed into it. He would fight it for a few miles then turn for home so it would be at his back just as fatigue was setting into his legs.

He decided against his familiar route along the edge of the river where the gusts were snapping the flags on the lifeboat shed and, instead, turned off the Esplanade and headed at an angle towards the main road taking the early morning traffic into Dundee. Even at 7.20 a.m., the cars from the eastern suburbs were hanging on to each other's bumpers.

As he ran, McBride thought of two things. Why did so many people who drove off-road vehicles only ever use them to go to the office or supermarket? And why did a killer or killers take the lives of their victims by different methods? The whole point about sequential homicides was their similarities, not their differences.

He was no nearer a solution to either of the riddles when the mobile he carried in the front zipped pocket of his running jacket chimed rhythmically to life.

McBride did not carry the phone at that time of day to receive messages. He did not know more than a handful of people who would be conscious at that hour and none of them would be alert enough to want a conversation. He took the mobile with him in case he lost an argument with an off-road monster and needed to call an ambulance. Besides, he did not permit a wide distribution of his number. That someone should interrupt him in the middle of his training unreasonably irritated him. Every run he ever undertook, even the ones that did not matter, was precisely timed and the full details written into a running log. It was of no relevance that he never looked at the entry again.

He drew reluctantly to a halt and extracted the mobile, touching the green answer button and pressing a finger against his spare ear so he might have some chance of hearing the caller over the cacophony of traffic noises surrounding him.

The woman who spoke to him was unknown yet familiar. 'Campbell?' The voice was gentle, accent-less, enquiring. He wondered why so many people seemed not to expect the person who owned the mobile they were calling to be the person who actually answered it. It was another of life's paradoxes. So, he reflected, was the fact that he could be at his most philosophical and fractious in the earliest part of the day.

'Campbell who?' he asked with mock awkwardness. It had the desired effect. Silence. He visualised the consternation on the face of the mystery caller.

After several moments. 'Oh, McBride . . . Campbell McBride. Is he there?' Her poise had vanished.

'You're in luck. This is he.' He immediately felt guilty. 'Sorry,' he hurried, 'just my little early-morning joke. Now, tell me who you are.'

'Anneke . . . Anneke Meyer. We met at Next Generation. Petra Novak introduced us.'

McBride's recall was instant. The face of the athletic blonde with the sensual nose sprang into his mind. He regretted his flippancy even more. He apologised again. As he gushed his words of contrition, he struggled to think of a reason she would be calling him and at 7.20 a.m. He knew it would not be for the purpose he might have wanted.

'I need a sample – DNA. Petra gave me your number so we could arrange it,' she said.

He had forgotten she was employed in the science lab of Tayside Police. 'No problem. When? Where? I'm completely at your disposal.' McBride grovelled in his attempt to atone for his off-putting levity at the start.

'ASAP. I'm going out of town before lunchtime. That's why I'm calling so early – sorry about that by the way but Petra said you were an early riser. Don't know how she knows that. Not even exactly sure what she meant by it!' Now it was Anneke Meyer who was being provocative.

McBride permitted himself a smile at how Petra might have reacted had she heard the last part of the conversation. He laughed at the thought and also at what he was about to say in response to her veiled enquiry. 'Are you asking how I stand with Petra?' This time both of them chuckled but it conveniently left the unasked question hanging in midair.

When Anneke spoke again, it was to arrange when she would enter his mouth with a swab. 'Your place or mine?' she offered. 'Whatever is most convenient. I'm based at headquarters in West Bell Street but I can drop round to your flat if it's better for you.'

McBride mentally debated the alternatives for one-tenth of a second.

'Make it my place in two hours, then.'

All the way home, he thought about women. Even when

he fought with the convoys of vehicles pouring through the confused Claypotts junction and its forest of traffic lights, he could not get three dead females and two very-much-alive ones out of his mind. The corpses should have taken up most of his deliberations but it was Petra Novak and Anneke Meyer who kept displacing them.

The two women were the same but different. Both magnetically attractive but one raven haired, the other blonde. Both athletic but one fragile like a ballet dancer, the other powerful with a well-defined physique. Both successful in their careers but one vulnerable and sensitive. He was attracted to each of them but knew which he preferred. He also knew he would move for the other one.

He was still struggling to work out the logic of that contradiction when he passed under the 400-foot twin wind turbines powering the giant Michelin tyre plant at Baldovie. The two whirling brutes, the most massive in a urban setting anywhere in the world, were said to resemble graceful pieces of industrial sculpture. Fine if you only had to view them on the journey home, not so satisfactory if your home sat in their endlessly rotating shadows.

When McBride finally turned out of the wind, he allowed the breeze at his back to help him pick up his pace. He ran away from the factories on either side of him and set off along a narrow road dividing a patch of countryside. As he pushed up an incline that would soon take him back to his apartment on the riverside, he realised he was within the telescopic range of Adam Gilzean. Idly, he wondered if the man who had been responsible for bringing him back to live in the area had his eyepiece focused upon him. He lifted a hand and waved in Gilzean's direction without knowing why.

When he was half a mile from home, McBride accelerated

again, this time to raise his heart rate as close as possible to its maximum 190 beats a minute. The only other occasions when it reached such a level were when he was engaged in a different kind of activity and always with a woman. He thought of Anneke Meyer and the light sweat that covered his body and wondered whether he should still be in his after-shower towel when she arrived to sample him.

Such musings disappeared the moment he opened the front door of his apartment. Lying on the carpet was a long white envelope, of the identical type he had recently passed to Detective Sergeant Rodger. The neatly folded piece of paper inside bore only two computer-generated words: 'Wrong library!'

37

This time he did not take the scenic route. He sped through the outskirts of the city behind the wheel of the Mondeo, unaware but indifferent that he passed the headquarters of the police traffic department at 20 mph above the speed limit in his haste to hit the motorway for Aberdeen. McBride may not have been a good driver but he was invariably a lucky one. Like every other occasion when he was in breach of the Road Traffic Act, which was most times he drove, he escaped a ticket.

His mind raced almost as swiftly as his driving. He could not believe his stupidity. Like a simpleton, he had naively believed the man he hunted would turn up on cue at the local library and walk straight into the arms of the detectives waiting in their disguises. Sure, he would show but not where he was expected. It was obvious now – just as it had been obvious to Petra that he wouldn't appear.

But, as he cursed himself, McBride had the satisfaction of knowing he was almost certainly correct in his prediction that his quarry could not resist leaving another message. He was convinced it would be waiting for him where they filed the newspapers in the main public library in Aberdeen.

He had other reasons to regret his dash north. When Anneke Meyer called with her swabs, she had been inclined to linger. Wanted another coffee. Wanted to discuss his fitness. Wanted to touch him when they spoke. Wanted intimacy.

He had wanted it too – but not then.

When they parted she thanked him for his co-operation and bade him a formal goodbye. She also took a notebook from her briefcase and wrote quickly on a page which she removed and placed on the small table near the door. McBride knew without looking that it was her home telephone number.

When he reached the library, he did not waste time asking for the recent files of *The Courier* but instead asked to be directed to those of *The Press and Journal*, the morning paper for Aberdeen. He was starting to get inside the head of the person who had silently sent him there – local murder, local paper. It was a pity the logic had taken so long to penetrate.

All libraries look the same even when the decor and shape are different. But unlike Dundee, there were no stunning breasts to captivate or sweaty creep to aggravate him. Just a friendly woman in her middle years who took his arm and led him to where he wanted to go. She left him alone to make his discovery.

The report of the press conference given by Detective Chief Inspector James Brewster was impressively lengthy considering how little the gag-a-minute cop had actually disclosed to the assembled hacks. McBride did not trouble to read any of it. He was riveted by the gap in the text – it had been left by someone with an obsessive predilection for neatness, manipulating an exceedingly sharp blade. He had fully expected a passage to be excised yet, when actually faced by its absence, it still had the capacity to startle him. Once again he reluctantly admired the meticulous craftsmanship of the deadly hand which had removed the words. It was not something he dwelt on. Of much greater importance was the nature of the words themselves. He needed to know where the trail of death was heading and if the journey was nearly over.

McBride noted the paragraphs on either side of the missing passage so he could ascertain what had been cut out. Then he travelled across the city to the headquarters of *The Press and Journal* to purchase an undamaged copy of a paper of the same date. As he entered the two-storey block off the Lang Stracht, McBride remembered that, only a few months earlier, his old employers, DC Thomson's, owners of *The Courier*, had purchased the rival Aberdeen Journals group in a £132-million deal that had taken the newspaper world by surprise. Not for the first time, he marvelled at the business acumen of the reclusive Dundee press barons who made little fuss but much money and still retained a contented and loyal workforce.

He had personal reasons for his sense of satisfaction at the takeover of the Aberdeen titles. As a junior *Courier* reporter, he had been sent as a one-man team into the disputed Mearns area to fight a circulation war with a rival six-strong pack of *Press and Journal* hacks.

Got you in the end, he said silently.

The receptionist who came back from the circulation department bearing the newspaper was polite but not really interested. She took his money and went back to picking at her cuticles.

McBride began reading the paper before he was out of the building. The story of the murder of Claire Bowman led the front page but the part of the report he was after was in the carry-forward contained in the main body of the daily. He stopped walking and pulled his notebook from a pocket to remind himself of the paragraphs he had jotted down. Then he scanned the words of the local reporter to locate the few words that had forced him to drive at speed from Dundee.

They had been spoken by DCI Brewster before he had lapsed into comedy mode – '. . . it isn't over yet – there is still some work to be done. Once it is complete, everyone will have a clearer picture of what this is about . . .'

A chill raced up McBride's spine and stopped at the collar of his shirt. The hairs on his neck jerked up. He felt a hand grab inside his stomach and the saliva in his mouth drained away. The passage referred to the routine early stages of police investigation and, in their context on the page, were unremarkable. But the message he was being given appeared to be unmistakable. *The killing of Claire Bowman isn't the end – it's part of the series . . . the deaths aren't being forecast to continue – they're being promised.* Uncomfortable as this thought was, it seemed the only logical conclusion McBride could arrive at.

38

In a small conference room off the main corridor in the headquarters of Tayside Police, three detectives sat looking at each other. On the table between them were six photographs. Three of the pictures depicted females smiling, relaxed and vibrantly alive. The remainder showed the same women after they were dead – two of them with the life choked out of them, the other lying in a pool of blood that had poured from her innards.

Although she was the junior officer, DI Petra Novak was directing the meeting because she had called it. She looked in turn at each of the two men sitting opposite and waited for them to say something. For the previous fifteen minutes she had spoken uninterrupted and had tried to persuade them that there was a good and urgent reason why they were there. Their silence and expressions told her they did not agree.

Detective Chief Inspector James Brewster stood up and took off the jacket of his polyester suit. Sweat stains darkened his armpits and the shirt that had once been white was now starting to stick to his back. He opened the button of the too-tight collar and slackened the knot of his unremarkable tie.

He was the first to speak. 'Sorry, dear,' he said, shaking his head and looking at Petra. His eyes were lifeless and betrayed a complete lack of interest. 'I just don't buy it. Serial killer? More like serial waste of time. You haven't even come close to making a case.' He waved a hand in the direction of the photographs. 'Where's your identical MO? Two of them strangled – by different methods – and the other so viciously assaulted up the jacksie that she bleeds to death.' He was dismissive. 'Did nobody tell you at police college that serial loonies always revert to type?' Brewster sat down and looked at the other man in the room for support.

Detective Chief Inspector Michael Law was everything that Brewster was not. In his perfectly pressed navy-blue suit, crisp shirt and fashionably discreet tie, he was cool, in control. He'd recently been made up to a divisional head of CID with Fife Police – the name had probably helped. He nodded slowly, wanting to disagree with his pedestrian opposite number from Aberdeen, to distance himself from him, but he was unable to. He spoke deliberately, reluctantly. 'I understand where you're coming from, Petra, but Jim's right. There's no evidence – just some coincidences,' he said.

The DCI from the south side of the River Tay picked up the photographs of Alison Brown, Ginny Williams and Claire Bowman. He leafed through them, studying their laughing faces again but taking no time over their death masks. 'The fact they all had fathers in the police is interesting but it's hardly a clincher,' Law said. 'Do you know how many policemen there are in the world? It's a coincidence – maybe a big one – but still just a coincidence.' He pressed on. 'All the women come from different parts of the country – one of them from a different part of the world – so where's your connection?' He spread his hands. 'There's not a single piece of evidence to indicate that their paths might have crossed, never mind them actually knowing each other. OK, there might have been sexual activity before they died but the DNA is different so we have different killers.' He looked at Petra, crossed his arms over his immaculate jacket, leaned back in his seat and waited for her to respond.

She did so at once. 'Surely they told *you* at police college that the victims of serial killers rarely know each other,' she said, defiance filling her voice. 'I'm not aware that the thirteen women Peter Sutcliffe hit with his hammer attended tea parties together. Or, for that matter, that the thirty-plus victims of Ted Bundy ever clapped eyes on each other. They came from different states across America, for God's sake. The thing that unites the victims is the person who put them to death. You both know that. I understand what you're saying about sex but who's to say that the person who left the DNA has to be the murderer? I can give you an explanation for that.'

'Give it,' Brewster and Law said in unison.

'Right, what about this?' Petra said. 'You have a perv – let's say he's a cop – who watches through the window as the victims have sex with their boyfriends. But he's not just a peeping Tom who gets his satisfaction by doing this and playing with himself – he's a homicidal maniac who has to do more. So he waits until the boyfriends leave. Then he goes in and pleasures himself in the way he likes best – by satisfying his blood lust. OK, I know you can easily pick holes in all that but it shows there are possibilities.'

Brewster and Law looked at each other but said nothing.

Before they could respond, Petra rose from her chair and walked round the table until she was standing beside them. She looked at them in turn again, this time not inviting them to speak but willing them to remain silent. 'It's because you can't cope with the idea that a policeman might be who we're after, isn't it? You just can't handle that, can you?' She knew she was being insubordinate but didn't care.

DCI Law looked up at her, ignoring her rebelliousness. His lips moved slightly. He smiled sardonically. 'And you can't manage the idea that your boyfriend from the press might be wrong, can you?' he said, his eyes not leaving her face.

Almost before he stopped speaking a crimson flush had rushed up from DI Novak's neck and into her cheeks. 'He's not my boyfriend – definitely not.' She spat out the last two words with firmness. 'Are you really saying the notes he was sent and the pieces cut from the newspapers in the library have no relevance?' She struggled to keep a mocking tone from her voice.

Brewster and Law fought to be first to reply. The detective chief inspector from Aberdeen won. 'How do you know someone's not just having him on? Taking the piss?' Brewster said. 'It has been known. Just because he's a flash investigative reporter from London doesn't mean somebody can't make a horse's backside of him.' Brewster laughed at the prospect.

The composed DCI Law waited for Brewster's mirth to subside. He brushed non-existent fluff from the razor crease of his trousers, smoothed down the silk tie with its shadow stripe. 'Look, Petra, just because poor Claire Bowman was raped and murdered by an ASP baton, it doesn't follow it was a policeman who was using it,' he said. 'They're not exactly impossible to acquire if you're a civvy.'

She had been saving some ammunition. 'It wasn't just a police baton,' she said softly. 'The tie used to strangle Alison Brown was black. So was the belt that throttled Ginny Williams. I've checked and the belt is identical to the kind

·issued to some forces. Sounds like parts of a police uniform to me.'

Law interrupted, 'The tie – full length, was it?'

'Yes, of course,' Novak answered, an unspoken question on her face.

'That rules us out then,' Law replied with a gleeful smile. 'All our guys wear clip-ons. Or is that something else they neglected to explain to you at police college? Can't have the villains strangling us when we're fighting them off!'

Law looked over at Brewster. They laughed together, simultaneously licking their index fingers before holding them up. 'One–nil,' they said in unison.

Petra remained silent, allowing them their moment of triumph. Her mind was in overdrive. She had a flashback to a semi-formal evening at the Scottish Police College at Tulliallan. 'Not quite, gentlemen,' she said slowly. 'Some senior officers still prefer proper length ties. Ask around and I think you'll find I'm right.' She wet the index finger on her right hand and lifted it. 'One–all, I think,' she said.

The three detectives continued to speak for another fifteen minutes. Despite their stated misgivings, the visiting chief inspectors from the forces on either side of the Tayside Police area promised they would work together with DI Novak. She listened to their assurances of co-operation and politely thanked them for their attendance. Inwardly, she sighed at their scepticism, forgetting that that was how she had felt when McBride had first revealed his theory of connected murder victims.

As the two men were about to leave, she made a suggestion. 'Since you're co-operating so helpfully, we'd best give the inquiry an operational name – you know how our superiors enjoy these things.'

Brewster shrugged. 'Please yourself. What do you fancy?'

'Something with "tri" in it – you know, for three, as in three police forces,' she explained.

Law made the first offer, 'What about Trichomonas?'

Brewster looked blank.

Novak smiled sweetly. 'Oh, nice. You want us to name it after a sexually transmitted disease.'

The chief inspector from Fife grinned but said nothing.

Brewster brightened. 'I know – Tripe!' He could barely get the word out for laughing.

'My turn,' Novak said. 'We'll call it Operation Tribune.'

The two chief inspectors nodded absently. 'Fine,' each of them said.

As she bade them farewell at the lift in the corridor outside the conference room, she allowed herself a private smile. *The name of a newspaper – how appropriate*, she told herself.

39

Nobody used to go to the gym, McBride thought to himself. That was because there weren't any. They hadn't been invented when he was growing up. Now the world was full of them – full of perspiring people trying to avoid heart attacks but probably inducing them, full of other sweaty people trying to look cool and wondering who was watching them. Men sneaking glances at panting women in tight Lycra. Women pretending they weren't doing the same at the guys.

From his position on his static bicycle, McBride had two viewing possibilities. He could observe the half-dozen incredible hulks at the top corner of the Next Generation gym working out with weights the size of tractor wheels or he could concentrate on the four ponytails jogging sensually on the treadmills in front of him. The hulks missed out. They had enough spectators anyway – themselves. They couldn't take their eyes off their own bulging bodies and moisturised orange faces in the banks of mirrors in front of them. And why did they have to grunt and curse all the time? So he watched the bobbing heads and bouncing buttocks on the running machines.

Occasionally, he glanced at the instrument on his wrist for a read-out of his heart rate. When it dropped below 142 beats a minute, he pedalled faster and kept turning the cranks at ever-increasing speed until it rose another forty beats. By the time his heart was hammering at a steady 182, he was no longer able to study the niceties of the varying body shapes of the ponytails. He could barely see them. Sweat cascaded like Niagara Falls off his forehead and into his eyes and his breath burst from his lungs in tortured gasps. He had looked more attractive on some other occasions – most other occasions.

He was between gasps when a voice spoke to him from behind. 'There must be better ways of keeping fit, Mr McBride,' it said quietly. He turned to look at the speaker but already knew the woman who made the words sound like an invitation was Anneke Meyer, the sample collector.

She had emerged from the small studio gym in the corner behind the spinning cycles. The water bottle and the towel she was carrying told McBride that she had just finished a session with her fellow body combat devotees. He would hardly have known it otherwise. The only trace of sweat was a small line of moisture above her upper lip which might have been caused by a tongue being drawn along it. Her golden hair was swept back in perfect symmetry. On top she wore a fitted purple vest with the indiscreet words 'Just Do It' discreetly placed over a small but firm breast. On the bottom, dove-grey Lycra pants stretched over her firm thighs and were even tighter on her backside. Only a wider than usual flare of her nostrils told him she had been breathing heavily.

He was glad Petra was not among her classmates that night. This was partly because he knew he looked a wreck but more because of the way he knew his eyes had inhaled the woman standing smiling at his side.

She spoke again before he could recover his breath or composure. 'So, this is how you keep that magnificent frame in shape.' She was teasing but, by the way she lingered in her undisguised study of his body, he knew that there was more than a trace of admiration in her comment.

'I could say the same to you,' McBride replied, pretending to breath normally. 'This is a bit of luck. I was going to be ringing you.' He did not know before he uttered them if the last seven words were true but knew as soon as he spoke them that they should have been.

'My good fortune too, then,' Anneke said. 'For what reason?' Her pale green eyes danced.

'For a drink or food – or both.'

'Being short-changed, am I?' She gave a low laugh. 'OK. Well, that will do for starters. When? Where? Isn't that what you said to me when I was arranging to do the stuff with your mouth?'

McBride nodded.

'And you said your place, didn't you?'

He nodded again.

'Best make it my place this time, then,' Anneke said. Her eyes stopped dancing and looked straight into his. She waited for a response, her gaze not breaking until he spoke.

'Tonight?' he asked.

'Perfect. How long have you got?'

He could not resist it. 'Never had any complaints!' He tried hard not to look like a smirking schoolboy.

She mimicked a seaside postcard. 'Oooh! You *are* awful!' She looked pleased. There was no embarrassment – just what seemed like anticipation.

For the second time on the three occasions they had met, Anneke Meyer dug into a bag in her possession, produced a notebook and then passed him the page she had written on. This time, the precise handwriting detailed her address.

'Nine thirty, OK?' she asked gently.

'Ideal. That will give me time to have a sufficient number of showers to get rid of this sweat,' McBride said.

She smiled at him, dropping her eyes theatrically. 'Sometimes sweat is good.'

The air that fills the Carse of Gowrie is all the calendar you'll ever need. It sweeps down the valley of the Tay in a gentle caress, coming off the river in an easy sigh and spreading across the flat fields all the way to the housing estates on the western boundary of Dundee. In summertime, it carries the scent of strawberries and raspberries and, in autumn, the smell of fresh soil from harvested potatoes. When winter turned to spring, it would bring the bouquet of new grass and wild flowers.

As McBride drove along the deserted country road taking him through Kingoodie, he lowered his window and allowed the cocktail smell of the river and hedgerows to fill his lungs. He sucked it in and breathed it out and wondered again why he'd ever swapped this place for the stench of London. Of course it was the job, the money – and the cosmopolitan women. But, whatever way he viewed it, he'd slowly come to understand what had kept people like Richard Richardson rooted in the place of his birth. The appreciation of the changing year – and with it the promise each new season seemed to bring – was largely absent for those who lived in major cities.

McBride's thoughts turned to the purpose of his journey and he felt a surge of anticipation at what the rest of the night held. He had not considered where Anneke Meyer might have chosen to stay. If he had, he would not have expected it to be in the heart of the Perthshire countryside. He convinced himself that it told him something about her but he did not know what – unpredictability, maybe.

Although evening had not yet extended into what he thought of as night-time, during the twenty minutes it took him to travel along the narrow local road running parallel to the main highway, he had not passed a single other vehicle. He squinted again at the address she had given him – 2 Cairnie Meadows, Glencarse. If there had not been an elegant sign pointing to a house 200 yards off the main road, he would not have easily found the place she called home. It wasn't what he had expected either. The two-storey stone building now caught in his headlights had clearly once been a farmhouse and almost certainly the abode of whoever had once owned the extensive fields on three of its sides. Since then it had been converted into what looked like two separate houses, each with new cottage-effect, white double-glazed windows. A garden with high hedges and the smell of fallen leaves extended off the rear. Two doors, each of them also white, led off the broad expansive of gravel in front of the structure. One was clearly the original entrance. The other, where a mock oil lantern glowed, was the access to the new residence that had been created by a sympathetic architect.

McBride swung on to the stone chips and the wheels were still noisily crunching over them when the most recent door opened and Anneke Meyer stepped out. As she stood there, framed in the light escaping from the front door, McBride realised it was the first time he had seen her legs. She was dressed stylishly but for casual effect. Mustard skirt in a soft suede fabric that stopped three inches above her knees. White drapey top that allowed the contours of her nipples to show. Silk scarf tied in a neckerchief. Black high heels. He couldn't be sure from where he was but McBride decided she wasn't wearing stockings. Make-up was minimal but skilfully applied. When she lifted a cheek to be kissed and he moved towards her to comply, he caught her fragrance. He did not recognise the brand but it was pricey. Groomed was what she was.

The interior of the house fitted its owner. Groomed it was too. All the walls he could see were the same – not white, not cream, just expensively in between. The floors that had once been stone were now laid in wood, real oak, immaculately sanded and varnished. Three rugs, different but matching, were carefully scattered. The sofa and chairs were buttercup yellow, timelessly modern. Probably designed in Denmark. Lighting was soft but bright enough to illuminate the Monet and Turner prints.

Music played from a hi-fi McBride could not see. He was astonished to recognise the CD as the *Isis Project*, the beautifully composed work of Englishman Guy Chambers which had been given French lyrics and sung so atmospherically by Sophie Hunter.

He could not conceal his surprise at her choice of entertainment. 'I'm impressed,' he told his hostess. 'I thought I was the only person in the whole of Dundee with that album.'

She smiled, gently nodding acknowledgement of his praise, but saying nothing.

'Do you know the story behind it?' McBride asked, desperate to explain.

'Yes, absolutely,' she exclaimed with an unexpected eagerness. 'He wrote it for his daughter Isis. It's the exploration of an imaginary woman's life and the journey goes from the innocence of childhood, through adolescence to the confusion and complexities of her life after that. I adore it – probably because I relate to it.'

McBride was starting to view her in a fresh light. He studied the woman whose physical appeal was magnetic and contemplated the depths that might be concealed behind the alluring exterior.

He quickly discovered that, among them, was an ability to prepare an exceptional meal at short notice. She described it as a light supper, indicating that she would have achieved more with greater notice, but McBride relished every mouthful of the mixed dish of smoked salmon and prawns.

As they ate, he delved into her background, probing conversationally but forensically. Her history unfolded piece by piece. She told him she was of mixed Dutch–English parentage and had grown up in Rotterdam but had attended university in the United Kingdom. After graduating from Durham, she had stayed on, working first of all in Birmingham before moving north to Scotland and Dundee.

She spoke lightly and with occasional bursts of laughter until McBride made a reference to how often she returned to Holland to visit her parents. It was not a subject for much discussion. At mention of them, her eyes filled and she struggled to hold back tears. They had perished together in an accident, she explained, and she was still having problems coming to terms with it. Then she adroitly steered the conversation away from herself and on to McBride's past. It was not a topic he particularly wanted to explore either. At least, that was what he believed.

By the time they had emptied a bottle of wine, he had surprised himself by telling her about the accident that had devastated his own life – of Simon, the little boy whose unfair death continued to haunt him. And he told her something of Caroline. How he had not understood how important she had been until she was no longer part of his existence.

He gave her the outline but none of the details of the two open wounds. No one ever got that close. When he became afraid that he might make an exception, he changed the subject.

'Tell me about the house,' he invited her.

'I'll do better,' Anneke responded, rising from the table they had shared for the last ninety minutes. 'I'll show you.' She walked behind him and ran her hand lightly over his shoulders. 'I'll give you a guided tour.'

He followed her, taking the hand she held out. They did not progress beyond the bedroom.

40

Most of the time McBride knew what he wanted from women. They were best when they were ladies out of bed and tarts in it. It was an acceptable combination for both of them. In the morning, they could pretend much of what had occurred hadn't – it made it easier over breakfast and the conversation was simpler.

Sometimes it didn't work that way. Sometimes the ones who were most willing were the ones who gave least. Their perception of sexual equality was not to share but to submit. In their own minds, they were the perfect partner, giving but asking nothing in return. They would never comprehend that, in bed, those who gave most were the ones who took most. It was a concept with which Anneke Meyer was fully acquainted. Her generosity was limitless and entirely to herself.

From the moment they entered the room at the back of the old farmhouse, she was no longer the possible prey but the undisputed predator. In her new persona, there was no compromise or surrender to convention. She assumed control from the outset. Without exchanging any words with McBride, she walked to a corner of the square-shaped bedroom and unhurriedly removed all her clothing. When she was naked, she placed it in neat folds over the back of a low chesterfield. Then she walked slowly back across the oak floor to the bed which was placed in the centre of the room and lay down, dropping her head on to one of four clinically white, newly laundered pillows placed precisely beneath the brass pillared headboard. She looked across at McBride, soundlessly inviting him to join her.

He hesitated – but only for as long at it took him to divest himself of what he wore. He did not follow her example for orderliness but left his garments where they lay on the floor.

What happened next and for the remainder of the night was not something McBride had experienced with a woman before. He was the entire focus of her attention but, for much of the time, he felt like a spectator.

Her first act was to inspect the part of his body she desired most – not to observe its dimensions but to examine it at close range. She held him firmly and squeezed intermittently, watching for the escape of any fluids. When none appeared, she appeared satisfied and without releasing her hold she reached into the drawer of a bedside table with her other hand and removed several packets of condoms. Continuing to gently massage him, she placed one of the sachets in her mouth and carefully tore the wrapping open with her teeth. She extracted the sheath and put it on him. Wordlessly, she moved over his body until she straddled him. Then she lowered herself on to his loins and covered him until their pelvises touched. Still she did not speak but her eyes never left his as she began to move rhythmically.

They only started to communicate verbally when she finally pulled away and rolled on to her back beside him, her appetite temporarily satisfied.

There was not much need for McBride's extensive sexual repertoire during the next few hours. She needed no guidance or instruction and actually added to his 'box of tricks' in one or two areas.

When daylight started to fill the room, it signalled the conclusion of her desires. She pulled herself on top of him once more but this time to sit on his chest. She gazed down at him and playfully patted the top of his head. 'Ten out of ten,' she declared with an approving nod. 'You've earned a hearty breakfast.'

McBride had only one question. 'OK, what was all the squeezing and inspection about before the outbreak of hostilities?'

She knew instantly what he referred to. Affecting the tone of a headmistress, she wagged a finger. 'A girl can't be too careful. My information is that you're a serial shagger. Just checking you out for any nasties. Same with all the condoms. Don't forget I'm a forensic scientist.'

A thought flashed through McBride's mind. He glanced at the top of the bedside table but could not be sure precisely what he saw. '*All*? Tell me how many – I think I lost count.'

'Four. Still, not to worry – there's always next time. Lots of opportunities for improvement.'

She slid out of bed and disappeared into the bathroom leading off the room. When she returned a few minutes later, she had showered and was wearing a white towelling bathrobe. She carried an identical one which she dropped on the bed beside him.

'His'n'hers!' she exclaimed.

When he prepared to leave after breakfast, Anneke accompanied him to his car. Apart from her own, it was the only one on the wide sweep of gravel extending the full length of the farmhouse.

'Your neighbours leave early, do they?' he asked absently.

'Don't have any, meantime. They split their time between here and Majorca. When the sun doesn't shine here, they go there to look for it.'

McBride opened his eyes wide, gasping dramatically. 'So no one would have heard my cries for help?'

'Only me. But I wasn't aware you needed any assistance. I thought you did very well all by yourself.'

They both laughed. But the knockabout wasn't quite over.

As he opened the door of the Mondeo he looked over at the nearest field and the remains of autumn crop which had been harvested. 'Potatoes?' McBride asked.

'No, rape.'

'Figures,' he said.

41

He was ten minutes into the drive home when his mobile sounded. He allowed it to ring several times while he conducted the usual debate with himself about whether to break the law and answer it while he drove or be sensible and pull over. A hands-free kit was never an option. They were only for people who wanted to look like someone off the Starship *Enterprise*.

It was a pleasant morning. A light frost was in the process of melting away under a struggling rising sun and a buzzard was circling over an unplanted field on his left. He wasn't in any kind of a hurry. He drew to a halt.

Petra's voice did not sing as usual. There was no melody – just a losing battle with irritation. 'You're up bright and early, aren't you?' It was not an observation, more a remonstration. 'I passed by round at your flat but you'd gone. Must be something important, I thought to myself, to get you on the road at such an uncivilised time.'

He knew he was being asked where he was. He also knew he could not tell her without indicating where he'd been. It was not something he wanted to do. So he sidestepped it.

'Pot, kettle, black,' he said lightly. 'What gets *you* out and about at this "uncivilised" hour?'

'Just thought we should have a chat but you're probably much too busy.'

'Never too busy for my favourite detective,' McBride said, trying to soothe her. 'Anything in particular on the agenda?'

'Bits and pieces.' Lightness was returning to her voice. 'DNA results are back. Can we meet?'

They arranged to join up in an hour to run together. It was just enough time to allow him to drive back into town and shower once more. He did not want the scent of the woman he had slept with to still be on him.

When he turned to lay his phone back on the passenger seat, McBride realised for the first time that he had stopped at the end of the narrow road leading to Castle Huntly half a mile away. He gazed across the flat expanse of fields at the sturdy fortress in the distance and thought about Bryan Gilzean. The 500-year-old castle had once been the home of the Earl of Kinghorne and later the first Earl of Strathmore but was now one of Her Majesty's open prisons, a sort of Scottish Colditz but without bars, machine guns and jackboots. Nor was it remotely escape-proof. It was for inmates coming to the end of their sentence and held lifers, among others, being prepared for their eventual release back into society. They'd left the bars behind in their previous institutions.

One day, McBride reflected, Bryan Gilzean would probably be scheduled for shipping down the motorway from Perth Prison a dozen miles away to finish his time in the splendour of the baronial halfway house. *Unless he was released beforehand with a fat compensation cheque in his pocket for a wrongful conviction*, McBride mused.

* * *

When they ran towards each other along the beach that separated their two houses, they raced to see who would be first to reach the bench at the end of the Esplanade where they had agreed to meet. The sprint was illogical but it made sense. Both were competitors. McBride knew he was. Petra pretended to herself she wasn't. She ran hardest and arrived at the seat first.

'What kept you?' she asked, her words coming in short gasps as she fought to regain her breath. 'I was about to go home.' She smiled at her triumph.

McBride took a long look at her. Studied the fashion-model, Slavic cheekbones, the slender neck, the light tan shining under the thin film of sweat her burst of acceleration had produced. He wondered how her bedroom was laid out and decided it was unlikely to be as clinically spartan as the one where he had just spent the night. He doubted, too, whether anyone lucky enough to share her bed would be subjected to a rigorous anatomical examination.

He was still deep in admiration when she spoke again. 'Do you need a rest or should we start out?' she asked.

McBride flashed a smile and, still without speaking, turned and ran away from her, sprinting quickly down on to the edge of the sand where it met the water and was firmest. 'Tell me about the DNA,' he called over his shoulder.

By the time she caught up with him, her breathing was coming in gulps once more. She drew level with his shoulder and matched him stride for stride. They continued to increase the pace together for another hundred yards then gradually eased back. Behind them, twin sets of footprints marked their route along the damp sand.

Petra's composure returned first. 'Clean as a whistle,' she said suddenly. 'The letters from your lethal friend contain a few prints and DNA traces but nothing unexpected. Needless to say, you're all over the envelopes. So's your local postman. We also took elimination samples from the delectable Janne at your publisher's and the receptionist at the Apex Hotel. Beyond them, nothing. Not unexpectedly, there's even less on the notes themselves. Apart from Janne's traces on the first one, we found nothing.'

'What about the stamps or envelope seals?' McBride asked.

'Stamps are self-adhesive – no spit required,' she replied. 'The envelopes had been moistened but not with saliva, with ordinary water.'

She waited for his reaction. He remained silent.

'You know what all this means, don't you?' she asked.

McBride nodded. 'Yeah, we're not dealing with an amateur – never thought we were.'

Petra turned to look at him. 'So?'

'So, if it's not an amateur, maybe it's a professional – like a cop or cops,' McBride said flatly. 'You might recall I've been trying to tell you that for some time.'

They had come to the end of the shoreline and had struck out along a stretch of grassland where a group of boys were doing their best to fall off a roundabout in a small playground. Two dogs broke away from their careless owners and charged in the direction of the runners. Without speaking Petra and McBride lengthened their strides to outpace them. By the time they succeeded, they had reached a path within touching distance of the main rail line connecting Aberdeen and London. An express thundered past, disturbing a large gathering of swans which had settled in an inlet. They rose in unison and started running inelegantly over the water before finally taking flight. Moments later, they swept over the heads of McBride and Petra in a perfect, unhurried, whispering formation of white feathers, as graceful as they had been awkward when they had fought to become airborne.

Petra had been trying to read his thoughts, imagining he was still chewing over his killer-cop theory. She broke his concentration. 'What if you're only half right?' she said quietly. 'What if that's what you're supposed to think?' She stopped speaking, looking at him, waiting for his reaction.

McBride said nothing until the swans had disappeared over a clump of trees on the other side of the rail line. When he spoke it was not, as Petra had expected, to protest. 'Been thinking about that too,' he told her. 'Could be an ex-cop. Could be someone who just hates them. Maybe the wrong person was banged up sometime. Maybe it's an elaborate red herring. The bastard may just dislike women. Maybe it's a load of old rubbish.' He covered another ten yards before he spoke again. 'So why involve me?' McBride asked, suddenly serious. 'I'm being played like some kind of monkey. What did I ever do to the organ-grinder?'

Petra swivelled her head until she was looking directly at him. 'Maybe you're supposed to solve it,' she told McBride. 'Then again, maybe he just likes making a fool of reporters.'

42

McBride sat watching the four men in the far corner of the public bar of The Fort. He studied their faces but there was no discernible reaction to anything that was taking place. They could have been playing poker instead of dominoes. He marvelled, as he always did, at the ability of the participants to hold so many of the oblong pieces in a single hand at the same time. Whenever he tried it, they fell on to the table – usually face up.

McBride preferred the public bar when he wanted time to think. No one tried small talk unless you encouraged it and, if you didn't, no one complained. Next door in the lounge they described you as peculiar if you remained silent any longer than five minutes. Nobody was ever going to chat you up in the wide room with the L-shaped public bar and you were unlikely to find anyone there who would make you feel like whispering sweet nothings in their ear.

He was still intermittently contemplating the tabletop athletes and the remains of his pint of lager when he was aware someone had soundlessly appeared at his side and was preparing to engage him in conversation. He turned to look at the intruder and recognised the small, neat figure of Adam Gilzean. All McBride thought at first was how out of place he seemed in a bar.

'I hope I'm not disturbing you, Mr McBride,' Gilzean said, 'but I was told I might find you here.'

McBride couldn't imagine who might have known he would be in the bar. He could think of nobody, far less anyone who also knew Adam Gilzean, but let it pass. He motioned to his visitor to take the empty stool beside him, asking, at the same time, if he wanted a drink. Gilzean accepted the seat but declined the refreshment. *So, it isn't exactly a social call*, he thought. *Not that Adam Gilzean was ever likely to make one on anybody. What does he want?*

McBride knew it would not take him long to find out. The precise man with the beard seated beside him was never anything other than direct but he was not normally as nervous. Maybe it was being in a bar that upset his composure.

'I'm anxious for a progress report,' Gilzean said. 'Bryan is too. I visited him yesterday and he was asking – he always asks.'

McBride did not know how to answer. There was a lot of progress – and none. And there was nothing he wanted to share meantime with the man who had come calling. What could he tell him, anyway? That another two women were also dead and that none of it made any sense? So, instead, he asked his unexpected companion a question. 'Tell me, the tie that was used to kill Alison – any idea where it came from?'

The response was swift, much faster than he had anticipated. 'None,' Gilzean said without pausing to think. 'It was black, wasn't it? It obviously belonged to the person who killed her. Bryan did not own a tie of that colour. I know because he had to borrow one of mine for his mother's funeral.'

McBride nodded, saying nothing. Before he could reply, Gilzean spoke again. 'It could have been part of a uniform, couldn't it?' His eyes never left McBride's face. He seemed anxious for a reaction.

McBride was left wrong-footed. It was not an experience he was overly familiar with. Whatever he had expected from Gilzean, it had not been a probing question. He would play it out. 'Hadn't thought of that,' he said lightly. Lying was easy when you had done it as often as McBride. 'What kind of uniform do you think?'

Gilzean hesitated, uncertain how to reply. He appeared to be turning something over in his mind. 'Well,' he said at last. 'Not a lot of people wear black ties. Bus drivers . . . naval officers . . .' He paused. 'And prison officers.'

'I can think of a few others,' McBride said.

'Such as?'

'Undertakers. And waiters in Italian restaurants.'

Gilzean smiled but only with his mouth.

'And we'd better not forget policemen,' McBride added finally.

The man perched uncomfortably on the stool to his left laughed – but still without his eyes. 'Yes, policemen,' he said softly.

Stay with it, McBride told himself. He raised his eyebrows, higher than was reasonable. 'You think it was a *cop*?' He tried to sound surprised.

'Stranger things have happened,' Gilzean said.

'Why would a policeman murder Alison?' McBride retorted.

'Why not? They're human like the rest of us – or inhuman.'

They fell silent. McBride drained his glass. He pondered a refill. Wondered what was in Adam Gilzean's mind.

Deliberated where to steer the conversation. Sometimes he wasn't as good at manipulation as he imagined. He decided to change direction. 'Is Bryan bearing up?' he asked.

Gilzean's intensity deepened. 'Just,' he said, 'but I don't know for how much longer . . .' His voice trailed away. He briefly turned his head away from McBride then looked back at him, fixing him with an unblinking stare. 'I did have a thought,' he said. 'Suppose Alison's killer had struck again. If the murder could be linked to hers, that would prove Bryan was innocent, wouldn't it? He couldn't have done it if he was in prison, could he?'

'You have a point?'

'Perhaps that's something for you to think about in your investigations.'

Gilzean rose from his stool. His visit was at an end. He extended a hand to McBride and apologised again for his intrusion. McBride shook hands and told him to feel free to do the same any time he felt like it.

As Adam Gilzean walked quietly from the bar into the street, McBride wondered if he had come to ask him something or to tell him something.

43

McBride had waited for daylight for the best part of two hours. When it came, it crept into the room the way a woman tiptoes into your head – softly at first so you don't hear the approach but then she's walking so loudly you can't think about anything else except the sound she's making.

He'd had noisy females in his mind the whole time he'd lain in the darkness doing his best to hurry the arrival of dawn. Two of them – one he'd slept with, the other he knew he wanted to. But it hadn't been Anneke Meyer or Petra Novak who had caused him to waken before he was due. It had been the man who had shared his company for a short time the night before – the man who wouldn't accept a drink. Adam Gilzean was troubling him. He was prodding tentatively at him but leaving marks that wouldn't go away.

When he rolled the blind open, McBride knew it was the kind of day that wasn't going to get much better – for the weather or anything else. Dawn hadn't been accompanied with a rising glow of sunlight or much else to feel optimistic about. It was dull and grey and dropped over him like a prison blanket.

On mornings like that he never wanted to run, especially if he also needed to think. These were the days when he oiled up the Trek and cycled with the weather. He didn't ride fast, didn't ride slow, just steady – and for several hours.

When he took the machine he preferred to most women he'd met down from its hook on the wall of the room that doubled as his office and went outside with it, McBride searched the sky for a patch of blue. He couldn't find any but somewhere in the north the shade of grey was paler. He settled into the saddle and pedalled towards it.

Fours hours later, Adam Gilzean still loitered in his thoughts but the expenditure of energy had caused the endorphins to kick into McBride's bloodstream and the familiar feeling of well-being they induced was permeating through him.

Kirriemuir had dropped away behind him and he rose out of his seat and stood on the pedals for the deceptive incline that would carry him into Glamis. Over his left shoulder he caught sight of the turrets of the castle where the mother of the queen had spent some of her childhood. It awakened long-forgotten memories of an assignment as a junior reporter when he'd stood in the wrong place and finished up in a line of dignitaries being introduced to Her Majesty by someone who had no idea who he was. It was a story Caroline used to delight in recounting whenever he was in danger of forgetting his humble journalistic origins.

He remembered other ways the woman who had once adored him used to keep his conceited feet on the ground. How she pricked his arrogant bubble but never with anything but gentleness – how she refused to take him seriously when he was at his most pompous. And he remembered Simon and the family they had once been.

So his long, lone journey into the hills behind Dundee

had been worthwhile, as he knew it would. By the time he negotiated the last rises and falls in the road that brought him in a gentle sweep into the outer suburbs of the city, his head was at peace – even if his heart wasn't.

The feeling of euphoria lasted for precisely one minute.

He passed a graffiti-camouflaged row of shops in a perimeter housing estate and glanced absently at the news-boards outside a dilapidated general store. An *Evening Telegraph* billboard screamed at him – 'Brutal Murder of Young Woman in City Flat'.

Instinctively he knew who had committed it even though he had no clue who that might be.

44

McBride cursed his foolishness at leaving home without his mobile. It was an illogical and pig-headed act he repeated every time he cycled. He knew he should carry it with the assortment of tyre levers and spare parts that filled the back pockets of his jacket. But it was a link with civilisation that seemed at odds with the sense of freedom he sought when he rode towards the best weather. It did not matter that it might be an invaluable aid for assistance in the event of an accident – or that it could be a hotline to the leading officer in a murder inquiry.

He muttered obscenities about himself to himself and dropped his hands low on to the hooks of the handlebars. Then he eased the slick Campagnolo ten-speed Chorus gears into the highest ratio he could handle that would enable him to arrive home in the shortest time possible. He tramped hard on the pedals and ignored the excruciating surge of pain caused by the sudden release of lactic acid into his legs.

Fifteen minutes later he was back in the Esplanade flat, sweat seeping from him, his thighs nipping in agony and his fingers stabbing out DI Petra Novak's number on his phone.

She responded immediately. 'Campbell? Where have you been?' she asked tetchily. 'I've been trying to raise you all morning.'

McBride did not attempt to explain his forenoon activities or his stubborn idiocy with his phone. 'Sorry – been out of contact,' he said pointlessly.

'You've heard?'

'Yes, just seen the billboards. Is it what I think?'

'Absolutely. No doubt whatsoever,' Petra said flatly. 'Our man's been busy.'

'How?' he enquired.

'Long story. Not pretty.'

'Who is – was – she?'

'Name's Ireland – Lynne Ireland. Lives – lived – in Broughty Ferry. Just round the corner from you, actually. Brook Street – the houses at the far end, just before you get to Esplanade.'

Before McBride could make a response, she spoke again. 'And, before you ask, yes, her father was a policeman – a chief super from Glasgow where the family used to live.'

McBride drew in his breath then gave a low whistle. He said nothing, taking in the thought that his tormentor had been within touching distance less than twenty-four hours earlier – might have driven past his apartment on the riverfront. He had a dozen questions but didn't ask one of them.

Petra spoke again. 'We're going to have to cut this short, for both our sakes,' she explained, talking quickly. 'I'm going into a briefing in three minutes and I presume you'll want to attend the press conference. It's scheduled for an hour from now.'

McBride looked at his watch. There was just enough time to shower and eat a sandwich on the move. He rang off.

Police officers who are in charge of press conferences view them with a mixture of anticipation and apprehension, mostly the latter. They stage them for two purposes. To boast following a successful conviction or to recruit the aid of the public whose assistance might allow them to brag in the future. No officer is truly comfortable sitting in front of rows of reporters. It is part of a police officer's natural inclination not to trust people but they trust members of the fourth estate least of all. However, for most of the time, especially on the major unsolved cases, they can't function fully without them. It presents them with an unhappy dilemma. They want to appear as if they are giving total co-operation to the journos they may despise but, if they could withhold every scrap of information in their possession, they would be happy. It is an uneasy relationship between two factions which feed off each other – both are vultures.

That afternoon, in the airless room in the headquarters of Tayside Police, he was, for once, in the unique position of not caring that he was about to be short-changed. He would play catch-up later with the attractive female detective inspector sitting next to Detective Superintendent John Hackett, who was doing his best to convince the hack-pack that he really was their best friend. The senior officer even managed to string out a meagre handful of facts into a statement that took all of eight seconds to read.

Lynne Ireland, a thirty-two-year-old administrator, had been discovered in the apartment block where she lived alone at around nine o'clock that morning by a colleague who had called to give her a lift to Dundee College where they both worked. She had suffered head injuries. Nothing appeared to have been removed from the flat. There was no evidence of a break-in.

The rest was the commercial – 'Anyone who was aware of Miss Ireland's movements after 9 p.m. the previous evening, when she was last seen alive, or who might have seen a suspicious person or persons entering or leaving the block of flats etc., etc.'

The Courier had two reporters in attendance – Kate Nightingale, looking fragrant in an unexpected white jacket covered in a pattern of red poppies which you either loved or loathed, and Richard Richardson, looking crumpled in a pinstriped suit covered with the customary ash.

Double Dick was the first to raise his hand with a question. 'Was a weapon used or was she punched to death?' he demanded.

'No comment,' the detective superintendent replied, feigning regret at his unhelpfulness.

'Had she been raped?'

'No comment.'

Double Dick tried once more. 'Are you linking it to any other murder?'

'No comment.' The detective superintendent looked uncomfortable.

The chief reporter of *The Courier* sighed. 'Do you think she knew her killer? I know – no comment.' Double Dick gave up. 'Waste of bloody time,' he muttered. 'I'm off.' He stood up and, on the way out, spoke to Kate Nightingale. 'See if you can charm something out of them. But don't hold your breath.' He looked over at McBride, nodded towards the door and raised an eyebrow.

McBride accepted the invitation and followed him into the corridor.

'We should boycott their bloody press conferences,' Richardson said. 'See how they manage without us.' He studied McBride for several moments before continuing. 'Didn't hear your dulcet tones in there. Not like you to be so reticent,' he said, making it sound like a question.

McBride lifted his shoulders. 'Not much point. I've seen you more dynamic yourself, come to that.'

This time Richardson shrugged. 'As you say, your head gets sore hitting brick walls.'

McBride recognised the sounds of the press conference winding up. He knew Petra would emerge into the corridor at any moment and wondered how he would get rid of Double Dick. A subterfuge was not necessary. His old colleague seemed happy to cut their conversation short.

'Must dash, Campbell,' Richardson said. 'Things to do, people to see.'

Trying to wind me up, McBride told himself. *Bastard wants me to think he's ahead of the game. Or maybe not . . .*

When Petra walked from the conference room, her superior officer was by her side, looking thankful his ordeal was over. She dropped half a pace behind the superintendent so he would not see her face. She glanced over at McBride and slowly shook her head from side to side, telling him it was not the time for a discussion. His return nod was just as imperceptible.

They met forty-five minutes later in the Bell Tree. She was waiting for him, seated at a table with a half-empty cup of coffee in front of her. She had arrived early because there was much she had to impart.

Lynne Ireland had indeed suffered head injuries but none that anyone at police headquarters had ever encountered before. The bone of her delicate nose had been smashed in two and the top half had travelled like a missile upwards at speed into her brain. She had died almost instantly. The murder weapon was a police hat. It had been placed peak first at the base of her nose, held firmly and then pushed with rapid force into her face. The cap had travelled no more than two inches but had been as lethal as a bullet. It could not have been anything other than a deliberate act of slaughter by someone who had set out to kill. Someone indifferent to the indescribable pain the victim would have momentarily experienced.

McBride already knew the answer to his first two questions but asked them anyway. Lynne Ireland was, of course, the daughter of a former police officer, an ex-chief superintendent who was retired and living in the west of Scotland. She had apparently also shared a bottle of wine with her killer.

Petra anticipated his next questions and gave him answers before he posed them. 'Yes, there had been sexual intercourse,' she said with something approaching resignation. 'We swabbed her for semen, found some and it's being checked out even as we speak. The hat carried no identification but should have been laden with enough sweat to give us all the DNA we wanted – except it had been scrubbed as clean as the proverbial whistle. From end to end. You want disinfectant traces? We could have filled a bottle!' Petra exclaimed.

McBride swore wearily. 'Thinks he's a clever bastard,' he said. 'And he's probably right.'

Petra paused for effect. 'Not quite,' she said softly. 'He missed a single hair clinging to the inside of the sweatband. Be interesting to see if it matches the semen.'

45

Police were all over Broughty Ferry like an east-coast haar. They were in the shops and on the street corners. They knocked on doors and ticked boxes on the questionnaires attached to their clipboards. They filled the betting shops and the coffee houses and, when they were done, they packed the bars. All the time they asked for help and all the time they failed to receive it. Not because the good citizens of the cultured seaside suburb were being difficult. How could you help when you had nothing to tell?

Lynne Ireland might have lived on another planet, as far as most of them were concerned. She left for work in the morning before the place was fully awake and by the time she returned in the evening the shutters were coming down. The ones who knew her best, her neighbours, didn't really know her at all.

She was 'a lovely young woman' who was 'decent and respectable' and she never made 'trouble' because she was 'quiet and private'. The subtext was they were hardly aware of her existence because that was how she liked it.

The door-to-door inquiries were productive only because they were non-productive. Whoever had visited the college administrator to take her life had been as 'quiet and private' as the occupant of the unremarkable flat herself. Death had arrived and departed unseen and apparently with an absence of sound. It was a brick wall.

None of it came as any surprise to Campbell McBride. Lynne Ireland symbolised a significant strata of her gender and generation. Financially independent. Emotionally uncommitted. Psychologically balanced. Socially anonymous. Everything about her said she would never finish up a murder victim – except her father's occupation.

Why should that be so important? It was a question McBride had asked himself a hundred times.

The same query had also been put to her father, ex-Chief Superintendent Thomas Ireland, who had finished a distinguished career as a divisional commander with Strathclyde Police, the largest force in the country. He had a high clear-up rate for most of his career but did not have the remotest notion why his job might have cost his daughter her life. Furthermore, he had rarely visited Dundee until his daughter had moved to a job in the city eighteen months earlier. None of it was particularly helpful.

McBride drew the Mondeo into the kerb in Gray Street after checking he was not parking on a yellow. It was an unaccustomed practice but, with the place swarming with uniforms, it seemed a sensible precaution. He realised he had pulled up outside two of his three most favourite places in the Ferry. After The Fort, he preferred to spend any spare time he had left browsing in Eduardo Alessandro's art studio, or sampling the extraordinary range of ice cream in Visocchi's parlour next door. He was in the process of contemplating a lightning visit to the latter when his mobile sounded.

Petra wasted no time with pleasantries. She told him the DNA test results were back and said he might be interested in what they showed.

He said nothing, waiting for her to expand.

Speaking with quiet deliberation that demanded no interruption, she explained that the profiles from the semen removed from Lynne Ireland and from the hair on the inside of the sweatband of the police hat had been compared. They did not come close to a match.

He remained silent, prompting her to repeat her announcement, which she did, this time with heavy emphasis on the 'not'.

McBride swore in disappointment

Petra spoke again. 'That was the good news,' she said, unable to keep a smirk from her voice. 'The hair belonged to a friend of yours.'

'Who?' he demanded.

'Bryan Gilzean.'

'What?'

'Bryan Gilzean, you know, the man doing life up at Perth,' she said, louder than she'd ever spoken to him before.

McBride swore again, this time with unexpected vigour.

He paused to consider the implications of the time bomb she'd tossed at him. No rational explanation surfaced. 'What in God's name does that mean?' he declared at last.

'It means the hair on the sweatband came from the head of Bryan Gilzean,' Petra said. 'No one else's head. That's it really. The rest we have to find out.'

'How?' McBride pressed.

'You're the investigative reporter.'

'And you're the detective inspector,' McBride said, exasperation overtaking him.

'Yes and we're both screwed,' she said, ringing off.

He sat behind the wheel staring at a signed Vettriano print in Alessandro's window but not seeing it. An avalanche of thoughts roared through the mind which, minutes earlier, had been wiped blank. None of them made any sense. Except one. The only certainty was that whoever killed Lynne Ireland, it was not Bryan Gilzean. *Is that the message?* he asked himself. *Is someone trying to prove he's an innocent man? Or is that just what we're supposed to think? Are we being informed or tormented? Or both?*

McBride was still wrestling with his thoughts when his mobile ran again. The caller did not identify herself. She did not have to. McBride instantly recognised the even voice that gave no hint of its geographical origins. Anneke Meyer was relaxed, playful – and inviting. She would be working out at Next Generation in a couple of hours. Was he free? Would he like to meet?

McBride told her he was tied up.

'That sounds interesting,' she teased. 'Feet or hands?'

He explained about Lynne Ireland – the story he needed to write about her murder for the next day's national paper he was freelancing for.

She reminded him of where she worked, told him she was aware of the tragedy, felt sick at the details.

McBride brightened. 'You'll have inside information, then,' he said. 'Maybe I should take down your particulars, after all?'

'My lips are sealed,' she said, sounding serious for the first time. 'But I imagine you know more than me. Petra will be keeping you informed.' She managed to make the comment sound like a question.

He did not oblige. 'Her lips are tighter than yours,' he said lightly.

'No comment – but maybe she needs more practice,' Anneke said, starting to laugh.

She allowed McBride to finish the call only after extracting a promise from him that he would be in touch within the next few days.

The mobile sounded once more. Petra said she was phoning because she knew he would suddenly remember to remind her of something she had remembered anyway.

'I'm confused,' McBride said. 'Remind me.'

'OK. We've staked out the Central Library. Same team. More cameras.'

He started to laugh. 'Not a chance in hell,' he said. 'There's more likelihood of Dundee United winning the European Cup than there is of our man showing up there. But do it anyway.'

46

Nobody buys newspapers for the good news. They don't know it and wouldn't admit it even if they did but people read papers to learn of the misfortune of others. If something ghastly has happened to someone else, it makes their own injustices seem more bearable. Life isn't so bad if it's worse for your neighbour. Death sells best of all. Not a hundred people perishing in an earthquake on the other side of the world but the last breath of a person you can identify with. It's even better when it has taken place in your home town and if the extinction of life has not been through natural causes.

On the day following the discovery of Lynne Ireland's corpse, *The Courier* was in danger of selling out. The morning daily carried words and pictures on the front and on two pages inside. Richard Richardson and Kate Nightingale might not have filled much of their notebooks at the obligatory but largely pointless police press conference but they had more than compensated in the background stories they had rapidly put together.

Double Dick was at his most eloquent and informed and he had painted a picture of Lynne Ireland with such deft strokes he could have known her all his life instead of them being complete strangers. Nightingale, hard-nosed but caring, was as elegant with her words as she was with some of her sexual practices. She had knocked out 750 words on the paradox of being able to live within the heart of a tight community yet still be a stranger in its midst. It was an impressive performance by both reporters.

McBride reread the articles for the second time then folded the paper and put it in his jacket pocket. He knew he would refer to it if the London news desk he was dealing with wanted a significant follow-up piece, which was probable if the story kept its legs. He did not doubt that it would.

Broughty Ferry still swarmed with police, uniformed and plain clothes, but the place was also starting to fill up with the rubbernecks who had made the short journey down from Dundee for no other reason than to gaze at the otherwise anonymous house where a young woman had died.

The *Big Issue* sellers, sensing a booming trade, had followed them out of the city centre and into the douce suburb. One of them, a female with a pinched face that stared dully out at McBride from underneath a low baseball cap, had taken up a pitch outside Woolworth's. She was probably about twenty but looked half as much again. She had been good-looking once but the decaying front teeth and acne spoiled any chance she had of making it on to the front cover of *Hello!* magazine. McBride looked at her with sadness as he passed by. Females like her stood on corners all over the country. Most of them were doing it to feed a habit. At least they were selling magazines and not their bodies. He fished into his back pocket and pressed a five-pound note into her hand, waving away the copy of her wares she offered him.

'Thank you, sir,' she said. The voice was unexpectedly cultured, like the well-cared-for hands. The politeness genuine. McBride had forgotten that addictions didn't only afflict those unlucky enough to be born into deprivation.

Luck, he thought. *Most folk would have said Lynne Ireland was lucky – until yesterday.*

He resisted the temptation to engage the magazine seller in conversation, to tell her life could be even worse if she fell in with the wrong people. She already had and they were waiting to take his fiver off her in exchange for some chemicals.

He walked on, feeling foolish. Not just because he had helped put money in some dealer's pocket but because he was killing time while he waited for the person who caused the temporary increase in Broughty Ferry's population to make his next move. He was convinced that would happen sooner rather than later. He sensed an acceleration in the events that were unfolding around him and cursed his impotence to do anything about it.

His thoughts could not extend beyond two subjects – both named Gilzean. The young man held in a prison twenty-two miles away whose hairs had been found on a tie used to strangle Alison Brown and again on the inside of the police hat which had been used so violently to propel a broken nose bone into the brain of Lynne Ireland. And his father, Adam Gilzean, who had seemed to set a whole chain of events in motion from the moment he had approached McBride in the High Street bookstore.

It was Adam Gilzean's most recent visit to him which troubled him most. *Christ sake,* McBride muttered silently. *He was practically forecasting another murder. Then it happens the same night. And a few hundred yards from where they'd spoken. It made no sense. But it made all the sense in the world if you were trying to make a point – and were prepared to kill to prove it.*

He needed to speak to Petra. Needed her input. Wanted to know where the police investigation had reached. He called her but was diverted to her voicemail. He left a message but did not say what was in his mind – just left an invitation to stop off at his apartment on her way home.

She did not arrive until 10 p.m. – fourteen hours after her day had begun. McBride did not need to ask if it had been a good day at the office – her face gave him the answer. The small amount of make-up she ever wore had disappeared, her mouth was taut and her hair was as untidy as his own. Even her fitted black jacket was creased. Only two things were familiar – the newly applied perfume and the fact that she still looked stunning.

She did not speak but took off her jacket, stepped out of her shoes, walked to the window overlooking the river and sat in the seat he had occupied for the last hour. She put her feet up on the window-ledge and uttered only two words, 'Wine, red.'

They were three-quarters of the way through the bottle of Châteauneuf du Pape before she started to give him a rundown on the day's events. Once she began, Detective Inspector Petra Novak paused only to have her glass topped up.

Much had happened, she told McBride. Operation Tribune was no longer a tolerated but ignored concept – it was in full throttle and a briefing room at headquarters had been cleared to accommodate the joint team of officers drafted in from Fife and Grampian to support the Dundee murder squad. No one was in any doubt now that a multiple killer was being sought – or that there was a high probability he would strike again.

'The brass admit to "probability",' she said wearily. 'I make it certainty.'

McBride nodded firmly. 'You can put money on it – as much as you've got. This is a game that isn't over.'

She looked at him earnestly. 'I've been asked to make a special plea to you,' Petra said. 'They're desperate that none of the joint operation details get out. If the public get the idea that a triple or quadruple killer is on the loose, it will create nightmares for us. They're also well aware that you hold some kind of fascination for the person responsible. They need your co-operation both ways – to keep them informed of any developments at your end and not to let the public in on any of it. Deal?'

McBride burst out laughing. 'Here we go again!' he exclaimed. 'Cheeky bastards. You use the rhubarb principle on the press – keep us in the dark and throw the occasional bucket of shit over us – then, when you're stuck, it's grovel, grovel.' He laughed louder. 'I suppose the request came from your superintendent, the "helpful" Mr Hackett? And I bet DCI Brewster from Aberdeen was backing him to the hilt? Two wankers.'

Petra nodded twice, looking apologetic. 'You can understand . . .' She didn't finish the sentence.

'Aye, I can understand. It's a one-way street until the police find themselves in another cul-de-sac.' McBride was enjoying himself but decided to put her out of her misery. 'OK,' he said eventually, 'tell them they have a deal. But the bargain is that, if this thing ever gets wrapped up, I get a day's start on the rest of the hack-pack with all the stuff you know but I don't. Deal?'

'No problem – I can guarantee it,' Petra said, her face brightening for the first time.

McBride had waited all night to discuss the subject that was starting to obsess him. He introduced it cautiously, anxious not to look foolish. 'Adam Gilzean . . .' he said slowly, 'any thoughts?' He was not sure what reaction he expected – curiosity, probably. It was not what he received.

'A few,' she said at once. 'As a matter of fact, I spent two hours with him this afternoon.'

McBride could not conceal his surprise. He raised his eyebrows but said nothing, mainly because he couldn't think of an appropriate response.

'We had him in,' Petra said simply. 'We needed to speak to him about the hair from the hat – his son's.'

'And?' McBride asked.

'And he didn't have a clue – not the faintest. He was staggered, to put it mildly.'

'You believed him?'

'Yes,' Petra said, nodding her head slowly. 'If he was putting it on, he should be nominated for an Oscar. It would be the performance of a lifetime.'

She looked at McBride, noting his disbelief. 'I know what you're thinking,' she said. 'I did too – for a spell. You know – that he might have killed Lynne Ireland and planted the hair so his son would look innocent.'

McBride recounted the visit Adam Gilzean had made to him in The Fort and the direction their conversation had taken. 'Lynne Ireland lived – and died – a few hundred yards from The Fort,' he told Petra. 'Adam Gilzean was in the area at the time, he had a warped motive and he was in the position to have had one of his son's hairs to plant as some kind of evidence of his son's innocence. What if Bryan Gilzean did murder Alison Brown and all this is some sort of elaborate killing spree to get him out of prison?' McBride demanded.

'Oh, sure! And what if the Pope's really a Muslim? Even for the fertile mind of a journalist, that's pretty far-fetched.'

McBride was about to protest when she raised a hand, turning the palm towards him as a silencer. 'Besides,' she said, a note of triumph rising in her throat, 'he's alibied, solidly. Lynne Ireland was seen alive and well by a neighbour at 9.20 p.m. Adam Gilzean reported for duty at 9 p.m.'

'For duty?' McBride asked, astonishment spreading over his face.

'Yes – as a Samaritan. He was on a night shift that evening and his whereabouts can be vouched for – every minute from nine o'clock until the next morning – long after Lynne died.'

'Samaritan?' McBride was still incredulous.

'Been one for a year or two. Giving something back, he said. He's an alcoholic and hasn't touched a drop for years. No chance of him sharing a glass of wine with Lynne Ireland – or anyone else. Not unless he wanted to topple head first off the wagon. And there's been no hint of that.'

McBride fell silent, absorbing what he'd heard. Petra drained her glass but waved away his offer to open a fresh bottle. McBride remained thoughtful for several more moments. Finally he said, 'So how come he seemed to think a policeman might be involved in an unsolved murder?' He started to explain the thrust of the conversation Adam Gilzean had had with him in The Fort.

Petra lifted her hand once more. 'He told us about that too,' she said. 'Your friend Richard Richardson had apparently been to see him and planted that seed in him. Don't ask me how he knew but he's obviously been ferreting around.'

It had not been a good night, so far, for McBride so, when

Petra rose from her seat to reach for her shoes and jacket, he decided against pushing his luck.

She asked for the phone number of the nearest cab company and, after a little hesitation, he gave it to her.

47

McBride woke early – even before his normal seven o'clock. It was becoming a habit he did not like but could do nothing about. He ran for an hour and, by 8 a.m., he had showered, breakfasted and worked his way through most of the morning papers.

He positioned himself at the main window of the apartment, faced west and waited. He knew the postman would appear at the far end of the Esplanade between 8.15 and 8.30 and arrive at his house about seven minutes after that. McBride also knew beyond doubt that he would carry a plain white envelope with his computer-generated name and address on it. Inside there would be only a single sheet of white paper containing a short message. It would be anonymous and, like the envelope, bear no fingerprints or traces of DNA.

McBride was right. He was also wrong. The postman delivered the letter at 8.22. It was white, without a signature and with a brief pronouncement. But, in addition, it included a page from the previous day's *Courier*. The communication was concise and unambiguous. 'Last message,' it read. 'No need to stake out the library.'

Page three of *The Courier* carried Richard Richardson and Kate Nightingale's sparkling prose about the background surrounding the killing of Lynne Ireland. The page was intact except for a small passage which had been painstakingly extracted with a sharp instrument. The precise handiwork was only too familiar.

McBride found the jacket he had worn the day before and removed the copy of that day's *Courier* from the pocket. He opened it at page three and scanned it quickly to locate the missing words. They were from the closing paragraph of Double Dick's report. He had been expounding his views about the consequences of a murder and its effects on a community. The entire paragraph read:

> It may have seemed like just one more killing. A big one. It will be all over the front pages for a few days then the circus will move on, another town, another corpse.

The sharp blade had extracted twelve words from the middle section – 'just one more killing. A big one. It will be all over'.

McBride scanned it several times but it was an unnecessary exercise. Its meaning was quite unambiguous. *Another murder was promised. It would be significant. Then there would be no more.* All that troubled him was what made a death 'big' in the eyes of the executioner. *Big in size? A fat person? A tall one? A big name. The Queen? Don't be ridiculous,* he told himself, *her father wasn't a cop.*

He was starting to lose it.

48

Whatever way he figured it, McBride had hit a brick wall – at speed.

Four dead bodies. All females in their thirties. All murdered in their own homes. All after sex and having shared a drink with their killer. All the daughters of policemen. All despatched to the next world by a piece of police equipment. All with clean records. So many similarities but also so many differences. None of them acquainted with the others. None who looked remotely like the others. None with any friends or colleagues in common. None of them with any grudge against the law. None of them put to death in the same way. None of them with the same sexual partner. Yet the last face they looked at on earth appeared to have belonged to the same person.

McBride knew a lot about killing. He'd seen plenty of it. Sat often enough in the Old Bailey listening to the extraordinary evil that apparently ordinary men were capable of. Knew there was no kind of wickedness that could go unexplored by people who considered themselves members of the human race. He'd seen other kinds of killings in places in the Middle East and Northern Ireland and Eastern Europe. The exterminators called themselves freedom fighters but they were still butchers. Whatever the act, the outcome was always the same. Someone died. And there was always a reason, however obscure.

So, what was the link between Alison Brown, Ginny Williams, Claire Bowman and Lynne Ireland? McBride asked himself for the twentieth time that day. *If they had never met, what or who did they have in common? What was the hellish bond that united them in their violent and untimely demise? Why was another cadaver promised? And why would there be no more after that?*

He was still agonising over the answers when a knock sounded on the door of the apartment. Like bell-ringers, McBride was a skilled profiler of door-knockers. This was not a stranger but someone he knew. It was that kind of knock. Not formal. Not heavy, demanding entrance. Not the uncertain tap of a salesman. It was cheery, familiar. An acquaintance. Someone who felt they had a right to be standing on the doorstep.

McBride opened the door to find Richard Richardson facing him. He was smiling, waiting to be invited inside. McBride threw the door wide, beckoned him to enter and led the way to the upstairs sitting room.

'So, this is chez McBride, is it?' Double Dick's eyes swept round the room, taking in the newspapers scattered on the floor, the white envelope and its single sheet of paper, a half-finished bottle of Budweiser from the night before. Without being asked, he sat down on the sofa positioned against the back wall. He could have taken either of the seats beside the window and its wide panorama of the estuary, which most folk would have done. The sofa seemed a defensive move.

There was no hint of self-protection in his demeanour. Double Dick was flippant, chiding, easy. He took control, pointing his toe in the direction of the Bud. 'Any more of those?' he asked. It did not matter that it was still morning – he could drink at any time of day.

McBride moved round the room, rearranging the mess and lifting the papers and the single item of that morning's mail. When he had done that, he brought his caller a chilled beer from the kitchen.

'To what do I owe the honour of this royal visit?' McBride asked.

'Nothing in particular – just passing,' Richardson lied. 'Thought I'd take a look at the place that's staged a hundred shag-fests.'

McBride laughed – genuinely. It never took Double Dick long to steer the conversation round to sex, usually the kind he imagined McBride was having.

'Had Katie Nightingale round yet?' Richardson asked. Then, without waiting for an answer, he added, 'Fantastic backside, eh? Missionary job, I reckon.'

McBride said nothing. Shook his head slowly. Smiled. Double Dick was not the sort who required encouragement.

They exchanged banter while the *Courier*'s chief reporter emptied his bottle. The swallowing of the last drop seemed to be the signal for Richardson to move on to the purpose of his visit.

'Read your piece in the *Mail*,' he said. 'Insightful – even if it was over the top, as usual.'

McBride inclined his head in mock acceptance of the half-compliment. 'Yours too,' he told his guest. 'Over the top, I mean – not insightful.'

'So, that's why you were reading it before I came in,' Richardson said. He was eager to let McBride know he'd noted the page from *The Courier* which had been lying on the floor. Richardson spoke again. 'Are you doing a piece for tomorrow?'

'Haven't decided. Not much is happening. Unless you know something I don't,' McBride said, throwing the question back.

Richardson shook his head. 'Not a dickie bird.' He wasn't aware of what he'd said.

'Still without a woman in your life, then?'

Richardson looked blank.

McBride persisted. 'Not a Dickie's bird!'

'Very funny.' The penny had dropped. He moved on, becoming serious. 'So, if you're stuck for a new line on the story, do you need help?'

McBride lifted an eyebrow but said nothing.

'Maybe you want to collaborate? Share? You tell me what you know and I'll do the same? Could work for both of us,' Richardson said.

Jesus. How can someone be so subtle when he writes but so obvious when he speaks, McBride thought. But he said nothing, trying to make it seem as though he was weighing up the offer.

After a few moments he responded. 'Thanks but no thanks. I'm not under any pressure from any news desks – meantime. When I am I'll let you know.'

Richardson shrugged. 'Up to you. You know my number.' He rose from the sofa. 'Thanks for the beer. Once this settles we'll get together in The Fort. Might even have Kate in tow.'

McBride accompanied Richardson downstairs. They said their farewells and Richardson started to walk towards his car when he turned and with a parting shot said, 'By the way, if you think it was a cop who did it, you can forget it.' He did not wait for McBride to reply before driving off.

Back inside, McBride nursed a coffee and sat at the window, gazing out over the river. Two bottle-nosed dolphins suddenly surfaced, hung suspended in a lazy arc, then dropped gently back into the water in perfect symmetry.

He thought about Richardson's final comment and nodded his head. *God knows how he knows but he's absolutely right*, he said to himself. *Whoever's out there slaughtering women, it isn't a police officer.* It had suddenly become obvious. *It's someone who hates the police – someone with a grudge. The bits of uniform weren't used as a smokescreen. They were used out of contempt for the people who wore them.*

49

That thought had not yet occurred to Superintendent John Hackett who was briefing his detective teams in the incident room of Operation Tribune on the upper floor of Tayside Police headquarters.

Behind him was a picture gallery of death. Photographs of four young women when they were alive and even more of them lying open-eyed but seeing nothing after their lives had been extinguished. In front of him were weary officers waiting for instructions on how they might work their way out of all the blind alleys they were lurching into.

Hackett was unable to illuminate them. Even when he was at his best, he was never burdened by inspiration. He was also charisma free and would not smile at another man in case it was misunderstood. His most distinguishing feature was a fish-and-chip-supper stomach which hung over a belt straining on its last notch.

Usually Hackett followed rule number one of detective school – put your best officers on to the potentially most productive lines of inquiry. Give the donkey work to the domestiques, the foot soldiers who knocked on doors, scrabbled on hands and knees searching for evidence and fed the computers.

He invariably ignored the reality that the biggest crimes were frequently solved by the most lowly soldier. Sometimes a junior typist keyed the words into a PC that unlocked the mystery that had perplexed the ones with all the scrambled egg on their hats. A dumb piece of equipment that didn't give a damn who had died or how, just clicked everything into place and extrapolated a name that had been hidden away.

With nothing else to go on, Hackett had ordered the soldiers to punch in every scrap of information they had and cross-reference it with the data held by the police forces in Fife and Grampian. They hooked up to HOLMES, the national investigations database for major inquiries that is based at Scotland Yard and which provides interaction between forces. It had been devised by IT anoraks to improve incident-room efficiency. The electronic genius could investigate, collate, analyse and interrogate quicker than some detectives could text for a pizza delivery. On good days, HOLMES solved more crimes than Sherlock ever did. On bad ones, it was an electronic irrelevance.

This was not one of its most memorable mornings. It was letting Hackett down. Badly.

He had asked it to search for someone with a pathological hatred of the police. Unsurprisingly, it had produced columns of names but none that connected with the Tribune victims. Then he demanded that it should consider if the fathers of the dead women may have made a common enemy among the criminal fraternity. Or was there someone psychologically flawed who committed crimes while dressed as a police officer? The soldiers flashed their fingers over the keys. They looked at the screens in expectation. The screens looked back, mute, indifferent, unhelpful. If Hackett could have disciplined them for insolence, he would have.

Detective Inspector Petra Novak entered the incident room and approached the morose superintendent to pass on the details of the telephone conversation she'd had with McBride ten minutes earlier. 'It's good news and bad news, sir,' she said cautiously. 'Campbell McBride has been notified that the killing spree is just about over. One more victim and that's it.'

'Asshole,' Hackett spat at her.

He caught her astonished look. 'Sorry. Not you, him – McBride,' Hackett said by way of explanation. 'What the hell has it got to do with him?' He was willing to lash out at anyone better informed than him. That meant no one was safe.

'He's just trying to be helpful, sir,' she said defensively, surprised by her rush of loyalty. 'It's not his fault. He's only passing stuff on.'

'Passing stuff on? How come he's up to his neck in it? Have we checked him out?' He started towards the computer terminals, thought better of it and returned to face Novak.

'OK, OK, give him our thanks. Tell him we're extremely grateful,' Hackett said, trying sincerity but failing.

When she called McBride, he was having the same debate he had with himself every day at that time – would he lunch on a KitKat or be sensible and have something green? The chocolate always won and every day he convinced himself that the next day would be different.

Petra saved him from once more breaking his promise to himself. She suggested they meet at Café Buon Giorno in the centre of town to catch up over a coffee. It would also give him an opportunity to hand over the contents of that morning's mail, she explained. 'Unless, of course, you would rather have another visit from Detective Sergeant Gavin Rodger?' she said mischievously.

'Mr Siberia himself? No thanks,' McBride said. 'I'll chill out with you over a bacon roll or something sensible, if you insist.'

They did not speak for long. Petra looked less strained than when he'd last seen her and was immaculately un-crumpled. But she was still under pressure. The relaxation she usually brought with her was absent. She drank two cups of Americano but couldn't finish her sandwich. He recognised the symptoms. They were the same kind that overtook him when a deadline loomed and his laptop screen was blank.

'Under the lash, then?' McBride asked.

'You could say that,' Petra replied. 'We're ticking all the boxes with the inquiry – sometimes twice – but getting nowhere. Hackett, if you'll pardon the pun, is hacking everybody off with his bad temper. He's getting pressure from every direction and taking it out on us.'

McBride gave an understanding nod. 'He knows he'll never make chief super if he screws up,' he said. 'His problem – and mine as well, come to that – is he knows the whole thing is staring him in the face but he hasn't a clue what it is.'

Petra looked disconsolate. Her shoulders drooped and she repeatedly brushed a nervous hand through her hair. She asked McBride for the envelope he'd had delivered that morning. He pulled it from his inside pocket and, from it, withdrew the single sheet of white paper and the page from *The Courier*. He reread the terse message on the crisp A4 sheet and handed it over.

Petra quickly scanned it. 'Short and to the point,' she said.

McBride spread open the newspaper page, glanced again at Double Dick and Kate Nightingale's reports, then passed it across the table.

Petra held the paper up in front of her face with both hands and peered at him with one eye through the tiny gap where the twelve words had been surgically removed.

'I spy with my little eye something beginning with M,' she said, starting to laugh. It was the first time she'd lightened up since her arrival.

McBride smiled. The adorable teenager he first knew was never far away. Two women, who looked as though they worked in a bank, glanced up from their panini but carried on eating in silence.

When Petra left him in the shopping mall outside, he advised her to get an early night. 'It will all seem much better in the morning,' he said attentively.

She smiled agreement. 'You're right. A quick visit to the gym on the way home, half an hour in the sauna, then tucked up by ten o'clock.' She put an arm round him, held him for longer than she needed, then placed a kiss that lingered on to his cheek. 'Be good,' she warned.

McBride nodded with mock solemnity. 'As always,' he replied, turning away and feeling conscious of his pleasure at taking her smell with him.

He had everything but nothing to do. McBride knew that, if he returned to his apartment, he would once more be alone with his thoughts. It was a situation he normally enjoyed. Today it was not the preferred option. He knew with absolute certainty that he would be consumed by the same kind of frustration experienced by Hackett at being unable to assemble the pieces of jigsaw that were careering hopelessly inside his head.

Even before Petra had disappeared into the crowd of shoppers bustling towards the Overgate shopping centre, he was becoming troubled by something he could not begin to identify.

He needed company and sought it in Waterstone's bookstore, the place where the appalling journey of slaughter had really begun for him.

Gordon Dow, the astute, likeable manager with the wardrobe of neatly ironed shirts, was elated to see him. *The Law Town Killers* was still the number one best-seller and canny Dundonians continued to seek signed copies in the hope of one day possessing a treasure. The idea amused McBride, especially as he was a collector of 'worthless' signed books himself. He hadn't even read a couple of them but still hung on to them for their investment potential.

So he sat for half an hour putting his signature to a stack of copies of the tales of murder he'd written about, wondering if one day someone might pen a book about the dead women now filling his thoughts. *Which category would they be in? he pondered. Solved or unsolved?*

When he'd finished, he spent some time with Gordon Dow in the downstairs coffee shop. The manager asked McBride if he'd seen the item in the previous day's *Courier* which had featured a photograph of Dow and his staff receiving an award for operating Dundee's best branch of any national chain of shops.

McBride shook his head absently. 'Sorry, missed it – been busy,' he said apologetically.

Dow left the table and returned a few moments later with a copy of the newspaper. He spread it open and began to turn the pages, pausing briefly at page three, which carried Double Dick and Kate's murder reports. 'Hellish business,' he said, jabbing a finger on their stories. 'Hope they nail the bastard, double quick.' He didn't wait for a comment but turned the page. He beamed proudly. In the middle of page four and spread over six columns was a large photograph of himself and his staff receiving their award from Dundee's Lord Provost.

McBride stared at it, saying nothing. He was transfixed. Not at the splendid picture and report of his companion's success but at the full significance of the item. He hastily congratulated the bookstore manager, ignored the half-finished cup of coffee in front of him and rose quickly to his feet, saying unconvincingly that he had suddenly remembered a pressing appointment.

In his haste to get out of the shop, McBride took the steps of the escalator two at a time. He hurried to the car park where he'd left the Mondeo. Then he drove home, his mind racing as fast as he was driving.

50

McBride desperately wondered if he had been unbelievably prophetic or was merely clutching at the first reasonable straw. He had predicted to Petra the answer to the riddle that was perplexing a large proportion of the country's police force was probably 'staring him in the face'. Less than a minute later, he had stared without seeing at a newspaper she had held light-heartedly in front of him. A newspaper that had looked ordinary but unusual at the same time. A newspaper that might have represented the first mistake a serial killer had made. Not for what it contained – for what it didn't.

When he had gazed back at Petra as she jokingly peered at him through the aperture left by the words that had been cut away, he had been aware that something had disturbed him about the page facing him. But what? It was unremarkable. It carried news of road accidents, a fire, the most recent decisions of the town council. Nothing unusual. Except . . .

Long before he arrived back at the flat on the Esplanade, McBride was toying with a theory so far-fetched he could not contemplate sharing it with anyone. But he knew he would not rest until he played it out.

Once inside the apartment, he took time only to remove his jacket before opening his laptop and accessing Google. He tapped a person's name into the search engine.

> No standard web pages containing all your search
> terms were found.

He tried again, this time just the surname but with an occupation.

> No standard web pages containing all your search
> terms were found.

He opened up a new window, the site of an organisation abroad, and repeated the process. Nil result. He keyed in a different set of queries. Interrogated every link. Nil. Nil. Nil. McBride sat hunched over the keyboard for more than two hours. If perseverance was all that was required, he would not have been defeated. But it wasn't and he was.

Finally, with a string of oaths, he logged off. He repeated the words over and over with increasing frustration before slamming the lid of the laptop shut.

He stared at the inoffensive little box for ten minutes, willing it to answer back. Then a thought entered his head – one so obvious he could not understand why it had not occurred before. Calmness returned. McBride opened the laptop up again and quietly communicated once more with Google. This time the enquiry was simple. He requested the telephone number of a large newspaper in a major European city and received an immediate response. He closed down the computer, picked up his mobile and keyed in the number he'd been given. He asked for the news editor and, after identifying himself, was put straight through. The voice at the other end spoke perfect English.

They talked for several minutes and, at first, the conversation was almost exclusively one-sided. McBride asked a series of questions and received a series of answers, all of them negative. Then the news editor put another journalist on the line, someone older, a man with a longer memory. The responses became less dismissive, more encouraging. 'What you are telling me is starting to sound familiar,' he told McBride. 'The details are sounding a bell, as you would say. But not the name. Give me time to do some research for you and I will call back.'

McBride paid him copious thanks, passed over his number and rang off with more expressions of gratitude. He sank deeper into his chair at the window, leaned his head back and closed his eyes. He realised it was the first time his mind had felt relaxed in weeks.

51

It was another three hours before the phone rang in McBride's flat. He had positioned it by his side and lifted it instantly. The same voice he had listened to with mounting excitement earlier spoke to him easily and with a hint of satisfaction. The caller had a story to tell, he informed McBride, and, although some of the details were still elusive, there might be enough information to be of assistance.

The journalist hundreds of miles away said the name of the person involved was not who McBride thought it would be but was almost certainly Charles Mikel, a middle-ranking police officer who, twenty years ago, had been one of his country's most promising officers. In furtherance of his career, which his superiors had hoped would develop and become international, Mikel had been sent to Scotland to attend a four-month course at the Scottish Police College at Tulliallan. His fellow students were other officers who had all been hand-picked by police forces in the United Kingdom and other parts of the world. Like Mikel, each of them had been identified as having the potential to reach the highest echelons of their profession.

The course had gone well for Mikel until two weeks before it was due to end. Then it had been suspected he'd become involved with a young male constable attending the college as part of the new recruits intake. The visiting officer had succumbed to the persistent advances of the attractive probationary policeman. Others on the course had been questioned about the suspected liaison and afterwards Mikel was ordered to return home, his studies incomplete. McBride had listened in silence, only nodding quickly from time to time and urging his caller to continue with his historic account.

When it seemed he had finished, McBride started to speak. But the voice on the other end of the line interrupted him. 'There is a little more, Mr McBride,' he said. 'Two weeks after Mikel returned home in disgrace a reporter from this newspaper learned of the story and published an account of what had taken place. Although it was not a sensational-style article, Mikel was devastated by the effect he knew it would have on his family. He committed suicide two days after the story appeared. His wife never recovered from his death and exactly a year later she also took her own life. It was a very sad thing for them.'

McBride asked several questions and the answers he received confirmed much of what he had bizarrely begun to suspect when Gordon Dow had proudly pointed out the photograph of himself and his award-winning staff earlier that afternoon. There was just a single question to be answered and the man speaking to him from one of Europe's best-known cities would not be able to enlighten him. McBride thanked his helpful fellow journalist, indicated that he might be in a position to repay his co-operation in the near future and rang off.

Without putting the phone down, he called Petra's number. She did not reply. The call clicked on to her voicemail and he remembered her promise of an early night. He did not leave a message. Instead, he rang police headquarters and asked if Superintendent Hackett was still on duty. To his surprise, he learned he was. To his greater surprise, he was put straight through.

Hackett was not especially delighted to hear from him. He struggled to sound friendly. 'How can we assist you, Mr McBride?' It would have been a reasonable question if it hadn't been laden with sarcasm.

McBride ignored the hostility. 'Might be the other way round, actually,' he said. 'If you can tell me what I need to know, I may be of considerable assistance to you.' He could sense the superintendent's battle to hold himself in check. The line was heavy with silence.

McBride pressed on. 'I need to know the names of all the officers who were on a particular course at Tulliallan twenty years ago.' He said it matter-of-factly – not making it sound like a ridiculous thing to ask just a couple of hours before midnight.

Hackett showed unexpected restraint. 'Don't be bloody stupid,' he almost hissed, pausing between each word for effect. 'How in God's name am I supposed to know that? You do own a watch, don't you? The college shut up shop about five hours ago. Get real, McBride.' Then, years of police training at last kicking in, he asked quietly, 'Why do you want to know?'

It was a fair question in the circumstances and McBride was about to tell him. Then, just as though he'd suddenly been caught in the headlamps of a truck hurtling towards him, he knew he had not needed to speak to Hackett. Hadn't required any assistance from him. Realising that he was already in possession of the information he thought he had wanted, a sudden chill ran the length of his spine.

McBride was also positive beyond doubt that he had to act on it without delay. 'Tell you tomorrow, Superintendent,' he said curtly. Without waiting for the acerbic Hackett to respond, he hung up.

Then, for the second time that day, McBride took a flight of stairs two at a time before throwing himself into his car and moving away at speed.

52

He headed east, out along the road that joined Broughty Ferry with Monifieth and past the low bungalows with their cropped, watered lawns and double-glazed windows where sometimes the curtains twitched. At that time of night, the bumper-to-bumper convoys that carried rush-hour commuters home to their smart houses had long disappeared.

McBride practically had the road to himself. He charged the Mondeo through the gears and put his foot to the floor for the long straight stretch that carried him into Monifieth. He took the last awkward bend into the centre of the small township almost on two wheels and sped through the deserted shopping precinct before braking abruptly to turn right into Tay Street. He drove for another hundred yards then swung left into the car park of the recently completed Grange apartment block that sat back from the golf course, looking out towards the North Sea.

Two cars were already there. He recognised them both. One belonged to Detective Inspector Petra Novak – the other to the person who had come to kill her.

McBride had not worked out what he planned to do when he reached his destination. All that had filled his mind was the need to arrive there. Quickly.

He was not sure if he was too late. *The other car's still there. Good sign,* he assured himself. He looked up at the top floor of the block where Petra lived. A light was on in one of the rooms where the curtains were drawn. He reasoned it had to be the bedroom. The sitting room would be on the opposite side of the building, facing the panoramic views of the sea.

Bad sign, he thought. *They should still be in the sitting room.*

He ran from the car and into the block. Looked at the stairs and threw himself at them – two at a time. *Christ. Third time today. Thank God for all the jogging.*

When he reached the top landing and the door to Petra's flat, he stopped momentarily to recover his breath. And think. He reasoned that he had two choices. *Kick the door open and charge inside. Or knock and see if anyone answers. Then what?*

He decided on the third option, the one he thought would be a waste of time. He pressed down on the door handle. Softly. Waited for it to lock out. It kept moving. Stopped at the bottom of its full length of possible travel. He pushed gently. The door eased open. He stepped inside on to an oatmeal carpet that ran the full length of a hall.

Music came from behind the door top left, the front-facing sitting room. Andrea Bocelli was duetting 'Somos Novios' with Christina Aguilera. Absurdly, he wondered why such an unlikely pair should join up. *Anything for a buck.*

McBride made his way slowly along the hall. Light shone from under the first door on his right, the bedroom. He stopped, listened. Silence. He nudged the bottom of the door with his toe. It swung open soundlessly. He pressed his back to the door. Stretched his neck and turned his head round its side. Peered with one eye into the room.

Petra Novak lay on the bed looking back at him, her brown eyes enlarging. Her mouth was wide open but there was no chance that she was about to shout out in surprise. The space between her lips was stuffed with something oyster coloured and McBride realised it was a pair of women's knickers. Nor was there any possibility that she would move towards him. She was stretched out in the crucifix position, each wrist manacled by handcuffs attached to the ends of the metal bedstead. He gazed at her, mesmerised, an absurd desire to laugh starting to rise within him. It was the kind of situation he might have dreamed of in his more perverted moments. Then monochromatic images of the heroine in a silent movie flashed into his mind. The urge to laugh was overwhelming.

McBride put a finger to his lips, pointlessly requesting her to remain silent. When he realised the incongruity of the gesture, he shrugged his shoulders apologetically and smiled. She tried to smile back, just as convincingly as anyone can with a mouth stuffed full of ladies' underwear. He wondered when she would work out that their inappropriate responses were a reaction to the fear they felt.

McBride was considering his next move when a voice spoke from the end of the passageway. It was soft, even, accentless and familiar.

He turned to face its owner. Anneke Meyer – or Mikel as she had been known before she changed her name – stood at the entrance to the sitting room. She had one hand raised, leaning against the door jamb. In the other, the one outstretched towards him, she held a pistol. Even from twenty feet McBride recognised it as a police-issue 9mm Glock 17.

'And you told me you were too busy to see me,' she mocked. 'Small world, isn't it? But then, I didn't know you and our friend in the bedroom were an item. We might have had a cosy threesome.'

McBride shook his head slowly. 'I came here for you, Anneke. I knew this is where I'd find you.'

She said nothing but inclined her head, inviting him to continue.

'Big mistake sending the page from *The Courier* to me,' McBride said, watching closely for her response.

She remained silent but nodded again, inviting him to continue.

'You should have bought it in Dundee, not your local shop. It was the Perthshire edition you posted off. Like most people, it never occurred to you that a big regional paper like *The Courier* would have several different editions, did it? Six, in fact. Just your hard luck that the piece about your last victim that you sent me happened to be on page three, the one before the start of the local news pages. Tough shit too that the Dundee edition that day was carrying a piece on page four that a proud bookstore manager forced me to look at. Took a little while to click but, after that, it wasn't too difficult . . . Who did I know in Perthshire? Who was a policeman's daughter?'

The last comment provoked a startled reply. 'You don't know anything about my father.' She almost spat the words.

'No, but a very helpful reporter on *De Telegraaf* in Amsterdam with a long memory brought me up to speed,' McBride said easily. 'So this is all about revenge? Get the daughters of the men who shopped your dad? Why them? Why not the fathers?'

She stared back at him. He thought of the last time they had been together in a house. It was a concept he was unable to grasp. Now she loathed him. Maybe she always had. Venom consumed her face. 'I lost a father – and mother. They should lose a daughter.'

'Why so elaborately?'

She threw back her head and made a sound that was meant to be a laugh. 'For fun. Police are stupid. Detectives no longer solve crimes. It is scientists – us. We supply them with the evidence. The fingerprints – the DNA. And we can use the same things to make them look foolish. Don't you think that's funny?'

'I'm pissing myself,' McBride said.

She gestured for him to come towards her. He complied, walking along the hallway as she backed into the sitting room, still extending the Glock in front of her. Inside the room, she waved her free hand in the direction of a low glass table positioned in front of a sofa. Two empty wine glasses and a bottle of wine with two inches left in it were the first things McBride saw. Then he noticed a white, folded cloth, the size of a handkerchief at one corner.

The woman he now knew as Mikel backed her way to the table and lifted the top of the material, throwing it back. Underneath were two condoms and a small hypodermic syringe.

'Recognise anything?' she asked, a note of triumph in her voice.

McBride did not reply.

She picked up a condom, swung it from side to side. 'Yours, I think. One of a set of four, if I remember. Though there wasn't much to get excited about in two of them.' She replaced it on the cloth and, still holding the pistol, skilfully lifted the hypodermic and inserted the needle point into the latex sheath. She pulled back the plunger of the syringe, glancing down briefly to be sure the semen from the condom teat was being drawn up into the barrel of the hypodermic.

'Maybe you'd like to be the one who injects this into the pussy of our friend next door,' she taunted. 'Or perhaps you would rather do it properly. Now, that could be interesting. I could judge your performance and give you marks out of ten. Either way, the clever detectives will imagine you were her visitor tonight.'

McBride sneered. 'The presence of semen isn't evidence of intercourse. You of all people should know that.'

'Clever boy,' Mikel said. She reached into a sports bag on the floor at the corner of the table and without taking her eyes off his face, extracted a large object that looked more like an instrument of terror rather than pleasure. She smiled at McBride's expression of surprise as she waved a vibrator at him.

'He's called the Emperor, though Brutus sounds a bit more appropriate, wouldn't you say?' She jerked the dildo up and down several times. 'That's usually enough to open up any unwilling passage,' she said. 'If Petra's mouth wasn't so full she'd tell you how it felt.'

McBride said nothing.

She was enjoying herself.

'In the unlikely event that some plod still isn't convinced, there's always the wine glass.'

She pointed down at the table. 'Familiar? The one on the left is the one you so enthusiastically handled when you paid your little visit out to Glencarse. Remember how many drinks you knocked back before joining me in bed? There's something else,' she said. She dug into her bag once more, this time removing a small, clear envelope used to carry forensic samples. Inside were half a dozen hairs.

'You left two of them on the pillow and the other four on your lovely white "his" bathrobe. Towelling is a wonderful material for holding on to hairs, don't you think? Place them in the right spot, though, and no one believes they didn't get there naturally. Causes no end of confusion among the thicko cops. Leaving Bryan Gilzean's hair on the hat that disposed of Lynne Ireland was a nice touch, don't you think?'

She stopped speaking, allowing McBride to consider what she'd said. After a few moments she asked, 'Anything else? Or is it all too complicated for the hotshot investigative reporter?'

'So how did you track your victims down?' McBride asked.

She shook her head pityingly. 'You really do disappoint me, Campbell. You, of all people, should know what the interrogation of a few properly selected databases can produce – that and some innocently worded questions in a handful of phone calls to the right people. Satisfied now?'

'One thing,' McBride replied. 'Why the "big one"? And why stop after it?'

Mikel looked at with him disgust. 'You're not really smart at all, are you? Petra's two for the price of one – with her, I also get you. The daughter of Detective Chief Superintendent David Novak, the tutor on my father's course at the police college, and you – a journalist. The same breed of parasite as the reporter who told the world about my father's indiscretion. If it wasn't for that bastard, my parents would still be alive. You'll do nicely in his place. Why stop? Only half true, I'm afraid. Next week I leave for nine months' study abroad at the University of San Diego. When I get back? Well, who knows . . .'

McBride dropped on to the sofa without asking permission. He folded his arms and looked across the room at the woman holding the gun.

'So, how was Petra going to get it? A bullet in the head? Hardly my style.'

She gave him a pitying stare. 'Nothing so crude.'

'So, how?'

'Just your style – "Shagger" McBride plays a sex game that goes wrong. The lovely Petra is handcuffed then choked for kicks. He should stop but doesn't. She dies. His semen is all over her, his prints on the wine glass, his hair on the pillow in the bedroom and on the back of the sofa. Twenty years minimum, wouldn't you say?'

'Neat. So, what next?'

'We play doctors and nurses.'

McBride raised an eyebrow.

'We go next door and you perform your little trick with the hypodermic,' she said. 'Don't suppose an athlete like yourself has ever used a needle before – unless, of course, it's been to improve your performance on your little bicycle. The lovely detective inspector so invitingly stretched out on the bed probably hasn't been on the wrong end of a needle either. She may even enjoy it. More than she did the Emperor, I imagine.'

McBride stared back at her, saying nothing.

She gave a short laugh and lifted the vibrator once more. Started to thrust it upwards several times. 'No, sadly, our friend here didn't go down too well or should I say "up" too well,' Mikel sneered. 'She should get out more. Meet more men. Get in some practice. Too much work and not enough play has made the delightful Petra a bit of a tight-ass.' She laughed again. She was starting to sound manic.

McBride eyed her coldly. '*You* got a lot of pleasure out of it though, didn't you?' he said, watching closely for a reaction.

Mikel dropped her gaze, a rush of colour filling her cheeks. She started to speak but changed her mind. She waved the Glock. 'Lift the syringe and lead the way into the bedroom,' she said, trying to sound scornful. 'Slowly.'

He picked the hypodermic from the table and moved towards the door. 'Another thrill awaits you, doesn't it?' he asked – not a question, a taunt.

Mikel ignored him and pointed the gun in the direction of the bedroom. 'Her too, perhaps,' she said.

When they entered the room, McBride saw at once that Petra had been silently crying. Smudges of dampness trailed down both cheeks. Vivid rings of red encircled both wrists where she had struggled against the handcuffs. She had never looked more distressed – or more in need of protection. He wanted to take her in his arms. Instead, he moved to the edge of the bed and gently ran the back of his hand over a cheek. 'Hi,' he said inadequately. Then, 'Not too easy getting to sleep with these things on, I bet.'

Petra's eyes crinkled at the corners, the way they did when she smiled.

The short exchange seemed to enrage Mikel. She moved to the other side of the bed. 'Get it over with,' she instructed McBride.

Petra wriggled the lower half of her body in protest at what was about to happen. The movement angered the woman with the gun even more. She lifted her free hand and swung it backwards. Hard. It caught Petra full on the right side of her face, the blow smashing into the opposite cheek from the one McBride had caressed with the back of his hand a moment before.

McBride instinctively stepped towards Mikel, as though to strike her in retaliation.

'Don't even consider it,' Mikel said. She lifted the pistol higher. 'As they say on the T-shirts, just do it.' She slid Petra's skirt up over her waist, exposing the naked lower half of her body, and gestured with the gun for McBride to inject the semen.

He complied as gently as possible. When it was over, he briefly stroked Petra's hair, doing his best to ease their shared awkwardness.

Mikel, who had watched the process intently, snapped at him, 'How touching! Right, you've done it.' She waved the Glock again, this time towards the sitting room. 'And take the syringe with you.'

McBride did as he was told. And as he left, he turned towards the bed and smiled gently at Petra who was staring nervously at his retreating figure. 'See you later,' he said softly, convincing neither of them.

Back in the main room, he stood facing Mikel. 'So, what now?' he asked. 'What do you have in mind now that I've messed up your grand plan?'

The question troubled her. For the first time since she had confronted him in the hallway after he had entered the flat, she appeared uncertain. The initiative had slipped from her. She remained silent. Thinking. Her eyes moved round the room.

McBride felt her hesitance. It did not give him the reassurance he might have imagined, or desired. With her carefully prepared scenario disrupted, Mikel would be unpredictable.

He cursed himself for not having phoned Superintendent Hackett before going in such haste to Monifieth.

The same thought appeared to occur at exactly the same moment in the mind of the woman standing opposite.

'I guess you neglected to call for reinforcements, Campbell,' she said. 'They would have been here long before now if you had. Tut-tut. Not such a clever boy, after all.' She shook her head in mock disgust and started to swing the Glock slowly backwards and forward.

McBride moved away from her and sat down on the sofa again.

She watched him closely but did not say anything. The tension between them started to reach deafening proportions.

McBride sat back. Put his hands behind his neck and rested his head in them. He had arrived at a strategy – a poor one but the only one he could think of.

'Before you shoot, there's something you need to know,' he said. 'Your father will be extremely disappointed with how you've turned out. Ashamed, even.'

The remark hit the target, slap in the middle.

Her eyes blazed and the nostrils he had once found so appealing widened. Her breasts lifted then dropped as she started to breath deeper. She took the three paces across the room she needed to be standing next to him at the side of the sofa. She did not speak but clenched her left fist, drew back her arm then punched him in the mouth with as much force as she could muster.

Blood sprang from McBride's lower lip. He reached cautiously into his pocket, removed a handkerchief and dabbed gently on the wound. 'You're losing it, Anneke,' he said. 'Where's all the control now?'

She did not reply but moved closer and stretched out her arm until the gun in her right hand was level with McBride's head. Then she eased a further two inches forward until the barrel was pressing into his temple. It was the coldest feeling he'd ever experienced. Worse than the chill that was filling his stomach.

The colour drained from Mikel's cheeks. 'My father loved me,' she said. 'He adored me. And my mother.' Her eyes flashed and what looked like tears began to well in them.

'He was an honourable, loving man – no doubt about that,' McBride said. 'He proved it by what he did to protect you and your mother from what he thought was the shame he'd brought on the family. Wasn't a lot of point though, was there? All he got for his trouble was a daughter who turned out to be a serial killer. That would make him real proud, wouldn't it?'

His words instantly produced the effect he sought. Mikel's face contorted. Her eyes swung from side to side then cast around the room. She stepped backwards, pulling the barrel of the Glock away from the side of McBride's head and allowing the pistol to drop almost level with her side. She was confused, agitated – torn between the love she felt for her father, her hatred of McBride and the self-loathing that was beginning to overtake her.

He pushed on, aware of the risk but accepting it. 'So what are you going to do now?' he asked. 'Problem you've got, as I see it, is how you wrap this up. Gunfire might alert the neighbours. You can always strangle Petra first, of course, then march me off for a firing squad somewhere quiet. 'Cept I might just object when you started the throttling bit. Or were you going to do that with one hand and hold the gun on me with the other? Even for a body combat instructor that might all be a bit tricky.' McBride rested his head on the sofa back. Waited for her to answer. His eyes never left her face.

She looked at him. Looked away. Looked back. Said nothing.

After several seconds McBride spoke again. 'There is another way, of course. Stop all this. Bring it to an end and make your father really proud. Give me the gun and we'll work things through together. Get help. We'll find a hospital where you'll be looked after.'

He rose slowly from the sofa and moved hesitantly in her direction. 'Your father had honour,' he said. 'You can get it too.' He held out a hand for the pistol. 'Let me have it.'

Mikel attempted speech once more. Changed her mind. Then made a decision.

She lifted the Glock, pointed it with slow deliberation, took aim and gently squeezed on the trigger. The bullet entered her right temple, blew her brain apart and exited to the left.

Hackett and the scene of crime teams arrived thirty minutes later. By that time the best-looking detective inspector who'd ever been on his force was free of her shackles and into another pair of knickers. In other circumstances, McBride would have been happy to have delayed both processes by a good hour – another time.

Novak had fifty questions she wanted to ask but not then either.

He had kept her in the bedroom and they hadn't said much. He had held her in his arms and she'd wept.

Later, she told McBride she needed to leave for a debriefing by Hackett and they both managed to laugh.

McBride drove the two miles back to his apartment slower than he'd driven in his life. He parked the Mondeo and started to walk along the beach. A white moon hung low overhead and the only sound was water breaking softly on to sand at his feet. He headed towards the lifeboat shed where he knew there was a seat.

He would occupy it and think of how he would describe the last few weeks of his life.

Then, when daybreak rose out over the river, he would call London and tell a news desk he had a story to write.